The Day the Queen Died

Thomas Brant

CHAPTER 1 - The News Comes In
Thursday 8th September 2022

Tony Kettlehurst was sitting at his desk at the Speke headquarters of Manic, looking at his computer, reading the latest updates from Buckingham Palace. The news was grim, though vague as ever. A brief statement issued earlier in the afternoon had mentioned "concern" for Her Majesty's health, and the internet was already ablaze with speculation. Tony had been in the business long enough to know when a story was about to break wide open, and this one had seismic potential.

Looking at his watch, he knew it was quarter past two, and that the news from the BBC had been announced that the Queen was under "medical supervision at Balmoral". As a producer at Manic Radio, he knew that the management, as soon as they heard that the Queen was under medical supervision, would be scrambling to prepare for what everyone feared was inevitable. Tony's job was to keep the ship steady while the higher-ups decided on their next moves. The "Royal Protocol Binder," a dusty relic of Manic Radio's planning department, was already open on his desk. Inside were detailed instructions on what to do in the event of a royal death—though nobody had updated it since Prince Philip's passing in 2021, and even that was a rushed job.

"Tony, are we running the protocol rehearsals or not?" shouted Sandra, his junior producer, from across the office.

Looking at the notes, Tony knew that the first requirement was to get, as soon as the protocol was activated, the

Manic Rock, Jazz, Blues, Metal, Classical and Soul teams to switch to a sombre and unified playlist. The instructions were clear: all stations were to abandon their usual programming and transition to reflective music. There were lists of pre-approved tracks: Elgar's Nimrod, Vaughan Williams, Adele's Hometown Glory, and even Bridge Over Troubled Water. But Tony couldn't help noticing that half the tracks had never been tested in live situations. Would a Metal station really go quietly into an Elgar requiem? He doubted it.

The next step was to get the most senior host in Manic employment, which happened to be the Dudley hub's Pete Smith, a 30-year veteran of radio, prepared. Looking at his roster, Tony knew that Pete was scheduled to do his regular drive slot on Midlands Manic, the Birmingham regional CHR station in the Manic Radio network, and that Pete would be required to, instead of hosting his own show, present rolling news on Manic Goldies, the Classic Hits station known for its nostalgia-driven playlist.

It was ironic, Tony knew, that Pete, as a CHR presenter, had spent decades cultivating a persona of upbeat, youthful energy, but was the most senior voice at the network. His experience, however, made him the natural choice for delivering the kind of gravitas and calm the situation demanded. Tony knew Pete was a 'shirt and tie, polished shoes, smart trousers' broadcaster, someone who could embody the solemnity required on such a historic day. But would Pete himself see it that way? The man had never hidden his disdain for corporate meddling, and Tony could already hear the grumbles about being pulled off his "bread and butter" CHR show for what Pete would no doubt call "the biggest downer of my career."

"Get Jane Spearmore on the phone, get her to alert him that he might not be doing drive but a network show," Tony muttered to Sandra, who was already halfway through dialling. Jane Spearmore, the regional director for Central England and the line manager of Pete Smith, would be the person he needed to get permission from to use here staff if the senior management in the building next door, where the executive offices were located, hadn't already made the call. Sandra gave Tony a quick thumbs-up as the call connected, leaving him to focus on the next steps.

Tony flipped through the binder again. The protocol also required the CHR network, made up of a mix of heritage stations that had come from Breeze Media and Manic prior to the merger with Lite Group a few months earlier, to stay fully CHR, with no deviation from the script, only allowing for the required national announcement, and then back to fully regular programming within an hour. Manic Dance, its sibling station, would also stay fully EDM and not shift into the sombre tone. The logic, Tony thought grimly, was that audiences for those formats weren't expecting reflective programming, and corporate research suggested they might switch off if the usual high-energy vibe was disrupted. "Heaven forbid we lose a few listeners on Spotify for five minutes," Tony muttered under his breath, rolling his eyes.

As Sandra wrapped up the call with Jane Spearmore, she relayed the response. "Jane says Pete's on standby, and that he's been keeping up to date, and that he's happy to do the planned show on Manic Goldies."

"Good," Tony said, nodding as he glanced at the clock. It was now 2:30pm, and he knew the next phase was to get presenters from one of Manic's Scottish brands to be heading from the Dundee hub to Balmoral, so live links could be broadcast directly from the scene if the worst was confirmed. It was a delicate operation, and Tony knew that missteps now would be remembered for years to come. "Sandra, is there any adults at Dundee?"

He had to chuckle, as most of the presenters there were under 30, and lacked the maturity of veterans like Pete Smith. Sandra grinned knowingly. "Well, it's the usual crowd. The only adults were on the Breakfast shift, and they're probably back in Ayr or some other little dump that's near Glasgow that they live in, and its 3 hours from Ayr to Balmoral, if traffic behaves."

Tony groaned. Of course, the two sane ones at Dundee would still live in Ayrshire and not Tayside where they worked. It was always the way with regional radio. "Right," Tony said, rubbing his temples. "Call Dundee, get someone to track down Robbie and Emma from Manic Radio Ayrshire's Breakfast Show. If they're willing to drive up to Balmoral, we'll need them reporting live from the scene as soon as possible. And remind them this is about as big as it gets—so no complaining about mileage."

Sandra raised an eyebrow. "You think they'll go for it? Robbie's been on a tear lately about how corporate is 'bleeding the soul out of local radio.' You think he'll play nice?"

Tony sighed. Robbie MacPherson was a well-known firebrand within the network, constantly at odds with the corporate suits and their directives. Emma Lee, his co-host, had a softer touch but wasn't far behind in terms of her disdain for the new corporate culture at Manic. Still, they were consummate professionals when the mics were on. "They might grumble," Tony conceded. "But this is history. Even Robbie will know when to rise above the politics."

Sandra nodded and picked up the phone, dialling the Dundee hub. Meanwhile, Tony turned his attention back to the binder. There was one section that he dreaded more than the rest: The Announcement. If Her Majesty passed, it would be up to Pete Smith to deliver the news across all stations in the Manic Radio Group.

He flipped to the page with the script, printed in bold capital letters.

"This is the Manic Radio Group across Britain. It is my duty to inform the nation that Her Majesty Queen Elizabeth II has passed away. The Queen died peacefully at Balmoral this afternoon. The King and The Queen Consort will remain at Balmoral this evening and will return to London tomorrow."

Tony read the words carefully, his mind racing with the gravity of what they represented. It wasn't just a script; it was the moment that would define not just the day's broadcast but likely the careers of everyone involved. There was no room for error. The delivery had to be flawless—calm, measured, and imbued with the right level of solemnity.

He scribbled a quick note to himself to remind Pete that under no circumstances was he to deviate from the script.

Pete might be a veteran, but Tony knew that live broadcasts, especially of this magnitude, had a way of throwing even the most seasoned professionals off balance. One slip, one moment of improvisation, and it would be headline news for all the wrong reasons.

Sandra interrupted his thoughts. "Got through to Dundee. They're... going to have to subcontract it to... ITN, our backup plan."

Tony knew that Manic contracted out their off peak news commitments to ITN, just like Bauer and Global using Sky News Radio for their news broadcast and breaking news. It was a standard industry practice, but it felt like a cop-out for such a monumental event. This was the kind of story that demanded local voices, not a generic national feed. He sighed. "Right, we'll use ITN for the immediate coverage if Balmoral breaks tonight but make it clear to them that we'll need our own presenters on the ground by morning."

Sandra hesitated. "Do you really think we'll get the go-ahead for that? You know how tight the budgets are, and management won't like us spending extra on travel and accommodation."

Tony waved her concerns away. "If they push back, tell them to call me directly. This is about credibility, Sandra. We can't claim to be the voice of Britain and then phone it in on the biggest story of the century."

Looking back to his notes, Tony knew that the Dudley studios were fitted with RCS's entire suite of tools, from Zetta and GSelector, to RCS News, whereas Speke, the Network Centre for Manic, had to rely on PlayoutONE, which was more suited for smaller stations. This discrepancy had always been a sore point for Tony. The flagship station of the network, using tools better suited for community radio, while regional hubs like Dudley enjoyed top-of-the-line tech. It wasn't just about the equipment—it was the marriage that Manic and Breeze had had, where the two halves of the same group still acted as though they were separate entities. Breeze Media's legacy, which favoured slick, high-tech operations, often clashed with the scrappier, cost-conscious ethos of Manic Radio.

And then there was the former Lite stations, which used Myriad, another system entirely, throwing yet another wrench into the works. Managing this technological patchwork on a normal day was hard enough; coordinating a unified response across all platforms during a moment of national significance was bordering on impossible. Tony scribbled down a note to check with IT about ensuring all systems were synced for the announcement.

"Any word on what the bosses upstairs are saying?" Sandra asked, breaking Tony's train of thought.

Tony glanced at the glass-walled office that housed the senior leadership team. Through the blinds, he could see shadowy figures gesticulating wildly, their phones glued to their ears. "Probably arguing over which department gets to take credit for the handling of this," he said dryly. "Or more likely, who gets to dodge the blame if it goes wrong."

Sandra smirked but didn't comment. Instead, she pointed to the clock. "It's almost three. If something's happening, it'll probably break soon."

Tony nodded grimly. The timing felt inevitable. The statement from Buckingham Palace earlier in the day had been the kind of thing you could read between the lines of, and every royal correspondent worth their salt had been hinting that the end was near. Still, the air in the office felt heavy with anticipation, like they were all holding their breath, waiting for history to happen.

****

Half an hour later, Tony received an email from management which meant he knew things were happening. It was just after 3pm, and the Palace had sent a message to all media outlets with the news, but informed them that they would not be permitted to release it until 6pm, or slightly thereafter.

The Queen had passed at 3:10pm.

Tony knew that the Palace wanted the near 3 hour gap between the email going out and the public announcement to ensure all key figures in government, the royal family, and Commonwealth leaders were informed. It was a sombre yet meticulously orchestrated process, befitting the gravity of the moment. The time was not just for courtesy—it was for coordination, giving broadcasters a narrow window to prepare for what would undoubtedly be one of the most-watched and listened-to moments in history.

"Sandra, tell Dudley to take control of Goldies. Harry, get all stations on Obit mode immediately, Karen, get the Manic Rock and Metal lot to hit the showers, and everyone, black ties, right now!"

The energy in the Speke office shifted instantly, an electric current of urgency replacing the tense anticipation. Tony's sharp directives cut through the murmurs of speculation, snapping everyone into action.

Sandra bolted to the phone, her fingers already punching in the Dudley hub's direct line. Harry, a junior technician, leapt from his seat, dashing towards the control room to initiate Obit mode across the network. Karen, Manic's head of niche stations, groaned audibly but moved swiftly to alert the Rock and Metal teams, who would likely not take kindly to being yanked off air mid-set.

Tony stood, straightening his tie as he surveyed the scene. The "black tie" directive was more than symbolic; it was a visual cue of professionalism and respect, an unwritten uniform for moments of national mourning. He glanced down at his own outfit—a crumpled shirt and no jacket— and muttered a curse. He'd have to grab something from his car. He knew asking the Manic Rock and Manic Metal crews at the Olympic Park studios to get showered was not a joke, as the smell their bodies emanated after long shifts in their famously chaotic and informal studios had become a running joke throughout the network. Still, today wasn't the day for jokes. Today was about precision, professionalism, and solemnity.

As Tony strode toward the door, Sandra called after him, "Do you think Pete's ready for this? He's good, but this is... something else."

Tony paused, his hand on the doorframe. "Pete's been doing this long enough to know when it's not about him. He'll deliver. I need to get on a Zoom meeting with our hub managers."

Tony strode out of the office, his mind a swirl of tasks yet to be completed. He knew the next few hours would define not only the day but possibly his entire career. There was no room for error. As he reached his car in the car park, he grabbed the black blazer hanging on the back seat and glanced in the rear-view mirror. His hair was a mess, and the tired lines under his eyes betrayed the long hours he'd already put in. He ran a hand through his hair and took a deep breath.

This was it.

Back in the office, the team had already sprang into action. Screens flickered with updates from across the network, and phones buzzed incessantly. Harry was hunched over the console in the control room, his fingers flying over the keyboard as he initiated Obit mode. Karen was on a conference call with the Olympic Park team, her voice calm but firm as she laid down the new programming orders. Sandra was pacing with her mobile pressed to her ear, coordinating with Dundee and Dudley.

Tony's laptop dinged with the link to the Zoom meeting with hub managers. He straightened his tie, threw on the blazer, and clicked to join. Faces popped up one by one on the screen—Jane Spearmore from Dudley, Tom Hargrove from the Huddersfield hub, Cardiff's Harriet Morgan, and a handful of other regional directors. Each wore the same mix of urgency and solemnity, their black ties and sombre expressions reflecting the gravity of the moment. The chatter on the call was subdued but efficient, a testament to the years of practice these managers had in dealing with crises, though none quite like this.

"All right, everyone," Tony began, his voice steady but firm. "You've seen the email. The Palace has confirmed, and we're under embargo until 6pm. This is not a drill. We have less than three hours to get every station in line. Updates?"

Peter Johnson, the Regional Director for London and the South East, based at the Olympic Park was the first to speak, his tone clipped but professional. "Olympic Park is ready. Lord Cedric Ashcombe is already on standby for Manic Classical. He's rehearsing the script as we speak. The Classical team is fully briefed, and we've prepped a playlist to match the mood. Cedric will go live at 6pm sharp."

"No, we're doing a fully networked announcement, Peter," Tony said with finality. "Pete Smith will deliver the announcement across all Manic stations. Cedric-"

"Really?" Harriet snarled with the force of a Welsh dragon. "Cedric's perfect for this. He's got the gravitas, the articulation—he's basically born for moments like this, Tony. Why use Pete?"

Tony sighed. He'd been expecting pushback, especially from Harriet and the regional directors who resented Speke's control. "Because it's not about gravitas, Harriet. It's about unity. Pete's been with us for 30 years... well, technically he started off under Woody Bones's banner, then Breeze's, then when we brought them ours, so he's been part of the wider network for 30 years. He's a recognisable voice to Midlands audiences on Midlands Manic, Birmingham's CHR station, and he used to listen to Ed Doolan and other BBC voices when he was younger, so he knows exactly how to approach something like this. We need a single voice to represent the entire network. Cedric is incredible, no doubt about it, but he's niche. This announcement is about every listener, from Cardiff to Carlisle, not just Manic Classical."

The tension in Harriet's face softened slightly, though her lips pursed in silent disapproval. The other directors exchanged glances on the screen but said nothing.

"Fine," Harriet relented. "But Classical will still go into Obit mode at six, right?"

"No, Obit mode tracks start now. No earlier, no later. CHR and Dance are to remain fully upbeat, even after the 6pm announcement, but every other station, including Classical, Rock, Jazz, Soul and Blues. Goldies goes fully rolling news as of now as per the protocol," Tony said firmly. "Staffing will remain as scheduled. The Anthem will play at 5.58pm, and then the Breaking News alert across all stations. No ads will play effective immediately."

****

CHAPTER 2 - Over at Classical
Thursday 8th September 2022

Lord Cedric Ashcombe of Durham was sat in the studio of Manic Classical in the Olympic Park studios of Manic Radio, his afternoon shift of timeless music nearly finishing. studio, usually a calm refuge from the corporate frenzy of the rest of the network, felt different today. There was an air of unease in the air, palpable even among the stillness of the grand symphonic compositions he adored.

Cedric had been with Manic for over two years, a card carrying member of the Conservative Party, a Eton man, and a former BBC Radio 3 host. He was, by all accounts, a man of old-school decorum and refinement, and in many ways, Manic Classical's brand was built around his steady presence, his reverence for the classics, and his unflappable approach to presenting. Today, however, he couldn't shake the feeling that something momentous was unfolding.

The programme had flowed as usual—Beethoven's Symphony No. 7 had just concluded, followed by a moving piece from Tchaikovsky—but Cedric couldn't ignore the news alerts popping up on his screen. His producer, Linus Roache, a recent Oxford graduate in Classics, because of course, only a love of true classical music could have convinced him to leave the lucrative world of finance behind, had been unusually quiet during the shift. Cedric noticed Linus's furrowed brow, and the odd silence hanging between them that had only grown deeper as the afternoon wore on.

The studio, with its heavy curtains and antique decor, normally provided a sense of detachment from the madness of the outside world. It was a haven for those who craved the delicate calm of Mozart, the serenity of Brahms, and the grandeur of Strauss. But today, the comforting embrace of the music seemed to have little effect. The backdrop of uncertainty hung like an invisible cloud over the proceedings.

Cedric adjusted his headphones, trying to maintain his composure, but the steady beat of his heart seemed to sync with the pulse of the outside world. He noticed the flickering of Linus's screen, a sign that something had changed. News was moving at a pace Cedric had rarely experienced. The quiet office had been punctuated with a few hurried phone calls, all of them short, clipped, and urgent.

"Linus, my dear fellow, is everything quite alright?" Cedric asked, his voice smooth, as though attempting to soothe the tension in the air.

Linus met Cedric's gaze, his face pale. "There's talk... Cedric, I think you ought to know—this isn't just another regular broadcast. I've been getting messages from the higher-ups at Manic. We've just been told to go to Obit mode."

Cedric's face tightened, and for a moment, the music in his headphones seemed to fade into the background. "Obit mode?" he repeated, the words tasting strange on his tongue. It wasn't a term he was accustomed to hearing outside of newsrooms or corporate boardrooms. The gravity of the situation began to sink in.

Linus nodded, his fingers hovering over his keyboard, as though unsure of what to do next. "Yes. We've been told that Her Majesty's health may be worse than what has been reported. Management, my Lord, have told us that the Palace has put an embargo on the full news, but Her Majesty... has passed. The announcement has been scheduled for 6pm, when Mary Thomas is scheduled to start show. She won't be doing the announcement on Classical though."

Cedric straightened in his chair, his hands instinctively moving to adjust the lapels of his blazer. The weight of Linus's words pressed on him, and for a fleeting moment, he felt a twinge of disbelief. The Queen—constant, enduring, the very essence of British stability—was no longer with us.

"I see," Cedric said, his voice steady, though there was a faint tremor beneath the surface. He reached up to remove his headphones, placing them on the desk with deliberate care. "Who's doing the announcement then, Linus? Surely someone appropriate has been selected for this most solemn of moments?"

Linus hesitated, his eyes flicking to his screen as another message came through. "Pete Smith, from Midlands Manic. He's the network's most senior presenter, and management thinks he'll bring the right mix of experience and calm authority."

Cedric raised an eyebrow. "Pete Smith? From a CHR station? I'm sure he's competent, but wouldn't someone more... seasoned in the nuances of such an occasion be more fitting? Someone like me, perhaps?"

Linus smiled faintly, recognising Cedric's trademark blend of self-assurance and diplomacy. "It's about unity, they said. One voice across all stations, and Pete's the one they've chosen. It's not about genre or individual flair— it's about familiarity, someone who represents the entire network."

Cedric leaned back in his chair, steepling his fingers as he processed the explanation. "I suppose there's logic in that. But still, I can't help but think that Classical, of all places, should set the tone for the nation in a moment such as this."

Linus glanced at the clock. It was just after twenty past three, and Cedric knew that the time before the announcement would pass in a flurry of preparations, yet would feel excruciatingly slow. For a station like Manic Classical, accustomed to precision and poise, this was an unusual moment. The weight of the occasion was palpable.

"Linus," Cedric said, breaking the silence. "If we are to relinquish the honour of making the announcement, then let us at least ensure that the lead-up on this station is worthy of the moment. Have you prepared the playlist for Obit mode?"

Linus nodded, sliding a piece of paper across the desk. "Here's what we've got: Elgar's Nimrod, Holst's Venus, and Vaughan Williams' Fantasia on a Theme by Thomas Tallis. It transitions into Mozart's Requiem just before the announcement at six."

Cedric picked up the sheet, scanning the selections. "A fine choice, though I might suggest swapping Holst for

Barber's Adagio for Strings. It carries an emotional weight that the occasion demands. And afterward, we must move to Beethoven's Symphony No. 3, the Funeral March."

Linus tapped the adjustment into his laptop, nodding. "Good call. And after the announcement?"

Cedric frowned slightly, considering. As a former BBC Radio 3 host, he knew that the publicly funded broadcaster would be planning something meticulous and dignified, likely reflecting the Queen's personal musical preferences. Manic Classical, though, had to strike a balance between its niche audience and the broader listenership that might tune in during such a momentous event.

"Do you know what Mary will be playing on her show?" Cedric asked, as he knew that the host who would follow him after his four hours of classical interludes and soft commentary would inherit a very different atmosphere, especially as she was a former Classic FM host, and so would bring a touch of commercial polish to the proceedings.

Linus glanced at his screen. "She's got Handel's Zadok the Priest lined up after the announcement, followed by Jerusalem and Rule, Britannia!—though I imagine management might ask her to tone it down, given the circumstances."

Cedric shook his head with an air of authority. "Indeed, Linus, we must tread carefully. Zadok is a coronation anthem—it speaks of beginnings, not endings. It may be too soon to transition to such triumphant fare. Perhaps we suggest something more introspective to begin her programme—Schubert's Ave Maria, perhaps?"

Linus made a note. "I'll flag it to her producer. It's a solid alternative."

The two men fell into a moment of reflective silence, the muffled hum of the studio monitors filling the air. It was a silence not of unease but of contemplation, the kind that arises when the weight of history bears down, demanding quiet respect.

"Cedric," Linus said after a pause, his voice softer now, "you've been doing this a long time. What do you think it'll feel like... when the announcement is made?"

Cedric leaned forward, resting his elbows on the desk. His expression was solemn, his voice calm but tinged with gravity. "Linus, I've been on air during royal weddings, jubilees, even state funerals. Each has its own gravity, its own rhythm. But this... this is something else entirely. The passing of a monarch—this monarch—marks the end of an era, not just for Britain but for the world. I was three when Her Majesty was crowned, and her reign has been the backdrop to all of our lives, a constant in a world that's changed beyond recognition. When the announcement comes, it won't just be history unfolding—it will be a profound shared moment of loss and reflection, something that transcends politics, class, and even our individual stations. It will be... unifying."

Linus nodded, the weight of Cedric's words settling over him. "And do you think we'll do it justice, Cedric? As a network, I mean."

Cedric allowed himself a faint smile, tinged with the wisdom of experience. "We can only do our best, Linus. That's all history will ask of us. The music, the tone, the words—they must all be chosen with care, but ultimately, it's the sincerity with which we present them that will matter. If we approach this moment with the dignity it deserves, I believe the nation will feel that, even though the static of their radios."

Linus tapped the desk lightly, his nervous energy showing. "Right, then. Let's make sure everything is perfect on our end. No margin for error."

Cedric glanced at the clock. It had been 10 minutes since the clock showed half past 3, the minutes slipping away faster than he had anticipated. The studio's calm stillness seemed to sharpen, every note of the music filling the air taking on added poignancy.

Looking at Zetta and GSelector, the Olympic Park studios preferences for playout and automation, Cedric saw Linus was adjusting running times, changing tracks and scheduling transitions with the precision of a conductor leading an orchestra. Cedric appreciated the young producer's diligence. It was a reminder that, for all his traditionalist sensibilities, the modern tools of broadcasting, when wielded by capable hands, could serve the same timeless purpose: to bring people together through the power of music.

Unlike the other Manic stations, the Classical station held no scripts, with presenters instead using their memories and their extensive knowledge to guide listeners through their journey. This meant network competitions, like the £500k Money Drop, excluded the Classical station entirely—its audience was deemed too niche, too serious for such frivolities. Advertisements were also limited to a 3 minute slot per hour, with the national news, presented not by Manic newsreaders but ITN, a contracted provider for the station, breaking the otherwise uninterrupted flow of music.

The few ads that did air were carefully curated to match the tone of the station—luxury cars, private schools, and the occasional mention of high-end retirement homes. The irony that most listeners to the station were Conservative Party members, or those leaning towards Conservative sensibilities, was not lost on Cedric as Liz Truss, a Conservative Member of the Commons, was the Prime Minister, and as Cedric was a member of the Lords, he had to maintain a careful balance in his on-air persona, avoiding even the faintest whiff of partisanship. Today, however, there would be no room for politics, no subtle nods or winks to his personal affiliations. Today, his duty was to the nation as a voice of calm and reflection.

Linus glanced up from his laptop, his brow still furrowed. "Cedric, I've just been informed that the central office wants all stations to synchronise for the national anthem at 5:58 pm. After that, Pete Smith will take over with the announcement."

"The national anthem? Who on God's green earth greenlit the idea of leading into the announcement with the national anthem?" Cedric asked, his tone caught between bemusement and incredulity. "It seems... a touch too ceremonial for what is, at its core, a moment of collective mourning."

Linus shrugged helplessly. "Apparently, it's part of the Royal Protocol Binder at Speke. They've been dusting it off since this morning, and everything is by the book. The national anthem is meant to signify respect and unity before the announcement. After Pete delivers the news, there's supposed to be a twenty-second silence across all stations, followed by reflective music... apart from our CHR network."

Cedric leaned back in his chair, his fingers steepled thoughtfully. "Ah, yes, the book. The hallowed tome of corporate radio etiquette. I suppose one must respect the process, though I do hope Pete delivers the announcement with the gravitas it deserves. A twenty-second silence, you say? Far too brief. Thirty seconds, at the very least, would feel more appropriate for the magnitude of the moment. And as for the Contemporary Hit Radio network, why are they not participating in Obit mode at all?" Cedric finished, raising an eyebrow at the absurdity of it.

Linus sighed, his fingers paused over his keyboard. "The logic, or lack thereof, is that CHR audiences 'expect escapism.' Management thinks reflective programming will drive them to Spotify or Apple Music. Apparently, keeping them upbeat will minimise audience drop-off."

Cedric gave a faint chuckle, though there was little humour in it. "Ah, yes. Heaven forbid we prioritise dignity over listener retention. Still, I suppose it's not my place to question corporate strategy. Our task is to guide those seeking solace through the power of music. The CHR lot can keep their escapism."

Linus nodded, clearly exasperated by the decision but choosing not to engage further. "Right, I'll make sure the transition to the anthem is seamless. After Pete delivers the announcement, we'll continue with the adjusted playlist. Shall we run through the plan one more time?"

Cedric gestured for Linus to proceed, his demeanour calm but his mind buzzing with the gravity of the situation.

"At 5:58 pm," Linus began, "we'll fade out whatever's playing and transition into God Save the Queen. The network announcement will follow immediately at 6 pm, delivered by Pete Smith. After the twenty—err, thirty—seconds of silence, Mary's show will commence with Schubert's Ave Maria, followed by your proposed adjustments to the playlist. Zadok the Priest will be held back for a later time, possibly during the King's official address or another suitable occasion. We'll stick to introspective, solemn pieces for the rest of the evening, with breaks only for short, reflective commentary."

Cedric nodded approvingly. "Excellent, Linus. That sounds suitably dignified. Make sure Mary is briefed thoroughly; she's a seasoned professional, but it never hurts to have a clear understanding of the tone required. And the transition from my programme to hers must be seamless—no chatter, no missteps."

Linus gave a thumbs-up, his fingers already flying over the keyboard to finalise the details. Cedric, meanwhile, rose from his chair, moving to the grand window at the far end of the studio. The muted sunlight streaming through the glass seemed oddly fitting, as if the very heavens themselves were dimming in anticipation of the news.

The familiar strains of Holst's Venus began to play softly through the studio monitors, and Cedric allowed himself a moment to breathe, to prepare mentally for the hours ahead. He was not just a presenter; he was, in many ways, a custodian of a cultural moment that would resonate for generations. It was a weight he felt acutely but carried with pride.

He knew that, as a Lord, he would be required to attend sessions of the House of Lords in the coming days, where tributes to Her Majesty would be delivered by peers and ministers alike. Cedric anticipated the sombre atmosphere that would envelop the chamber, a stark contrast to the often-contentious debates that characterised British politics. The Queen's passing would bring about a rare unity, a collective pause to reflect on her remarkable reign and the continuity of the monarchy.

Looking at his screens, Cedric knew that he had 7 minutes until the next transition, so he grabbed the notepad that was on the desk and started jotting down his speech for the Lords, where he would speak on the Queen's enduring legacy. His words would need to encapsulate not just his personal admiration for her steadfastness and grace but also the collective gratitude of a nation. He would draw on her constancy in times of upheaval, her quiet sense of duty, and her unique ability to bring people together, even in moments of great division.

The pen moved steadily over the notepad, his thoughts coalescing into carefully chosen phrases.

"Her Majesty was more than a monarch; she was a symbol of continuity in an ever-changing world. Her reign witnessed monumental shifts in society, technology, and

23

geopolitics, yet she remained a steady hand, guiding the nation with quiet dignity and resolve.

"I was a three year old child when Her Majesty was crowned, and though I could not fully comprehend the magnitude of the moment then, it has stayed with me throughout my life. She was the nation's grandmother, a constant presence in the fabric of our collective identity. Whether through her steadfast Christmas broadcasts or her quiet gestures of solidarity during times of crisis, she embodied the best of Britain: resilience, grace, and a deep sense of duty.

"In this chamber, as we reflect on her life and her legacy, we do so not merely as members of the Lords but as citizens who have been privileged to witness a reign that spanned seven decades. It is incumbent upon us now to uphold the values she championed: unity, compassion, and service to others. And as we look to the future, to His Majesty King Charles III, we do so with the same hope and faith that Her Majesty inspired in us all."

Cedric paused, re-reading his words. They felt appropriate, capturing both the personal and the universal. Folding the notepad shut, he placed it carefully into his briefcase.

The gentle conclusion of Venus stirred him back to the immediate task at hand. He donned his headphones again and leaned into the microphone, his voice smooth and measured as he transitioned seamlessly into the next piece.

"That was Holst's Venus, a celestial meditation of rare beauty, perhaps a fitting accompaniment to a day that feels, in its own way, like a pause in the heavens. Coming up next, we'll hear Barber's Adagio for Strings, a piece often described as a lament for the soul—a composition of quiet strength, reflective and deeply moving. I remember attending a fine performance by the BBC Symphony Orchestra in my youth where this very piece brought the room to an almost reverent stillness. Let us embrace its solemnity together."

Cedric's voice carried the transition with the poise he had honed over decades, his words laced with the kind of gentle authority that calmed even the most restless of spirits. He removed his hand from the fader and sat back, letting Barber's mournful strains fill the room.

****

CHAPTER 3 - Rocking All Over The World

Thursday 8th September 2022

Bradley Turner had to chuckle at the demand his team at the Olympic Park studios in London had received from Speke.

"Shower, black ties, Obit mode."

As the brand manager for Manic Rock and Manic Metal, and a true rock enthusiast, he knew that any rocker who didn't smell like they'd come out of a mosh pit was probably doing it wrong. He imagined the scene now: his crew, a dishevelled bunch of long-haired, leather-clad rockers, being ordered to wear black ties and to get cleaned up before going on air. The thought of it made him snicker, though he also knew he couldn't exactly blame them. The protocol was the protocol, and this was a moment that transcended the usual chaos of the rock station.

It was quarter to 4 and the atmosphere in the Manic Rock studio was already buzzing with anticipation. The usual banter about festival line-ups and legendary riffs had given way to hushed conversations about the news trickling in from Buckingham Palace. Even in the irreverent world of rock and metal, there was a sense that something monumental was happening.

Bradley was sat in the control office, reading a book about Iron Maiden, their biography, when a runner burst through the door, looking flustered and out of place amidst the rock memorabilia plastered on the walls.

Bradley glanced up, his finger still marking his place in the book.

"Speke's on the line again," the runner said, breathless. "They want to make sure we're fully prepped for the announcement and the transition to Obit mode."

Bradley sighed, placing the book down gently. "Prepped? What do they think we're doing, playing darts and headbanging to Enter Sandman? We've got it covered."

The runner looked unconvinced. "Karen said she needs confirmation that all the stations are in sync. They're pushing for total coordination."

Bradley rolled his eyes. "Fine, fine. Let's confirm. Skinny Jim's got Zetta on the Manic Rock side of things set up with Sex Pistols leading after the announcement, God Save The-"

Bradley froze mid-sentence, catching himself before finishing the title. Even for a station known for irreverence, God Save the Queen by the Sex Pistols wasn't exactly the track you'd want to follow a royal death announcement. He gave a low chuckle, shaking his head. "Okay, scratch that. Let's make sure Skinny Jim isn't pulling one of his stunts. If I find that queued up, I'll have his head—and not in the fun, Ozzy Osbourne way. Anyway, George has got the Manic Metal side set up on Zetta, even though an Obit playlist for Metal music is like trying to find a lullaby in a Slayer album. But we'll make it work."

Cassie "Riff Queen" McAllister, the producer of the 4pm to 7pm slot on Manic Rock, and her counterpart for Manic

Metal, Jeff "Doomhammer" Carter, whose shows would carry on the mantle of their respective genres into the evening, entered the control office, looking like they'd been pulled straight out of a gig. Cassie's leather jacket was scuffed, her eyeliner smudged from a long day, while Jeff, clad in a Cannibal Corpse t-shirt, had a coffee cup in hand that he looked ready to smash into the nearest wall.

"Tell me we're not actually going full Obit mode," Cassie said, her voice heavy with disbelief. "I get it—big moment, national mourning, all that—but reflective rock? What even is reflective rock? Stairway to Heaven?"

Bradley spat his coffee across the desk, the idea of Stairway to Heaven being on the prepared Obit playlist catching him completely off guard. He laughed so hard his chair nearly tipped over. "Cassie, I swear if I see Stairway to Heaven on the list, I'm calling the lawyers. I think Led Zeppelin would agree it's not exactly royal protocol."

Jeff leaned against the wall, rubbing his temple. "Look, I get the need for respect, but this is Manic Metal. Reflective? Our listeners think reflection means staring into a pool of blood while listening to Raining Blood. What's next, you want me to play Nothing Else Matters?"

Bradley raised an eyebrow. "Actually, that's not the worst idea. Metallica's got a sombre edge when they want to. It's reflective without being too... polite."

Cassie groaned, slumping into the nearest chair. "Brad, if you make me play Metallica tonight, I'll quit. Again. And this time, I won't come back after two weeks."

Bradley chuckled, waving her off. "Relax. We'll stick to the script Speke sent, but we're making it ours. Let's be real—our audience isn't tuning in for Vaughan Williams. They want something that resonates, and we can deliver without sounding like we've abandoned who we are."

Jeff crossed his arms. "So, what's the plan? Just play all the slow tracks from Pink Floyd and call it a day?"

Bradley leaned forward, pulling a printed playlist from the stack of papers on his desk. "Here's what we've got so far for Rock: Brothers in Arms by Dire Straits, The End by The Doors, Wish You Were Here by Pink Floyd, and yes, Jeff, Nothing Else Matters is on there. For Metal, we're looking at tracks like Fade to Black by Metallica, Planet Caravan by Black Sabbath, and maybe In My Darkest Hour by Megadeth."

Cassie raised an eyebrow. "Wow, this might actually work. But I swear if anyone slips Sweet Child o' Mine in there, I'll riot."

Jeff smirked. "Could be worse. Could've been Free Bird. Imagine the calls we'd get—'This isn't reflective! This is karaoke fodder!'"

Bradley clapped his hands together, drawing their attention. "Right, jokes aside, this is serious. We've got to stick to the tone but keep it authentic. Our listeners might love chaos, but even they'll know this is different. So, here's the deal: we follow Speke's guidelines, but we add our spin where it fits. And Jeff, no Slayer tonight. Sorry, mate."

Jeff sighed dramatically but nodded. "Fine. But if anyone complains, I'm telling them to take it up with Speke."

Cassie glanced at the clock. "So, what's the timeline? When do we make the shift?"

Bradley tapped the schedule. "We go into Obit mode at 5:58, with the national anthem across all stations. Pete Smith will deliver the announcement at 6. After that, we start the playlist. Keep your links tight, minimal chatter. Let the music do the talking."

Cassie frowned. "What about after the announcement? Do we keep it solemn all night?"

Bradley nodded. "For the most part, yes. But we'll gradually build back into the usual vibe by tomorrow morning. The big bosses want us to maintain the reflective tone tonight, but they know our audience won't tolerate it for too long. We'll ease back into regular programming carefully."

Jeff tilted his head. "And what if we get calls asking for God Save the Queen by the Sex Pistols? After all, Hank's show at 10 is an all-request show."

Bradley smirked at Jeff's question. "If anyone calls asking for God Save the Queen by the Sex Pistols, tell them we're fresh out of irony tonight. And Hank's all-request show is suspended—he'll run a curated playlist like the rest of us. No exceptions... well, apart from the CHR lot of ours. Anyway, Kerrang and Kiss'll be playing similar stuff to our Obit mode, so I doubt we'll be alone in navigating this minefield. Let's just not be the ones to make headlines for all the wrong reasons."

"You mean Bauer are actually going to do Obit mode properly?" Jeff asked, a smirk tugging at the corner of his mouth. "I thought they'd just keep smashing out Bring Me the Horizon and hope no one noticed."

Bradley leaned back in his chair, shaking his head. "Bauer know what they're doing when it comes to moments like this. They'll lean on their Greatest Hits network for the reflective stuff, just like Global will use Smooth and Classic. The rock world, though... that's where we step up. We're leading the charge for the guitar crowd."

Cassie tapped her fingers on the desk thoughtfully. "Alright, but what if we do get backlash? You know how our listeners are—they thrive on rebellion. They might see this as us selling out."

Bradley leaned forward, his tone serious. "Cassie, this isn't about selling out. This is about respect. Even the most rebellious rocker has someone they look up to, someone they mourn when they're gone. This is one of those moments where we set aside the riffs and the anarchy and recognise the magnitude of what's happening. We do it our way, sure, but we do it right."

Cassie nodded, her defiance softening. "Fair point. Alright, let's make it happen."

Bradley glanced at the clock. It was approaching ten minutes to four, and the weight of the evening ahead hung over the team like an ominous riff from a doom metal track. The usual chaotic energy of the Manic Rock and Manic Metal studios had been replaced by a strange quiet, punctuated only by the low hum of monitors and the occasional buzz of phones. Even the runner, who had been rushing back and forth between Speke's directives and Bradley's crew, seemed subdued.

"Right," Bradley said, breaking the silence. "Let's get into gear. Cassie, Jeff—make sure your hosts are prepped. Minimal chat, focus on the music. No jokes, no stunts, and absolutely no deviating from the playlist without clearing it with me first. And I want them showered and wearing black ties... orders from the top."

"Shower? Black tie? What do you think this is, a Royal Variety Performance?" Cassie quipped, rolling her eyes.

Jeff smirked. "I'll tell Skinny Jim to wear a tux. Maybe even polish his boots while he's at it."

Bradley chuckled, but his tone quickly grew serious again. "Look, I know it feels weird—hell, I'm not thrilled about it either—but this is one of those times when we need to play ball. If Speke wants black ties, we'll give them black ties. Just make sure everyone's on the same page. Apparently Management know we don't use deodorant or polish our leather jackets, but they still want us to look respectable for once."

Cassie and Jeff exchanged knowing smirks, the tension in the room easing slightly.

"Fine, boss," Cassie said, standing up. "I'll make sure Riff Queen Radio looks like it's hosting a funeral instead of a gig. But if anyone cracks a joke about me wearing heels, I'm blaming you."

Jeff stretched, groaning theatrically. "Guess I'll go break the bad news to the Metal team. Shower and ties... they're gonna think I've lost my mind."

Bradley gave a small laugh. "Just tell them it's either that or a conference call with Speke explaining why Metal's playlist turned into a Slayer tribute. Trust me, they'll choose the showers."

As the two producers left to rally their teams, Bradley leaned back in his chair, the weight of the evening settling over him once more. He glanced at the playlist again, mentally rehearsing the transitions and imagining how each track would land with their audience. There was no manual for moments like this in the rock world—no protocol binder could account for the balancing act they were about to perform.

Putting his headset on, Bradley tuned into the Manic Rock feed that Studio 16 was broadcasting, catching the final few minutes of the afternoon slot hosted by Darren "The Axe" Reeves. Darren, with his gruff, smoky voice and knack for pulling off impromptu rants about everything from subpar guitar solos to corporate meddling, had been treading a careful line for the last hour. Bradley could tell that even Darren felt the weight of the moment.

"Ok, Rockheads, it's the last 5 minutes with me, The Axe, here on Manic Rock, and I've got a bit of Sex Pistols with God Save the Queen lined up for you," Darren said with his upbeat rockstar fever. "I remember when this first came out, and man, did it stir the pot. Radio 1 banned it, and Woolies didn't stock it, but damn, for a 9 year old like I was then, it was the best thing ever. Changed my life, that song did. Anyway, here's to the fascist regime."

The opening riffs of Sex Pistols' "God Save the Queen" blasted out, and Bradley's heart sank as the anarchic anthem roared through the speakers. He yanked off his headset, scrambling for the studio phone to call Darren's producer, Lisa, before things spiralled any further.

"Lisa! What the hell is Darren playing?!" Bradley barked, his voice cutting through the line.

Lisa's voice came back, equally panicked. "He slipped it in without telling me! I had The Who queued up on Zetta but he'd-"

"That's why we don't give the jocks playlist overrides!" Bradley snapped, cutting Lisa off. "He's fucking ex-Kerrang, and Bauer would never have allowed that level of chaos. Pull it now. I don't care if you cut to silence—yank it, or we'll be explaining ourselves to Speke and probably the Palace."

There was a beat of hesitation, then Lisa's hurried acknowledgment. Bradley sank back in his chair as the offending track was abruptly replaced by a mid-play cut into The Who's Behind Blue Eyes. The awkward transition was far from seamless, but it was better than letting Johnny Rotten scream through a moment meant to be solemn.

"Who the fuck did that?" Darren's voice on the live streamed feed of Manic Rock cut off mid-rant, was quickly muted as the producer killed his mic, leaving a moment of dead air before seamlessly transitioning back to The Who. Bradley exhaled sharply, running a hand through his hair. The damage was minimal, but it was a stark reminder of how precarious this evening was going to be.

Bradley called Lisa directly, bypassing the studio phone. "Lisa, I need you to rein Darren in. He cannot go rogue like this. One more stunt, and I'll have to pull him off air."

Lisa sighed audibly, her frustration apparent. "He's fuming, Bradley. Says he's 'making a statement' or some bollocks like that. But I'll handle it. Promise."

"Good," Bradley said firmly. "And remind him that if Speke gets wind of this, we'll all be in the firing line."

Before he could say anything else, the red phone, the one that Speke used to communicate their most urgent directives, lit up like a warning beacon. Bradley groaned inwardly, knowing this wasn't going to be a congratulatory call.

He grabbed the receiver. "Bradley Turner, Manic Rock."

Tony Kettlehurst's clipped voice crackled through the line. "Bradley, care to explain why the Sex Pistols were just blasting through the Rock feed? We're getting calls from senior management, and let me tell you, they're not impressed."

Bradley pinched the bridge of his nose. "It was Darren going off script, Tony. I've already yanked it, and his producer's been told to keep him on a tight leash."

"Not good enough," Tony snapped. "And he's swore live on air too, which means OFCOM will have our heads if this escalates. You know how sensitive this situation is, Bradley. Do you want the Palace calling us directly? Or worse, a front-page headline tomorrow screaming 'Manic Rock mocks royal death'? Get your house in order, or I will."

Bradley sighed heavily, gripping the phone tightly. "Tony, it's handled. I've already dealt with the producer, and Darren's being pulled into line as we speak. I'll make sure he doesn't deviate again."

"You'd better," Tony growled. "The spotlight is on us, Bradley. One more screw-up and the only playlist you'll be managing is in a hospital waiting room."

The line went dead, leaving Bradley to stare at the receiver. He slammed it back onto the cradle and leaned back, exhaling slowly. The gravity of the evening ahead loomed even larger now. He knew that Darren's shift was ending shortly, which meant that Cassie, along with Simon "Dr Rock" Foster, the host of the drivetime show, would be taking over. Both were reliable, seasoned presenters who understood the magnitude of the moment. Bradley felt a shred of relief, knowing that the next segment of the night was in capable hands.

As the control room settled again, Bradley reached for his headset and tuned back into the studio feed. Cassie's voice, calm and steady, replaced Darren's chaotic energy.

"That was Behind Blue Eyes by The Who, a track that reminds us of reflection and resilience. As we transition into this evening, we'll be bringing you a selection of music that speaks to the gravity of the moment. Thanks for being with us, Rockheads—this is Manic Rock with Dr Rock and me, Riff Queen, Cassie McAllister. We've got a jam packed show for you guys, but first it's the news with Sarah Ingram."

Bradley turned off the feed and leaned back in his chair, allowing himself a rare moment of relief. Cassie's measured tone was exactly what the station needed to steer things back on track. If anyone could navigate the tricky waters of a reflective rock playlist while keeping the audience engaged, it was her.

Looking at the paperwork that he needed to do, Bradley sighed and pushed it aside. Tonight wasn't about paperwork or the usual administrative grind. Tonight was about ensuring the station didn't just survive but delivered something meaningful, respectful, and true to its identity in the face of an extraordinary moment.

Suddenly another email came in, this time from the compliance team, and Bradley knew that, at 4 in the afternoon, there may have been young listeners tuned in during Darren's slot. The Sex Pistols' stunt and the profanity that followed might already have triggered complaints. OFCOM wouldn't take kindly to any breach of the Broadcasting Code, particularly not on a day as sensitive as this. Bradley opened the email and skimmed it quickly.

From: *Sally.Harper@manicradio.group*

To: *Bradley.Turner@stratford.manicradio.group*

Subject: *Compliance Alert – Darren Reeves Incident*

Bradley,

It has come to our attention that Darren Reeves deviated from the pre-approved playlist during his segment and aired the Sex Pistols' God Save the Queen, followed by on-air profanity. As you know, this is a serious breach of both corporate directives and OFCOM regulations, particularly given the sensitivity of today's events.

We've already received a preliminary count of five listener complaints and are preparing an internal incident report. Please ensure Darren is fully briefed on the gravity of his actions and document the steps you're taking to prevent further issues during the transition to Obit mode. Additionally, please confirm whether Cassie and Simon's shifts have begun without incident.

We'll need a written statement from both you and Darren by 9am tomorrow.

Regards,

Sally Harper

Head of Compliance

Manic Radio Group

Bradley groaned, running a hand through his hair. The last thing he needed right now was a compliance report on his desk, but Sally was right—this couldn't be ignored. Darren's stunt had not only jeopardised the station's reputation but risked drawing unnecessary scrutiny from OFCOM, which could lead to fines or worse.

****

CHAPTER 4 - The Huddersfield Hub
Thursday 8th September 2022

Huddersfield, a West Yorkshire town where the sound of the radio often echoed through the streets like an old friend, was a place where local communities found solace in their airwaves. As the North East England hub, where every station from Manic Radio North East, the Newcastle station of Manic's contemporary hit radio network, to Manic Radio Lincolnshire, their Lincoln area station, broadcast from, the mood in the Huddersfield hub was one of quiet tension. The usual hum of the newsroom, the chatter of producers, and the slap of headphones were replaced by hushed conversations, phone calls, and a sense of waiting.

"We've got to what?" Tom Hargrove, the Regional Director for the North East said as he heard the news from his counterpart at Cardiff on the internal Zoom call. His tone was incredulous, as if he couldn't quite comprehend the gravity of what was being asked of him.

"Yes, you heard right. All CHR drives are to run as normal." Tony Kettlehurst's voice crackled through the Zoom call, the clarity of the connection belying the confusion that was settling in Tom's chest.

"You're asking me to keep the drive-time shows running, as usual, while... well, while this is happening?" Tom couldn't believe what he was hearing. The voice of a nation had just gone silent, and now the radio network, the very pulse of contemporary pop culture, was being told to carry on as if nothing had changed.

"That's right. For the next few hours, at least," Tony's voice was firm, yet tinged with the frustration of a man who knew he had no real choice in the matter. "Play the script, get the national announcement out there, but don't deviate from the format otherwise. This is the directive. Bauer and Global will be Obit obsessed for the next 24 hours, so senior management have decided we're to keep to our CHR format at all times. The 18-35 demographic are going to want continuity, not Funeral Hits FM."

Tom stared at the screen, his fingers tightening around the edge of his desk as the weight of Tony's directive sank in. He had seen the business of corporate radio compromise local culture many times before, but this was different. This was an unprecedented moment, and yet they were being told to act as though it was business as usual. He struggled to make sense of it, even as his mind raced through the logistics of how he could possibly maintain any semblance of normality with a country in mourning.

As a former Hits Radio Network employee who had been on duty when Prince Phillip had passed, he had been in the position where his Newcastle stations, along with the rest of the country, had shifted into sombre programming. He knew that his successor at Bauer would hate that Manic had decided to buck the trend, sticking to its CHR guns while the rest of the industry adopted a more traditional approach. Tom's memories of that day at Hits Radio—a playlist filled with Adele, Sam Smith, and other reflective pop tracks—made this directive from Manic feel even more surreal.

"Will it be up to the stations to announce or are we having one voice across the network?" Tom asked, as he knew

Bauer did the latter, a common practice for major announcements of this kind. A single, unified voice lent gravitas and consistency, ensuring that the message was delivered without deviation or error.

Tony's response was immediate. "One voice. Pete Smith on Manic Goldies will read the announcement, and all CHR stations will simulcast it. After that, it's back to regular programming. No deviation, no special programming. Just the announcement, then business as usual."

Tom exhaled slowly, trying to process the directive. It felt jarring to shift from the weight of a historic moment to the light, upbeat tone of a CHR drive-time show. Then he remembered.

Pete Smith.

A CHR host on the Birmingham Manic feed, Midlands Manic.

Doing Goldies? Of all the things to make sense of today, this felt like the oddest. Pete Smith, one of the Drive hosts at the Dudley hub, a regional voice and not a national figure, now tasked with delivering the announcement across multiple stations. It seemed an unusual choice, but Tom couldn't deny that Pete had the gravitas required for a moment like this. Despite the strangeness of the situation, there was something comforting about the fact that Pete, a voice Tom trusted, would be delivering the news.

It was twenty past 3, and he knew that time was ticking away, bringing them closer to the national announcement at 6pm. Tom looked around the Huddersfield hub, where his team was busy coordinating with presenters and producers across the North East region. Normally, the CHR stations thrived on their upbeat energy, full of irreverence and cheeky banter. Today, however, the air was heavy, the usual laughter replaced by the low murmur of strained conversations.

Looking back at his time at Bauer, when he managed TFM, the Teesside station, and Metro Radio, both co-located at the Metro Radio studios in Newcastle, Tom couldn't help but reflect on the differences in approach. Back then, although they were part of the Hits Radio Network, local managers had some element of discretion when it came to if ever the Obit mode was enacted for smaller moments in the royal calendar. Prince Philip's death had seen TFM and Metro fall in line with the network's reflective programming seamlessly, the playlist adjusted to reflect the nation's sombre mood while still keeping a local flavour. This directive from Manic to ignore tradition felt almost rebellious, but it wasn't the good kind of rebellion. It was the kind that left people shaking their heads and questioning the leadership.

What made it worse was that, unlike the Hits Network, which used regional hubs for stations in a similar area, Manic had gone one step further and centralised operations to the point of absurdity. The Huddersfield hub was tasked with running everything for the North East, from Newcastle to Lincoln, a swath of stations so broad it made regional nuance nearly impossible. His counterpart in Dundee was in charge of the whole of Scotland, Exeter had control of the South West, Dudley had control of the entire ITV Central region, as well as Mid Wales, Cardiff covered the South Wales, Somerset, Gloucestershire, Herefordshire and Worcestershire areas, Stratford Olympic Park the South East, London and South Central regions, Manchester the Greater Manchester stations, as Manic and Hits Radio were locked in a fierce battle for dominance in the UK's CHR market, and finally Speke, the Network Centre and North West region hub, coordinated the overarching network directives while maintaining a tenuous connection to the localities it purported to serve. The centralisation, while cost-efficient, had eroded much of the regional identity that made radio a lifeline for communities.

Tom knew that he was no stranger to networked formats and corporate mandates, but today felt like an entirely different beast. The directive to maintain regular CHR programming, even in the face of national mourning, had placed him in an unenviable position—trying to balance the tone of stations that thrived on irreverence with the gravity of the moment.

The mess of Manic's current position being a merger of two entirely different broadcasting philosophies gnawed at Tom. The original Manic Radio ethos was about being scrappy, hyper-local, and unapologetically authentic, while the legacy Breeze Media half of the company leaned into slick professionalism, polished branding, and a near-obsessive focus on market research. The merger in 2019 and subsequent Lite Group acquisition had created an unwieldy hybrid that often felt like it was trying to be two things at once.

Huddersfield itself was a former Manic station, White Rose Vibes, itself a 2019 amalgamation of Wool City

Echo, White Rose Classics, Ridings Heritage FM, Colne Valley Vibes and Calder Gold, which had been implicated in a gender pay gap scandal during its ownership under the pre-Breeze era, had been designated a Lite hub, as Tees Retro Radio, which had become Manic Radio Teesside only 2 months earlier, Humber Echo FM, which had become Manic Radio East Yorkshire & North Lincolnshire, Fenland Echo, which had become Manic Radio Lincolnshire, Dales Vibes had become Manic Radio York & North Yorkshire, Tyne & Wear Tune, the competitor to Metro Radio in Newcastle, becoming Manic Radio North East and a mega merger of the South Yorkshire stations, Danum Beat, Rother Gold and Steel City FM to create Manic Radio South Yorkshire, had all fallen under its purview. The hub now controlled a patchwork of stations that had little in common except for their forced branding under the Manic banner. Tom often felt like he was overseeing a Frankenstein's monster of radio, pieced together from the remnants of what had once been thriving local stations with distinct identities.

As it was before 4pm, the schedule was that it was a network show, which, because Huddersfield and Exeter used Myriad, Speke, Dundee, and Cardiff using PlayoutONE and Dudley and Stratford using the RCS suite, meant that the technological inconsistencies between hubs added another layer of complication to an already fraught day. Tom sighed, watching the various screens in the control room display a patchwork of playlists, studio feeds, and network schedules. Each hub was tasked with syncing to Speke's directive, but the outdated and fragmented systems across the network made seamless coordination a challenge.

Then, after 4pm, Manic Radio North East, Manic Radio South Yorkshire, Manic Radio York & North Yorkshire and White Rose Vibes would switch to local drive presenters, each tasked with continuing their usual upbeat CHR programming while adhering to the strict directives from Speke, while Lincolnshire, as well as East Yorkshire, would remain with the standard network show that was slated, Danny O'Neil, a Speke based presenter who was known for his cheeky humour and ability to handle high-energy slots, even under challenging circumstances.

As all 4 stations were Huddersfield based, Tom knew that Then, after 4pm, Manic Radio North East, Manic Radio South Yorkshire, Manic Radio York & North Yorkshire and White Rose Vibes would switch to local drive presenters, each tasked with continuing their usual upbeat CHR programming while adhering to the strict directives from Speke, while Lincolnshire, as well as East Yorkshire, would remain with the standard network show that was slated, Danny O'Neil, a Speke based presenter who was known for his cheeky humour and ability to handle high-energy slots, even under challenging circumstances.

Unlike his colleagues, Tom preferred to keep up to date with each of his crews in person, something that had been an oddity, even at Bauer, where regional directors were often more hands-off, leaving the day-to-day interactions to station managers. In Huddersfield, though, Tom believed in face-to-face leadership, even if it meant crisscrossing the sprawling hub during moments of chaos like this.

He stepped out of his office, clipboard in hand, and made his way through the maze of studios and offices. The quiet hum of the hub felt different today, the usual buzz of upbeat radio personalities replaced by a subdued professionalism. As he walked, he passed the North East crew preparing for their local drive-time shift. Jess Taylor, the voice of Manic Radio North East's drive slot, was poring over her show notes, her usual cheeky grin replaced by a focused expression.

"Jess, we've got some changes to your show."

The 21 year old presenter looked up from her notes, her eyes narrowing slightly as she adjusted her headphones. "Changes? What's happened? Don't tell me there's been a major incident in Newcastle?"

Tom hesitated for a moment, choosing his words carefully. "Not exactly, Jess. It's... well, you've probably seen the news about the Queen. The announcement will come at 6pm, but until then, we're under strict instructions to keep things as normal as possible. That means your drive show goes ahead as planned, no reflective programming, no deviations from the usual tone. Just the announcement, and then back to CHR. Is your producer around?"

"No... he's... well... erm... fucking one of the runners," Jess said, frowning.

Tom knew that Zane Harris was a former Bee Manic breakfast producer who had come over with some of the Manic staff when the Lite-Manic acquisition took place, and there was rumours that the former Manic hubs had a habit of being hedonistic, a stark contrast to the more

48

polished professionalism of the former Lite Group stations who, despite being a network, had retained fully local programming during the daytime until July, when the merger happened and they took the Manic national feeds for mid-morning and early afternoon, with Tom having been responsible for enforcing the Day 1 Integration, despite being new at the time to Manic.

The cocaine habits that the Manic side brought from Speke and Manchester had also brought a level of chaos that the former Lite hubs were unaccustomed to. For someone like Tom, who prided himself on a balanced yet professional approach, managing a team with such contrasting work cultures was like walking a tightrope.

Tom took a deep breath. "Jess, you know the importance of this evening. I need you to focus, and if Zane isn't around, I'll get someone else to step in as your producer. You're the voice of Newcastle for the next few hours, and that means you need to keep the tone upbeat without being tone-deaf."

"I'll try, but... well, I'm having problems logging into Myriad. It's not matching what the running order and script from Speke says," Jess said, her frustration clear. "I tried calling IT, and instead of logging a ticket, they're trying to hook me up with their manky mates for a date. I'm engaged and yet they're trying to get me to go out with some bloke from Leeds who they say 'can fix any tech problem.' Honestly, Tom, this hub's like the bloody Wild West sometimes."

Tom rubbed his temples. The technological inconsistencies between hubs were frustrating enough, but the chaotic work culture left over from the Manic-Lite merger often compounded these issues. IT flirting with presenters instead of doing their jobs? Not ideal.

"Right," Tom said, his tone firm. "Leave the tech issue with me. I'll get someone from Speke to remote in and sort Myriad for you. You focus on prepping your links. Keep it light, keep it positive. Just stick to the running order as best you can. And if Zane doesn't show his face in five minutes, I'll find someone else."

Jess nodded, though her frown didn't entirely fade. "Got it, Tom. I'll do my best. But this whole 'business as usual' thing feels... weird. Oh, I forgot to mention... Samantha's on the warpath as Timmy tried to grope her."

Samantha Greene, a former Wool City host who had left in 2019 for Heart as a national host based in London, but had then returned two months earlier to helm the White Rose Vibes drive show as her father, Alan, had died during her time at Global, wanted to be closer to her family in Leeds. Samantha was known for her sharp tongue and zero tolerance for nonsense, so Tom wasn't surprised she'd already handled the situation. Still, he couldn't ignore the deeper issue of inappropriate behaviour festering in the hub.

"Right, Jess," Tom said, determined to deal with these layers of chaos. "You focus on your show. I'll have a word with Samantha and get this sorted. And I'll make sure HR deals with Timmy."

Tom left Jess to her preparations and headed down the corridor to find Samantha. She was leaning against the doorframe of the White Rose Vibes studio, arms crossed, her expression a storm cloud.

"Samantha, what's happened?" Tom asked, already bracing himself.

"That little git, Timmy, tried to grope me in the kitchen while I was grabbing a coffee," Samantha said, her voice sharp. "He's lucky I didn't slap him then and there. Instead, I told him to sod off, and now he's sulking in the lounge like a child. Honestly, Tom, this hub needs a bloody reality check."

Tom sighed. "You're right, and I'll handle it. Timmy's behaviour is unacceptable, and I'll make sure HR addresses it immediately. In the meantime, are you ready for your show? You know what's happening at six."

Samantha nodded. "Yeah, I heard. Just got off the phone with Tony at Speke. He's adamant about keeping things normal, but honestly, Tom, this whole 'no reflective programming' thing feels wrong. People are going to tune in expecting us to acknowledge what's happening, not just pretend it's another Thursday."

"I agree," Tom said, his voice low. "But this directive comes from the top. We have to follow it, at least for now. Just keep the tone light but not frivolous. No jokes about the situation, no speculation. We'll have to tread carefully."

Samantha frowned but nodded. "Alright. I'll stick to the script. But if one more idiot tries to grope me, I'm going straight to the police."

"You won't have to," Tom assured her. "I'll deal with Timmy personally and make sure this hub gets the professionalism it needs. Thanks for keeping it together, Samantha. I know it's not easy."

She gave a tight smile and returned to her studio, leaving Tom to handle the fallout. He made a mental note to call HR immediately after the announcement at six. For now, his priority was ensuring the Huddersfield hub stayed on track during this unprecedented evening.

As Tom moved through the hub, he couldn't help but feel the strain of the day pressing down on him. Between technical issues, cultural clashes, and the monumental news about to break, it was clear this day would go down as one of the most challenging in his career. Yet, amidst the chaos, he felt a deep sense of responsibility to his team, his stations, and the listeners who relied on them.

At 4 pm, the local drive shows began, and the Huddersfield hub hummed with activity. Tom paused outside the control room, listening as Jess Taylor kicked off her show with a cheerful energy that belied the tension in the air.

"Good afternoon, Newcastle! It's Jess Taylor here, bringing you all the hits to get you through your Thursday. Coming up, we've got brand-new music from Harry Styles, a throwback from Dua Lipa, and your chance to win tickets to see Ed Sheeran live. Stay tuned as we've got the latest headlines for all you Tynesiders with Josh Griffiths."

****

CHAPTER 5 - Over in Ulster
Thursday 8th September 2022

Weston O'Rourke was sitting in his flat in Belfast, his shift as a producer for Bauer Media's Cool FM, a station which was technically part of the Hits Radio Network, but had fully local programming, had ended a few hours earlier.

Working as part of the Breakfast team at the Ulster hub, Weston was accustomed to early starts and the relentless pace of live radio. By the afternoon, he usually relished the quiet of his small Belfast flat, sipping a mug of tea and catching up on the news. But today felt different. The updates about the Queen's health had cast a shadow over the usually lively streets of Belfast, and the city seemed to be holding its breath.

Being in his early 20s and a product of Bauer's training program, the Bauer Academy, Weston was no stranger to the intricate dance of local radio. Cool FM was a powerhouse in Northern Ireland, blending its local charm with the polished professionalism of the Hits Radio Network. Despite the station's pop-heavy playlist and cheerful vibe, today, the weight of history loomed large.

He had to chuckle, however, that, unlike Bauer who insisted on keeping their Northern Ireland stations on the Emerald Isle, Manic had moved their station, Ulster Vibes, to a hub in Liverpool, the complete opposite side of the Irish Sea. The decision still baffled him. How could a station claiming to represent Northern Ireland's unique voice operate from a city that, while vibrant in its own right, had no direct connection to Ulster's culture or community? It was one of the many quirks of corporate radio that Weston often found himself questioning.

He glanced at his phone, where notifications from his colleagues at Cool FM were lighting up. The group chat was buzzing with discussions about the protocol for handling the unfolding news. Bauer, like most major networks, had shifted into "Operation London Bridge," their detailed plan for broadcasting during a royal death. Cool FM would soon be moving into reflective programming, blending soft pop with tributes to Her Majesty—a far cry from their usual upbeat fare.

As a Catholic and a Unionist, a unicorn in Ireland because of the delicate balance of identity politics in the region, Weston often found himself navigating a unique space in Belfast. He knew that the Queen's passing would evoke a complex mix of emotions across Northern Ireland. For many Unionists, it would be a moment of profound sorrow and respect, while for some Republicans, it might be met with indifference or even quiet defiance. Weston respected both perspectives, understanding that the island's history was as layered and intricate as the patchwork of its radio landscape.

Peter O'Shea: *Wes, mate, guess what?*

Peter, Weston knew, was one of his friends from Ulster Vibes who had made the move from his native Belfast to Liverpool after Manic's controversial decision to base its Northern Ireland operations there. Seeing the WhatsApp chat pop up made Weston smile. Peter's messages always had a way of cutting through the noise, even on a day as heavy as this one.

Weston O'Rourke: *Let me guess, you're going Obit mode for Drive?*

Peter O'Shea: *Nope. Normal CHR all night, even Toni Green's show is fully CHR with no downers.*

Weston raised an eyebrow at Peter's reply. No downers? On a day like today? The absurdity of the situation hit him like a wave. While Bauer, Global, and almost every other major network in the UK and Ireland were carefully orchestrating sombre tributes and reflective programming, Manic Radio seemed determined to stick to its high-energy CHR formula, as if nothing monumental was unfolding.

Toni Green, Weston knew, was one of Manic's network hosts, their evening Queen who was as Mancunian as Hattie Pearson, as vibrant as Adele Roberts, and as sharp as Sara Cox. She was known for her quick wit and infectious energy, the kind of presenter who could light up a room—or a studio—with her charisma. But imagining her chirping away with the usual upbeat banter on a day like today felt almost surreal.

Weston O'Rourke: *Seriously? No shift in tone? No tributes?*

Peter O'Shea: *Nada. The memo says, "Keep the vibe alive." Corporate thinks the young listeners won't want a funeral on the airwaves. It's all about continuity, mate. And get this... Brum's Drive isn't even staying regional... they're taking Danny and the Network feed.*

Weston nearly choked on his tea. Taking Danny and the Network feed? That was a bold move, even for Manic.

Birmingham's drive-time show was usually local, like Cool FM's setup, catering to the unique personality of the Midlands. Yet now, they were opting for a networked show with Danny O'Neil, who usually did a network drive for Manic Radio's smaller markets, such as Londonderry, Dublin, the Wirral, Warwickshire and Kent, not big key markets like Birmingham. It was a puzzling decision, to say the least, but it seemed to be part of Manic's broader strategy of unifying their CHR programming, no matter how tone-deaf it might appear on a day like today.

Weston shook his head, baffled at the contrast between his own station's approach and Manic's. Bauer's Cool FM, firmly rooted in Northern Ireland, had always taken pride in being reflective of its audience's emotions. Even in the middle of the most upbeat pop tracks, there was a sense of connection, of knowing what the listeners needed at any given moment. And today, they needed something that matched the gravity of the day—something soothing, respectful, and unifying.

Weston O'Rourke: Mate, that's... bold. Reckon the listeners will notice?

Peter O'Shea: Oh, they'll notice, alright. Whether they care is another thing. The younger lot might just carry on like nothing's happened, but the older crowd? They'll be fuming. But hey, corporate knows best, right? And Goldies... its turning into News 24 Lite.

Weston chuckled dryly at Peter's last message. Goldies turning into News 24 Lite. That wasn't surprising. Manic Goldies, the group's nostalgia-driven station, would naturally bear the brunt of the day's historic weight. It was designed for an audience that likely felt a deep connection to the Queen, many of whom had grown up with her as a constant presence in their lives. But Peter's tone hinted at something more than just programming choices—it spoke to the absurdity of balancing corporate directives with real human sentiment.

Weston O'Rourke: *Who've they got for it?*

Peter O'Shea: *Pete Smith. Midlands guy, been around forever.*

Weston raised an eyebrow, a wry smile tugging at the corner of his lips. Pete Smith—of all people. A CHR presenter who'd spent decades cultivating an upbeat, affable persona, now tasked with delivering one of the most solemn announcements in modern British history. It wasn't that Pete wasn't capable; his professionalism was well-known. But the juxtaposition of his usual style with the gravity of the moment was enough to make even the most seasoned radio professional do a double-take.

Weston O'Rourke: *Pete Smith? Doing that? Well, I'll give it to them; it's not boring.*

Peter O'Shea: *Aye, it's a choice. To be fair, Pete's solid. And guess what our Protocol says for Goldies?*

Weston O'Rourke: *What's that?*

Peter O'Shea: *Rolling News only until after the funeral.*

Weston spat his drink out of his mug, laughing despite himself. Even Bauer wouldn't take Greatest Hits Radio off their classic hits playlist for rolling news only, he thought. It seemed Manic Goldies was leaning so far into the gravitas of the moment that it was practically becoming a news channel.

Weston O'Rourke: *Rolling news on Goldies? Isn't that the one place where you'd expect them to lean into nostalgic tributes instead of turning it into BBC Radio 5 Live? What about the music?*

Peter O'Shea: *Gone. All the classics pulled until after the funeral. They reckon it's 'what the audience expects'. Tune into the Manic Prime app and you'll hear Pete umming and erring, as if he were Huw Edwards trying to keep from spilling the news before the Palace releases the embargo.*

Weston looked at the clock and noticed that it was quarter to 4, and that the messages from his colleagues at Bauer had stated that Cool FM would begin its transition to reflective programming within the hour. While Weston's station was embracing the gravity of the moment, Manic's approach seemed like a surreal caricature of corporate radio priorities.

The stark contrast between the two networks' handling of the situation left Weston shaking his head. Bauer, with its localised and thoughtful programming, clearly understood the nuances of the Northern Irish audience. Meanwhile, Manic seemed to be following a "one size fits all" directive from Speke, which somehow managed to miss the mark in almost every possible way.

He looked back at his phone, scrolling through the group chat with his Cool FM colleagues:

Aoife O'Donnell: *Weston, you'll love this. Our playlist for the next hour is mostly stripped-back acoustic versions and ballads. Feels right, though, doesn't it?*

Weston O'Rourke: *Better than what the other lot are doing.*

His phone pinged with the same question from everyone at Cool FM, no matter if they were a Breakfast host, an Evening show host or even Evanna Maxted, the Saturday late host on Cool who had only recently joined the Bauer Media Audio team after graduating from Queen's University the previous year.

Evanna Maxted: *Go on, what have the Ulster Vibes lot got planned for their Belfast drive?*

Weston O'Rourke: *Nothing special. Business as usual. Not even a nod to the news until 6 pm, and after that? Back to CHR like nothing's happened. Its Richie and Alfie for their usual Belfast show, and Derry and Dublin get the general network*

Evanna Maxted: *"Seriously? Richie and Alfie, doing their usual banter? Can you imagine them trying to steer around the news? Bet they'll go off-script the first chance they get."*

Weston O'Rourke: *"Wouldn't surprise me. Richie's not exactly one for following orders, is he? And Alfie... well, let's just hope he remembers to turn his mic off before cracking one of his 'edgy' jokes."*

Aoife O'Donnell: *"Meanwhile, here at Cool, we've got Louise on Drive. She's starting with 'Fix You' by*

Coldplay and transitioning into 'Run' by Snow Patrol. Reflective, respectful... and very Northern Irish. Exactly what people need today."

Weston O'Rourke: *"Yeah, well, Manic doesn't do nuance. If it's not in the directive from Speke, it's not happening. And the weird thing? Their audience is going to notice."*

Weston leaned back in his chair, letting his colleagues' messages wash over him. Cool FM's thoughtful approach to programming wasn't just about following corporate guidelines—it was about understanding the pulse of their listeners. Northern Ireland was a place where history and identity ran deep, and radio stations like Cool played a pivotal role in reflecting that.

He thought about Richie and Alfie, the Ulster Vibes drive duo. They were good lads, in their way—energetic, cheeky, and quick with a joke. But today wasn't a day for their usual banter about Belfast traffic or the latest TikTok trends. Weston couldn't help but wonder how they'd navigate the announcement at 6 pm. Would they rise to the occasion, or would their natural irreverence get the better of them?

The irony wasn't lost on him that Cool FM, part of Bauer's Hits Radio Network, had somehow managed to retain its local identity, while Manic's Ulster Vibes, ostensibly a station for Northern Ireland, felt like it was broadcasting from another planet. The decision to base its operations in Liverpool had been controversial from the start, and today, it felt more disconnected than ever.

Aoife O'Donnell: *So, Dublin Vibes and Western Ulster Vibes get the Manic network feed, but Richie and Alfie are doing Belfast? How does that even work? Surely, they should all be local today?*

Weston O'Rourke: *It's Manic, Aoife. Logic doesn't apply. Dublin and Derry get the same network as Hull and Warwickshire, while Belfast gets the local lads. It's chaos disguised as a plan. And you wanna know the best bit... Birmingham gets a network show today.*

Weston shook his head, scrolling through the stream of incredulous messages from his Cool FM colleagues. The surreal patchwork of Manic's approach seemed to get more ridiculous with each revelation.

Evanna Maxted: *Wait, Birmingham—one of the UK's biggest cities—is getting the network feed? I thought they'd at least keep it regional for a day like today! Our Mike and Gemma will demolish the network ratings if that's the case.*

Weston knew that Bauer's Mike Toolan and Gemma Atkinson, the Hits Network drive duo based in Manchester, had a loyal following and an uncanny ability to strike the perfect tone, even in challenging times. Compared to the Manic network feed, which was probably packed with generic pop tracks and chirpy chatter, Mike and Gemma's reflective yet warm approach would resonate far better with listeners.

Aoife O'Donnell: *Honestly, it's almost funny if it weren't so tragic. Birmingham gets the network while Richie and Alfie wing it in Belfast. Who's making these decisions?*

Weston O'Rourke: *Some execs in Speke with a spreadsheet, probably. I bet they think the Queen's passing doesn't resonate with CHR audiences, but they're in for a shock According to a mate at Manic, the Brum drive host is helming Manic Goldies and doing their network announcement of the Queen's passing.*

In contrast, Manic's insistence on keeping CHR upbeat felt disconnected, almost disrespectful. Weston knew the younger listeners would likely appreciate the escapism, but he also knew many would find the lack of acknowledgment jarring.

He glanced at the clock. It was 4 pm. Cool FM's drive-time show had just begun, but Weston really wanted to hear the dumpster fire that was Manic's Ulster Vibes. Picking up his phone, he opened the Manic Prime app, selected Ulster Vibes, and pressed play. The station's usual jingles—bright, punchy, and unmistakably CHR—filled the room, followed by the upbeat tones of Richie O'Connor.

"Good afternoon, Belfast! It's Richie and Alfie here, bringing you all the biggest hits to get you through your Thursday. We've got some cracking tracks lined up, and later, we'll be chatting about the weirdest excuses people have given for missing work—trust me, you don't want to miss this!"

"Yes, we've got the biggest hits and some smashing throwbacks, but first, it's the news with Sean Peterson," Alfie's voice picked up seamlessly, his cheerful tone at odds with the weight of the day. The usual upbeat news jingle played, and Weston braced himself for how the bulletin would navigate the tightrope of acknowledging the Queen's condition without stepping on the embargoed announcement.

Sean Peterson, Ulster Vibes' newsreader, came on air with a measured tone that contrasted sharply with Richie and Alfie's buoyant delivery.

"This is Sean Peterson with the latest news. Buckingham Palace has released a statement expressing concern for Her Majesty the Queen's health. Members of the Royal Family are currently at Balmoral. Manic Radio's Scottish correspondent, Angus McKinley is at Balmoral, Angus, what's the latest?"

"Thank you, Sean. Here at Balmoral, there's a sense of quiet anticipation as members of the public and press gather near the gates. We've seen several senior members of the Royal Family arriving throughout the day, which has added to speculation regarding the Queen's condition. While official details remain sparse, it's clear this is a significant moment, and the atmosphere here reflects that. Sources close to ITN... I mean, Manic Radio, state that the Queen is under medical supervision, and all updates will come directly from Buckingham Palace. Back to you, Sean."

Weston picked up on the slip, of Angus referring to the sources as being "close to ITN," rather than Manic Radio, and chuckled, as it was obvious that, unlike Bauer and Global, who used Sky News Radio for their network of bulletins, Manic's reliance on ITN for news production was showing cracks in coordination and tone.

Sean Peterson resumed, clearly aware of the fine line he had to tread. "Thank you, Angus. We'll bring you more updates as we receive them. In other news, Belfast City Council officials have announced plans for a major redevelopment project in the Cathedral Quarter, aiming to boost tourism and local businesses. The project, expected to begin early next year, has already sparked a lively debate among residents and business owners. More details on our website."

Sean's voice faded, and the station's jingles returned, leading seamlessly back into Richie and Alfie's banter.

"Thanks, Sean," Richie said, his tone as cheerful as ever. "Right, Alfie, let's talk about these work excuses. Did you know someone once claimed they couldn't come in because their cat 'refused to get off their lap'? I mean, honestly, who's running the show in that house?"

Alfie laughed. "Sounds like my kind of pet. Anyway, let us know what your work excuses are, our WhatsApp is 028 9649 6010, drop us a voice note or a text, and we might just play it on air!"

Weston winced. The shift in tone from a historic moment to light-hearted banter about work excuses was jarring, to say the least. It wasn't Richie and Alfie's fault—they were just following the directives from Speke—but the disconnect between the gravity of the situation and their usual CHR programming was glaring.

The segue into a dance anthem, Destination Calabria by Alex Gaudino, only heightened the surreal contrast. Weston shook his head, muttering to himself, "Business as usual, huh? Sure, feels like it."

The Ulster Vibes broadcast rolled on, an odd juxtaposition of national anticipation and corporate obliviousness. Richie and Alfie carried on their usual banter, occasionally dropping hints that "something big" was happening but never fully addressing it. Meanwhile, the upbeat hits continued, as if the world outside wasn't holding its breath.

As the saxophone based groove of Destination Calabria played on, Weston couldn't help but feel a deep sense of dissonance. The upbeat track was infectious, yes, but it felt tone-deaf in the face of what was unfolding. He leaned back in his chair, the sound of Richie and Alfie's banter washing over him like white noise, disconnected from the reality outside his flat.

Weston glanced back at the Cool FM stream. Louise Harper's voice came through, warm and soothing, perfectly matching the tone of her show.

"That was Fix You by Coldplay, a song that reminds us of resilience and unity. Stay with us for the latest updates as we navigate this historic moment together."

****

CHAPTER 6 - Legal Eagle
Thursday 8th September 2022

James Jenkins was sat at the headquarters of Global Media, a towering modern building in Leicester Square that exuded the polished professionalism of one of the UK's biggest broadcasters.

Unlike his first foray into radio as part of Brookes Vibes, acting as a runner, then the sole 'Vibes Hunk' during his Oxford University days, James was now a corporate lawyer specialising in media and broadcasting law. His career had brought him full circle, from the chaos of student radio to the polished corridors of the country's most influential media company. But today, his usual calm confidence was tinged with unease. The news about the Queen's health had cast a shadow over the building, and the hum of Global's operations was unusually subdued.

Seeing the name on his phone, he saw that it was his wife, Carly, a former Brookes Babe who, like him, had been part of the infamous Brookes Vibes street team during their Oxford University days. Carly had joined Emap after University, as a HR assistant and, now, was a speaker on Women's Rights following the pay gap scandal at Wool City Echo, having assisted Samantha Greene and her female colleagues there in their struggle against a deeply ingrained culture of inequality. Carly had transitioned into a role as a consultant on diversity and inclusion, working with media companies across the UK, including Global. Her sharp wit and fierce dedication to her principles had made her a formidable advocate for change.

James answered the call, his tone softening as he greeted her. "Hi, love. How's the day going?"

"Tiring. I've been working with News UK and their radio team all morning, delivering a session on diversity and inclusion. For a Murdoch-owned company, they're surprisingly receptive—well, at least on the surface. How about you? I imagine Global must be in overdrive today."

James leaned back in his chair, glancing out of his office window at the bustling Leicester Square below. "You could say that. They're preparing to activate Operation London Bridge. Every station's been briefed, from Capital to LBC. The lawyers are just making sure all the compliance angles are covered. It's all very... clinical. But I can't help feeling a bit removed from it all."

"Wait... Operation London Bridge? The Queen's not...?" Carly's voice softened, her usual sharpness replaced by a tentative unease.

James shook his head, though he knew she couldn't see him. "Not yet, but the Palace has issued a statement about her health. Everyone here is working under the assumption that it's imminent. Global's preparing for the announcement at 6 pm, but the embargo means we're all in a holding pattern until then. I've just had to review the legal framework for the embargo and ensure that none of our stations jump the gun. If anything leaks early, it could be a PR disaster—and worse, a breach of trust with the Palace. I mean, remember two years ago when Prince Phillip passed away, and the BBC got skewered for their handling of the initial announcement? No one here wants a repeat of that."

Carly sighed on the other end of the line. "That's a lot of pressure, even for a company as seasoned as Global. How are the presenters handling it? I can't imagine someone like Roman Kemp switching effortlessly from his usual Capital banter to a moment of national mourning."

James chuckled softly, though it lacked his usual warmth. "It's going to be a challenge for everyone. Roman and the Capital lot will hand over to news coverage as soon as the announcement breaks. LBC will go wall-to-wall with analysis, and Classic FM's already queued up a playlist of reflective music. It's the smaller stations I'm worried about—Heart 80s, Smooth Chill—they've got automation running most of the time. One wrong cue, and we've got Wake Me Up Before You Go-Go playing right after the announcement. Remember how Brookes Vibes got blasted about their 7/7 coverage? We were in our final year, and we'd been dating over a year and half, and were heading to lectures, you your sociology and me my law tutorials, when we heard the news?"

"Oh, yeah, Mark had graduated from being an electrician to being a cover host, and he'd been on the Breakfast show when the news broke. Instead of handling it with any sense of decorum, he played Don't Stop Me Now by Queen immediately after the bulletin. The complaints flooded in before the track even finished. That poor guy— he meant well, but it was a disaster." Carly's voice softened with nostalgia, tinged with the memory of those chaotic student days. "You know, he and Clarissa are planning to invite us over to Oxford for the weekend, if we're not busy."

James smiled, appreciating Carly's light-hearted attempt to lift the mood. "Ah, Clarissa and Mark—the Brookes Vibes legends. I wonder if they still argue over whose idea it was to run the mud wrestling promotion in Freshers' Week. But yeah, let's hope things don't go down like that today. Global's processes are robust, but even the best systems can falter when the stakes are this high. Speaking of which, I'll probably be tied up here late tonight. Ashley's called a late all-hands meeting."

James knew that his ultimate boss, Ashley Tabor-King, the Executive President of Global, would be on high alert today, monitoring every facet of the company's response. Ashley was known for his meticulous approach to crisis management, and James could already imagine the intensity of the meeting: protocols reviewed, contingencies discussed, every department tasked with ensuring that Global's output was seamless and respectful.

"Late-night meeting with Ashley?" Carly's tone was a mix of amusement and sympathy. "That sounds... intense. Make sure you grab some dinner beforehand. You know what he's like—once he starts talking about brand alignment and 'keeping Global's edge,' you won't escape for hours."

James laughed softly. "I'll try to sneak a sandwich beforehand. But honestly, I don't blame him. This is the kind of moment that defines a company like Global. If we handle it well, we reinforce our reputation as the gold standard in British broadcasting. If we mess it up, we'll be the subject of tomorrow's headlines for all the wrong reasons. And with the BBC on their A-game, the margin for error is zero."

Suddenly James's phone went off, a text from a friend who worked in the Legal Department at Manic, and he read the message with curiosity. It was from Daniel, a university friend who had ended up at the legal team in Manic Radio after a few years of corporate law.

Daniel: *Mate, you'll never believe the circus over here at Manic. Speke's got everyone running around like headless chickens. Word is they're making the CHR lot stick to their usual bangers right after the announcement. Absolute madness. Also, heard Pete Smith's doing the announcement. Pete. Smith. Thoughts?*

"Hey, Carly, just had a text of Daniel, you know, my mate who was at Oxford with us, one of the Balliol lot. Guess how Manic are treating London Bridge?"

James heard Carly chuckle from the other end of the line. "Oh, I can only imagine. Let me guess—something completely tone-deaf and chaotic? They've got a reputation for making even the simplest things absurdly complicated."

James smirked. "Bingo. According to Daniel, Speke's decided that the CHR stations are to stick to their usual playlists, even right after the announcement. Imagine Dua Lipa's Don't Start Now blasting out minutes after Pete Smith breaks the news."

"Pete Smith, isn't he that grumpy old-school presenter who Manic employ in Birmingham. I think I met him when they employed me to do a DEI workshop last year and he said that corporate radio was the death of creativity and local authenticity?" Carly finished James's thought with a knowing laugh. "Yes, I remember him. Grumpy or not, he's solid behind a mic. But putting him in charge of the announcement for the whole network? That's a choice. Do they think his Midlands accent is going to magically unify the nation?"

James chuckled, though the absurdity of it all wasn't lost on him. "It's so Manic, isn't it? They probably think having someone 'authentic' will soften the blow of sticking to their regular programming. But honestly, they're setting themselves up for backlash. The Queen's passing isn't just news—it's a seismic cultural moment. People don't want Dua Lipa or Harry Styles immediately after hearing about it. They want dignity, reflection, connection."

Carly sighed, her tone shifting to something more contemplative. "It's a missed opportunity for them to show they can handle a moment like this with the seriousness it deserves. And it's not just about listeners— it's about their people, too. How's Pete supposed to deliver the announcement and then pivot back to his usual style? It's not fair on him, either."

"I'll text Daniel, see what he has to say about the pivoting. You know his wife used to work here... Pete's that is, not Dan's?" James said, chuckling. "She used to work with Nigel Freshman over at Brindleyplace on Smooth Breakfast for the Midlands."

James quickly typed out a reply to Daniel, his amusement tinged with disbelief.

James: *Pete Smith? Doing the announcement? That's bold even for Manic. How on earth is he supposed to go from delivering that news to pivoting back to CHR banter? Also, aren't the listeners going to freak out when they hear Dua Lipa or Calvin Harris right after? Feels like they're setting themselves up for a disaster.*

As he sent the text, Carly spoke again, her voice thoughtful. "You know, it's moments like this that really expose the difference between broadcasters. Global, Bauer, even the BBC—they've all got their flaws, but they understand how to handle a moment of national significance. Manic's approach sounds like a car crash waiting to happen."

James nodded, though Carly couldn't see him. "It's not just the listeners who'll notice. The Palace will be paying attention to how the media handles this. If they feel that any network is treating the announcement without the proper gravitas, there could be repercussions—not legal, of course, but reputational. And for a network like Manic, which is already teetering on the edge of credibility, this could be a defining moment."

Daniel: *He's staying on Goldies for his shift, doing rolling news until 7 and then handing over to the regular shift for the 7-10 slot, which'll be more rolling news. We've got, and you'll love this, Danny O'Neil... hang on, there might be a change.*

A few minutes later, Daniel sent another message which made James laugh.

Daniel: *Right, it seems that Midlands Manic's drive won't be networked instead of Pete's show... one of the Manc lot* *is going to be presenting remotely from Piccadilly Gardens for the Brum show. Hallie Young, one of the former Breakfast lot for Brum is doing the Midlands Manic drive show now.*

James shook his head in disbelief as he read Daniel's messages. He knew from his counterparts at Communicorp, the franchisee who ran XS Manchester and Smooth North West on behalf of Global due to Ofcom regulations, that Hallie was one of Bee Manic's drive presenters alongside a former Capital presenter, JJ Dennison, who had joined when Manic had brought the Lite Group network's Manchester and Cheshire stations under the Manic banner. Hallie was known for her polished delivery and vibrant energy, but the idea of a former Bee Manic presenter handling a moment of such gravity was another level of surreal.

"Well, love, do you want a laugh or what?"

Carly's chuckle crackled down the line. "Always. What now? Did Manic decide to follow the announcement with a game of Guess the Banger?"

James smirked, shaking his head. "Not quite, but close. So, Pete Smith's doing the announcement on Goldies, right? Well, he's being covered by a presenter on Midlands Manic by... a Manchester presenter."

James smirked, shaking his head. "Not quite, but close. So, Pete Smith's doing the announcement on Goldies, right? Well, he's being covered by a presenter on Midlands Manic by... a Manchester presenter. She's the Brummie girl who used to do the Midlands breakfast and moved up there when Toni Green got the network evening show. Hallie Young. She's apparently doing Midlands Manic's drive show today, broadcasting remotely from Manchester. You know, if we tried that at Global, we'd have OFCOM knocking on our door, as Manic's big city stations are required to do 7 hours of in-Approved Area, whereas we've got it at the legal minimum of 3 hours local and the rest networked, but within Ofcom guidelines. Honestly, Manic's compliance team must be having kittens trying to justify all these odd workarounds."

Carly laughed, the kind of laugh that spoke of both disbelief and amusement. "Let me get this straight. They've got someone presenting Birmingham's drive show from Manchester on the day the Queen's passing is expected to be announced? That's some next-level corporate gymnastics. Imagine how that's going to go down with listeners. 'Oh, by the way, your local Brummie show is coming live from a completely different city.' How do they even sell that?"

James leaned back in his chair, the absurdity of the situation sinking in. "I doubt they'll mention it at all. They'll probably just plaster Hallie's face on the website with 'Birmingham's Favourite Presenter' in big letters and hope no one notices she's not actually in the city. But honestly, it's this patchwork approach that shows how out of touch they are. They're trying to centralise while pretending to stay local, and it's a mess."

Carly sighed, her tone softening. "It's sad, really. There was a time when radio meant something—when it was about community and connection. Now it's all spreadsheets and metrics. Even Global, for all its polish, isn't immune to that. But at least they know how to rise to the occasion when it counts."

James nodded, his thoughts returning to the weight of the day. "Yeah, this isn't just any day. The Queen's passing isn't just news—it's history. It's the kind of moment people will remember for the rest of their lives, and how broadcasters handle it will stick with them. For some, it'll be a comforting voice on Classic FM, or a thoughtful discussion on LBC. For others, it'll be Dua Lipa on loop while they wonder if the station even cares."

Suddenly there was a knock on the door, and Ashley Tabor-King, the Executive President of Global, stepped into James's office. Ashley was impeccably dressed as always, exuding the air of authority that came with leading one of the UK's most powerful media companies. His expression was focused, but there was an underlying tension in his movements.

"James," Ashley began, his voice low but steady, "I need you in the boardroom. We've got about 90 minutes before the embargo lifts, and I want all departments aligned. This is one of the most significant broadcasts we'll ever handle, and it has to be flawless."

James nodded, quickly ending his call with Carly. "Understood, Ashley. I'll be there in a minute."

Ashley lingered for a moment, his sharp eyes taking in the room. "You've been reviewing the legal frameworks, yes? Are we watertight on the embargo compliance? I don't want a single station jumping the gun."

"We're solid," James assured him. "I've double-checked every directive to ensure the stations adhere to the timeline. I've got a call back waiting from the Communicorp compliance team to confirm everything is aligned with their simulcasts on the franchised side. They've confirmed Smooth is taking the network feed as normal, and their local Heart and Capital stations, as well as XS Manchester, are awaiting confirmation from their local teams."

Ashley gave a curt nod, satisfied with James's response. "Good. Communicorp's simulcast alignment is crucial. The last thing we need is a rogue station breaking the embargo and dragging us into a scandal."

James stood, gathering his notes and slipping them into a sleek folder. "I'll update the board on everything, including Communicorp's compliance. We're leaving nothing to chance."

As he followed Ashley out of his office and into the corridors of Global's Leicester Square headquarters, James felt a renewed sense of purpose. The hum of activity around them had reached a crescendo, with staff from every department moving with the urgency and precision of a well-oiled machine. It was a stark contrast to the chaotic picture Daniel had painted of Manic's operations.

"Oh, by the way, OFCOM sent another email this morning about Nick and his show on LBC," James said as they passed the news team preparing the 4pm news. Ashley's brow furrowed slightly, his focus momentarily shifting from the impending announcement to James's comment.

"What now?" Ashley asked, his tone calm but with a sharp edge that signalled he wasn't in the mood for distractions.

James adjusted his pace, falling in step with Ashley as they made their way to the boardroom. "It's about some of the calls Nick Ferrari took on Breakfast the other week. They've had 3 complaints, but I've listened to the audio of the show and had a chat with his producer."

"Great, let me guess, one of the callers decided to be wildly inappropriate, and Nick handled it in his usual blunt style?" Ashley finished, his tone dry with a hint of amusement.

"Nope, it's the guest he had in the second hour—Boris Johnson," James said, sighing.

"Great," Ashley shook his head, a wry smile flickering across his face as they reached the boardroom doors. "Let me guess, Boris managed to stir up enough trouble to keep OFCOM busy for a month. What was it this time? A joke gone wrong? Or did he decide to wax lyrical about Partygate during breakfast radio?"

James opened his folder, extracting a neatly printed sheet of notes. "A bit of both, actually. He made a quip about 'surviving more crises than the BBC,' and followed it up with a rather clumsy analogy comparing himself to Churchill. OFCOM received complaints claiming the segment lacked impartiality. Nick, to his credit, pushed back and steered the conversation back on track, but it's caused a minor stir. I asked Nick what he thought, and he said Boris was just being Boris, but he reckons the listeners took it the wrong way because of the timing. The

Ofcom complaint is mostly procedural; it doesn't look like anything that will escalate further. Still, I'll have a formal report drafted before the end of the day to keep everything above board."

Ashley nodded, his expression a mix of mild irritation and amusement. "It's typical Boris. He has this knack for walking into trouble and dragging everyone else with him. Make sure the report's airtight; we can't have Ofcom breathing down our necks with everything else going on today."

As they entered the boardroom, James was greeted by the sight of Global's senior leadership team gathered around the long, polished table. The room was alive with the hum of quiet discussions and the shuffle of papers, every person present acutely aware of the historic moment they were preparing to broadcast.

Ashley took his place at the head of the table, commanding the room's attention with a glance. "Right, everyone, we've got less than ninety minutes before the embargo lifts. I want a final check-in from each department. Programming, legal, news—let's ensure we're all aligned."

****

CHAPTER 7 - Penny
Thursday 8th September 2022

Penny Carmichael, like her friends, were sat in the training room of one of Bauer's many Bauer Academy locations across the UK, this one nestled in Manchester's bustling MediaCityUK. Penny was a hopeful young presenter who had grew up on the Wirral listening to Radio City, Bauer's flagship station for Liverpool and the surrounding areas and Cheshire & The Wirral Vibes, Manic's local station for the western side of the River Mersey.

Her love for radio had blossomed in this rich cultural tapestry, with the contrast between Bauer's polished professionalism and Manic's chaotic charm offering her two distinct visions of what radio could be. Now, as a trainee in Bauer's Academy, she was on the cusp of joining the industry she had adored since childhood.

Having sat through a training session earlier that day that had been led by Wes Butters, one of Bauer's most seasoned presenters, Penny found herself inspired by his anecdotes about how things go wrong on live radio, and how to remain calm under pressure.

The 19 year old knew that she was on a two year program, with the first year studying how Bauer worked, then a year placement as a cover presenter on one of Bauer's many stations. Her dream was to land a role at Radio City or at the main Hits Radio in Manchester or working on one of their digital brands like Absolute, Kiss or Magic. But for now, she was focused on soaking up every ounce of wisdom she could from the seasoned professionals around her. The training day was winding down when Penny noticed a distinct shift in the atmosphere. The trainers, usually bustling with energy, were exchanging hushed words by the doorway, their expressions sombre.

Her fellow trainees began whispering among themselves, speculating on what might be happening. Penny leaned over to her closest friend in the programme, Alex, a 21-year-old from Hagley who had dreams of joining Free Radio.

"Do you think it's something serious?" Penny asked, her voice low.

Alex shrugged, but his brow was furrowed. "Could be. Wes looked pretty rattled when he left earlier. I overheard one of the staff saying something about 'Operation London Bridge.' Doesn't that have to do with the Queen?"

Penny's stomach tightened. The idea that the Queen's health might be at the centre of all this suddenly made the tension in the room feel heavier. She glanced at her phone, but there was nothing new on social media apart from the earlier statement from Buckingham Palace expressing concern for Her Majesty's health.

Before anyone could speculate further, a senior trainer, Clara Morris, entered the room. Clara was known for her no-nonsense demeanour, but today her usual briskness was tempered with a softness that immediately drew everyone's attention.

"Right, everyone," Clara began, her voice steady but solemn, "we've just had confirmation that Bauer is moving into Obit mode across all stations. As you've probably guessed, this is in response to concerns about the Queen's health. While no official announcement has been made, we're working under the assumption that significant news may break in the next few hours. For now, we're asking all trainees to stay in this room until further notice. This is an important moment for the industry, and we need to ensure everything runs smoothly."

The room fell silent, the weight of Clara's words settling over the trainees like a heavy blanket. Penny felt her heart race. This was the kind of moment they'd been taught about in abstract terms—how radio reacts during national emergencies, the protocols for sombre occasions—but experiencing it in real time was entirely different. The magnitude of the situation wasn't lost on her; the Queen had been a constant presence her entire life, a symbol of stability and tradition.

Clara continued, her tone calm but firm. "For those of you who haven't yet encountered Obit mode, this means every station in the Bauer portfolio will shift to reflective programming. Local presenters will deliver the news with sensitivity, and our playlists will feature appropriate music—think Adele, Coldplay, and other reflective artists. From Hits Radio to Greatest Hits Radio, to Absolute and Magic, all brands are aligned. This is one of those rare moments where every decision we make, every word we broadcast, truly matters. Now, for those of you who are planning on joining regional or national Sales teams, this is what we call Hell for you, as there is little to no adverts allowed during Obit mode. Advertising breaks will be replaced with extended news coverage and music chosen for its reflective tone. This decision isn't about revenue—it's about respect, dignity, and serving our listeners."

Penny noticed a few trainees exchange wide-eyed glances. The idea of cancelling ads—an essential revenue stream for any commercial radio station—underscored the gravity of the situation.

"Now, usually, all of the networks, the BBC, Bauer, Global and Manic, opt to do similar programming during a national event of this scale," Clara continued, her gaze scanning the room, "but there are always exceptions. We've heard that Manic has decided not to follow the traditional approach for their CHR stations. They're keeping upbeat playlists and only airing the announcement when it breaks, then going straight back to regular programming."

The outbreak of laughter, Penny herself included, over what Clara just described as "Manic's approach" was a welcome break in the tension, though it quickly gave way to incredulous murmurs. Penny couldn't help but chuckle at the absurdity of the situation. The idea of upbeat CHR playlists blasting Dua Lipa or Calvin Harris immediately after a historic announcement was almost too much to process.

Alex leaned over to Penny, shaking his head in disbelief. "I mean, can you imagine? 'The Queen has passed, now here's Levitating!' Manic's branding really is chaos incarnate."

Penny stifled a giggle, whispering back, "It's so tone-deaf, it's almost impressive. They've made a brand out of being the class clown of radio."

Clara raised an eyebrow at the ripple of laughter but allowed it to pass, recognising the need for a brief release of tension. "Yes, Manic's decision is... unconventional. But it serves as a reminder of why we at Bauer take these moments so seriously. This is about trust, about being the steady voice our listeners need during uncertain times. That's why we're here, why we train you the way we do. Because when the world stops, radio keeps going. Now, there was a reason Wes has been here today, and it's not just to give you anecdotes. Since half twelve, three hours ago, we've been prepared just in case Obit mode was needed. Obviously, you can all assume what will happen with Cash Register."

The mention of Cash Register, Bauer's popular on-air competition, drew a fresh wave of murmurs from the trainees. It was a staple of many stations, a high-energy segment that brought a sense of excitement and anticipation to the day. Penny knew that pulling it, even temporarily, would be a significant departure from the usual programming.

Clara continued, addressing the unspoken questions in the room. "Yes, Cash Register has been suspended across all relevant stations. Competitions like this, which rely on upbeat and high-energy interaction, are entirely inappropriate during Obit mode. Instead, airtime will be dedicated to reflective programming and extended news coverage. It's a decision that wasn't made lightly, but it's the right one."

Penny raised her hand tentatively, catching Clara's attention. "Clara, do we know if presenters will be addressing listener reactions? I imagine people will be texting and calling in with all sorts of emotions."

Clara nodded, her expression softening. "That's an excellent point, Penny. Yes, presenters will be trained to handle listener interactions with sensitivity. On-air calls and texts will be screened carefully, and any listener comments that reflect the gravity of the situation will be included where appropriate. We're not just broadcasting to inform; we're here to provide comfort and connection."

Penny nodded, feeling a sense of pride in the thoughtfulness of Bauer's approach. It was moments like these that reminded her why she wanted to work in radio—to be part of a medium that could adapt, respond, and connect with people on such a profound level.

Clara paused, letting the room absorb the information before speaking again. "For now, I encourage you all to observe how this unfolds. Listen to how different stations approach the transition, how they strike the balance between being reflective and being relevant. These are the moments that will shape your understanding of what it means to be in this industry."

As Clara stepped aside to answer a trainer's question, Penny leaned back in her chair, her mind racing with thoughts. She felt a sense of awe at the responsibility that lay ahead for the industry, a responsibility she would one day share. But there was also a sense of unease—how could a station like Manic justify its decision to stick to regular programming during a moment of national mourning?

Alex nudged her gently, pulling her from her thoughts. "You know," he said, his voice low, "this is the kind of day that'll stick with us forever. Years from now, we'll be telling people where we were when the Queen passed, and for us, it'll be here, in training, watching it all unfold."

Alex nudged her gently, pulling her from her thoughts. "You know," he said, his voice low, "this is the kind of day that'll stick with us forever. Years from now, we'll be telling people where we were when the Queen passed, and for us, it'll be here, in training, watching it all unfold. I'm going to have a look on Digital Spy, see what the gossip columns in the Forum sections say. You know, there's a load of insiders not just from Bauer but from Global, Communicorp, BBC, and even Manic who spill the beans there. I bet it's already buzzing with speculation about how everyone's handling today."

Penny smiled, appreciating Alex's knack for finding levity even in tense situations. "You do that, Alex. Just don't get too caught up in the drama—Clara will have your head if she catches you on forums instead of paying attention."

Alex grinned, his phone already in hand. "Noted. But if I find out anything juicy about Manic's chaos, you'll be the first to know."

Penny shook her head, stifling a laugh as she turned her focus back to Clara, who was now deep in discussion with one of the trainers. She glanced at the clock on the wall. It was just after 4 pm. The next few hours would undoubtedly be some of the most significant in British broadcasting history, and she was grateful to be witnessing it from the inside.

As the trainees settled back into quiet chatter, Penny couldn't help but feel a swell of anticipation. This was the kind of day she had dreamt about when she first applied to Bauer Academy—not the sombre nature of it, of course, but the chance to be part of something bigger. To see the industry she loved rise to the occasion, to learn from the best, and to one day be one of those trusted voices on the airwaves.

Suddenly Alex chuckled. "Penny, looks like Nation have dropped a clanger."

Penny turned to Alex, raising an eyebrow. "Oh no, what now?"

Alex grinned, holding up his phone. "Look at this post."

Steepdrop: *Nation Stations after news played Heaven Is A Place on Earth and Easy played Heaven Must Be Missing An Angel presumably not having altered the playlists.*

Penny shook her head, trying not to laugh as Alex showed her the post on Digital Spy. It was too absurd to be true—two Nation Radio stations inadvertently playing "heaven" songs right after the sombre news bulletin.

"Nation really living up to its reputation, huh?" Penny said, stifling a giggle.

Alex grinned. "I mean, how do you not double-check your playlist on a day like today? It's like they had one job."

Their quiet laughter drew a glance from Clara, who quickly returned her focus to her discussion with another trainer. Penny leaned in closer to Alex, lowering her voice as she saw it was nearing ten past 4.

"Okay, but what about the gossip from Manic? Anything about how they're planning to handle this disaster they're calling a strategy?"

Alex scrolled through the forum, his expression a mix of amusement and disbelief. "Oh, you're going to love this. Apparently Manic Rock just played... God Save The Queen.

Penny nearly choked on her water. "Wait. The Sex Pistols? You're joking, right?"

Alex grinned, holding up his phone as if it were a prized relic. "Nope. Someone on the forum says they caught it live. A rogue presenter apparently thought it'd be 'ironic' to play it. Management scrambled to cut it off mid-track, but not before Johnny Rotten's voice declared, 'God save the Queen, the fascist regime!' Absolute chaos."

Penny shook her head in disbelief, torn between laughter and horror. "Manic Rock really knows how to live up to its name. Can you imagine the calls they're getting right now? Ofcom's probably already drafting their complaint letter."

Alex smirked. "Apparently, it wasn't even intentional. A producer claims the presenter loaded the track as a placeholder during the Queen's health updates and forgot to take it out before hitting play. Honest mistake or sabotage? You decide."

Penny leaned back in her chair, shaking her head. "If nothing else, Manic will make sure this day goes down in radio history—for all the wrong reasons. Meanwhile, Bauer's over here making sure not a single note of Fix You is out of place."

Clara, who seemed to have radar-like hearing for trainee mischief, glanced their way. "Everything alright over there, Penny? Alex?"

They both straightened up immediately, although Penny had to laugh. "Oh, just Manic dropping God Save The Queen before the news and before their drive show."

The laughter from the others in the room drew Clara's attention fully. Her brows furrowed in a mix of confusion and mild amusement. "God Save the Queen... the Sex Pistols version? Before the drive show? Please tell me that's a joke."

Penny grinned, her face alight with both disbelief and mirth. "Not a joke. Apparently, someone at Manic Rock thought it was a brilliant idea. They cut it off halfway through, but not before Johnny Rotten had his say."

Clara sighed, pinching the bridge of her nose. "That's... well, I'd say that's unbelievable, but it's Manic. At least it makes a good case study for what not to do during a moment like this."

The room erupted in laughter again, the trainees finding some relief in the absurdity of Manic's missteps. Penny noticed that even Clara's lips twitched, though she quickly masked her amusement with a stern look.

"Alright, everyone," Clara said, her tone firm but not unkind. "Let's focus. This is a historic moment, and while it's tempting to poke fun at the competition, our job is to learn how to do better. Penny, Alex, since you're so keen on discussing playlists, let's turn this into a teaching moment. What would you have done differently if you were producing that show at Manic Rock?"

"I'd have Zetta locked down quicker than a Covid quarantine zone," Penny quipped, earning a ripple of laughter from her fellow trainees. She quickly followed up with a more serious response, her tone thoughtful. "I'd have made sure that the presenters can't access the playlist, only the production teams and management, so they can ensure the music aligns with the tone of the moment. I'd also have prepared a curated set of reflective tracks beforehand—songs like Brothers in Arms by Dire Straits or Wish You Were Here by Pink Floyd. Tracks that resonate emotionally but don't feel out of place during a sombre occasion."

Alex nodded in agreement, adding his own thoughts. "And I'd make sure there's a clear chain of command. If a presenter has any doubts about what's appropriate, they need to run it by someone senior before it goes live. Also, I'd be monitoring everything in real time—no room for rogue decisions."

Clara smiled approvingly, nodding at their responses. "Good thinking, both of you. It's all about preparation and control. This is exactly why we emphasise the importance of planning and teamwork in situations like this. When the stakes are high, there's no room for improvisation or assumptions."

Alex then chuckled, and Penny noticed he was distracted. "It seems Bee Manic has accidentally said the Queen has passed."

Bee Manic, Penny knew, was the Manchester based station of Manic Radio, one of the CHR stations in the Manic network. It was notorious for its chaotic energy and occasional mishaps, even on ordinary days. Penny raised an eyebrow at Alex, her interest piqued.

"Wait, what? Bee Manic announced the Queen's death already?" she asked, her voice hushed but tinged with disbelief.

Alex nodded, still scrolling through his phone. "Yep, according to Digital Spy, it wasn't even a formal announcement. It's only one presenter according to DS, that JJ Dennison. Apparently Hallie, the other presenter, is doing Midlands Manic drive as their usual Midlands guy, get this... is doing a Goldies rolling news special."

"Wait... Hallie Young is doing a drive show for Midlands Manic remotely from Manchester?" Penny interrupted, her voice tinged with both amusement and incredulity. "How does that even make sense? I get remote shows in an emergency, but today of all days? And what about Bee Manic? Didn't they have protocols in place?"

Alex shrugged, grinning at the absurdity. "Looks like JJ went off-script. He made a comment about 'a moment of history' and then straight-up said, 'This marks the end of an era—the Queen has passed away'. Obviously, without Hallie there, he hasn't got someone to keep him from derailing completely. Someone's uploaded it to SoundCloud."

Penny couldn't help but cover her mouth, half-laughing, half-horrified. "SoundCloud? Are you serious? Ofcom is going to have a field day. Can you imagine the fallout? Saying something that monumental before the official announcement? Speke must be on fire right now."

Alex shook his head, his grin widening. "Oh, it gets better. Apparently, JJ said it during an ad-lib between tracks, and the producer didn't cut the feed fast enough. He followed it up with, '...and now, let's keep the energy going with a classic banger from Joel Corry.'"

The room erupted in laughter, and even Clara, who had been valiantly trying to maintain her composure, let out a small chuckle. She quickly composed herself, though, raising a hand to settle the group.

"Alright, that's enough," Clara said firmly, though her eyes betrayed a flicker of amusement. "As amusing as Manic's chaos may be, this is exactly why preparation and discipline are key in moments like this. The last thing you want is to be remembered for mishandling a historic announcement. Now, let's refocus. Penny, Alex, what do you think Bee Manic should have done differently?"

Penny straightened in her seat, her tone thoughtful as she responded. "For starters, they should have had strict protocols in place for ad-libbing during a day like today. Presenters should have been briefed extensively about what they can and cannot say, with clear boundaries to avoid speculation or premature announcements. And if Hallie was scheduled for Midlands Manic, Bee Manic should have had a fully staffed team in Manchester—not just JJ winging it solo."

Alex chimed in, his voice confident. "And the producer should have been actively monitoring the feed. If JJ went off-script, they needed to cut to a pre-recorded segment or even silence the mic. It's basic crisis management. This is a textbook example of why you don't leave inexperienced—or overconfident—presenters unsupervised during a high-stakes broadcast. You'd leave big announcements to either IRN, the Head of News or a senior network presenter—someone with the authority and gravitas to handle it properly."

Clara nodded, her approval evident. "Exactly. Bee Manic's situation is a reminder that even in an era of centralised operations, human oversight is irreplaceable. Technology alone won't save you if the people running it aren't prepared. This is why we hammer home the importance of teamwork and clear communication."

Penny couldn't help but feel a swell of pride at how far she'd come since starting the Bauer Academy programme. While the day had been a whirlwind of emotions and revelations, it had also reinforced why she was pursuing a career in radio. For all its challenges, the medium had a unique ability to connect, comfort, and inform in moments of both joy and sorrow. She hoped that one day, she'd have the privilege of being one of those trusted voices that listeners turned to when the world seemed uncertain.

Clara glanced at the clock and addressed the room one final time. "Alright, everyone, keep observing and take notes. We'll reconvene shortly to discuss how different networks are handling this moment. In the meantime, if anyone spots any other... interesting... developments, keep them to yourselves until the next session."

The trainees chuckled as Clara left the room, leaving them to process what they'd just witnessed. Penny leaned back in her chair, exchanging a knowing look with Alex.

"You know," she said with a wry smile, "today might just be the best lesson we'll ever get in this business. Who needs textbooks when you've got Manic to show you what not to do?"

Alex laughed, nodding in agreement. "True. But hey, if nothing else, we'll have some cracking stories to tell when we're the ones running the shows."

As the trainees turned back to their discussions, the sombre weight of the day mingled with their laughter, creating a sense of unity among them. They might have been witnessing a historic moment in radio from the sidelines, but Penny knew that one day, they'd be the ones in the driver's seat—ready to rise to the occasion with professionalism, empathy, and maybe even a little humour.

****

CHAPTER 8 - Auntie
Thursday 8th September 2022

As part of the management team, Jack Harper knew that BBC Local Radio was the beating heart of the communities it served. Sitting in his modest office at BBC Radio Merseyside, Jack was acutely aware of the responsibility that came with the job, especially on a day like today. The Queen's health had dominated the news, and now, as rumours swirled and official channels remained tight-lipped, it felt as though the nation was holding its breath.

BBC Local Radio, affectionately known as "Auntie" to insiders and listeners alike, was uniquely positioned to bridge the gap between national gravitas and local sentiment. Unlike commercial stations bound by corporate directives or rigid playlists, BBC Local Radio prided itself on its flexibility and its connection to the communities it served. For Jack, that connection was everything.

A former member of Manic Radio's marketing team, back when it was a smaller network and based in Garston, as opposed to Speke, he had joined the BBC in 2018, initially as the Deputy Head of Marketing for the BBC station, having moved from Bauer's Radio City where he had been the Marketing Manager. Jack's journey to his current role as the manager in charge of BBC Radio Merseyside had shaped by his desire to move away from the commercial pressures of ad sales and playlists and toward something more meaningful. He had always believed in the power of local radio to inform, connect, and reflect the communities it served. And today, with the nation on edge, he felt the full weight of that responsibility.

Sitting in his office, he was watching the coverage on BBC News 24 that Huw Edwards was anchoring with his characteristic calm and gravitas. Huw's voice was steady, his every word chosen with precision. The camera occasionally cut to live shots of Balmoral, the gates adorned with bouquets of flowers left by members of the public. Jack knew that this level of composure was what the BBC excelled at, especially in moments of national importance. It was a reminder that, no matter how chaotic things became, "Auntie" would always find a way to provide calm amidst the storm.

"The time now is 3 o'clock, and we're continuing to bring you coverage of the latest updates on Her Majesty the Queen's health. Buckingham Palace has stated that the Queen is under medical supervision at Balmoral, with members of the Royal Family travelling to be by her side. We will, of course, bring you any further news as we receive it."

Jack let out a breath he hadn't realised he was holding. The measured tone of Huw's broadcast was a masterclass in journalistic restraint. He turned his attention to the email that had just pinged on his screen. It was from the Head of BBC Local Radio, outlining the directives for all regional stations during this sensitive time.

From: *helen.archer@bbc.co.uk*

To: *jack.harper@bbc.co.uk*

Subject: *Urgent: Local Radio Protocol for Reflective Programming*

Dear Jack,

As we navigate this historic and sensitive day, I want to remind everyone of our responsibility to our listeners. Please ensure the following:

1. ***Tone****: All programming must reflect the gravity of the situation. Avoid light-hearted or overly casual content.*
2. ***Music****: Transition to reflective tracks immediately. Use pre-approved playlists with a focus on classical, acoustic, and soothing selections.*
3. ***Local Connection****: Encourage presenters to share listener stories and reflections where appropriate, ensuring a balance between personal connection and national significance.*
4. ***Preparedness****: Be ready for an official announcement at any moment. Ensure all staff are briefed on protocol.*

Thank you for your dedication. Today, we embody the best of what BBC Local Radio represents: a trusted, unifying voice in uncertain times.

Best regards,

Helen Archer

Head of BBC Local Radio

Jack knew that his manager's directives were exactly what was needed. BBC Local Radio stations thrived on their ability to adapt and provide a personal touch, and today would be no exception. His job now was to ensure that BBC Radio Merseyside lived up to that standard.

Looking over to where the studio was, he could see the presenter, Laura Bennett, carefully going through the pre-approved playlists and briefing notes. Laura was one of BBC Radio Merseyside's most experienced voices—a trusted figure in the region and someone who understood the delicate balance required on a day like this. Known for her warm tone and natural empathy, she was exactly the person Jack wanted on-air when navigating a moment of national significance.

Through the glass window, Laura caught Jack's eye and gave a small nod, signalling she was ready for any updates. Jack stood up, grabbed his clipboard, and walked over to the studio.

"How's it going?" he asked as he stepped inside, keeping his tone low so as not to disrupt the live broadcast.

Laura muted her microphone momentarily, her face a mixture of calm and focus. "All good so far. I'm about to start my request show-"

"No, no request show today," Jack said, looking at Laura with a tone of quiet authority. "We're transitioning into reflective programming for the rest of the day. No requests, no light-hearted segments. Stick to the pre-approved playlists and follow the briefing notes closely."

"No, no request show today," Jack said, looking at Laura with a tone of quiet authority. "We're transitioning into reflective programming for the rest of the day. No requests, no light-hearted segments. Stick to the pre-approved playlists and follow the briefing notes closely."

"Wait, why, what are we expecting?" Laura asked, her voice tinged with concern as she glanced at the clock. It was 3:04pm, and Jack could see the newsroom had finished their extended bulletin and was getting ready to throw to Laura. Jack quickly unmuted the microphone and loaded up a standard playlist.

"Good afternoon, Merseyside," Jack said, quickly trying to calm any tension Laura might have felt while maintaining a smooth handover. "You're with BBC Radio Merseyside, and I'm Jack Harper. Laura will be on, straight after this," he said, clicking to load Bridge Over Troubled Water by Simon & Garfunkel, a staple of the BBC's reflective playlists during sombre times. The familiar, soothing melody filled the studio, and Jack turned to Laura, who was still processing the sudden shift.

"Jack, what the hell, you're not a presenter, you're the station manager, you've never done an on-air handover before," Laura said, her voice a mix of confusion and frustration. "What's going on? Do we know something?"

Jack held up his hand to calm her. "Not yet, Laura. But we need to be prepared. The Palace has been quiet, and Huw Edwards has been anchoring nonstop on News 24. Now, what do you think that means, Laura?"

Jack held up his hand to calm her. "Not yet, Laura. But we need to be prepared. The Palace has been quiet, and

Huw Edwards has been anchoring nonstop on News 24. Now, what do you think that means, Laura? I'll give you a clue - you was at Manic on the 9th of April last year. Another clue is Operation London Bridge."

Laura's eyes widened as she pieced it together. "The Queen... This is about Operation London Bridge, isn't it? You think it's about to happen?"

Jack nodded solemnly. "We don't know for certain, but all the signs are there. Huw's saying that the Queen is under medical supervision at Balmoral, with the Royal Family gathering by her side, and the tone of the coverage across the BBC is unmistakable. Laura, we're treating this as imminent. We need to be the trusted voice for our listeners right now."

Laura took a deep breath, her professional instincts kicking in. "Alright, Jack. Reflective tracks, calm tone, and no requests. Got it. What about listener interactions? Do we still take calls and texts?"

Jack nodded. "Yes, but only if they're appropriate. Neil will screen everything, so whatever he sends to you has been cleared with me personally. Salford will program the system with the new playlist," he said, working from memory as he knew the Operation London Bridge protocols were finely tuned across the BBC network. Jack continued, "So you'll have tracks coming through automatically, and I'll be monitoring everything from here. If anything feels off or too emotional, I'll intervene. We're in this together, Laura."

Laura nodded, her initial hesitation replaced with determination. She had been through high-pressure moments before—local tragedies, breaking news stories—but this was different. This was history in the making.

"Right," she said, straightening her posture. "Let's do this. Do we have an official announcement prepared in case it comes through?"

"Have you ever read the protocols for what happens? We hand over to Radio 4 as they do the national announcement," Jack explained, as he knew that he was responsible for remembering off by heart the official process, a cornerstone of Operation London Bridge for all BBC local stations. He continued, "Once the announcement has been made, we stay with Radio 4's coverage until Salford tells us to return to local programming."

"Oh, of course, we must obey Salford as if it were the God of all radio," Laura quipped sarcastically, and Jack felt the sting in her tone. He knew she had worked at Manic's Preston station, one which, in 2010 had come under controversy when Rob Trowbridge, a breakfast host and 25 year veteran of the station, had been arrested for possession of indecent images and sexual assault, the first of two well-known presenters in the commercial sector, the other being a Bristol based presenter who had worked in both the BBC and commercial sectors.

Laura's disdain for overly centralised management was understandable, given her experience at Manic, where chaos and poor leadership had often led to disastrous consequences. However, Jack also knew that the BBC's protocols, while sometimes rigid, existed for moments like this—to provide structure and avoid the very chaos Laura detested.

As the studio filled with the sound of *Bridge Over Troubled Water*, Jack could feel the weight of the moment pressing on him. The Queen, a symbol of constancy for so many, was gravely ill, and the world was waiting for news. Jack understood the significance of the day, and he knew that BBC Local Radio, with its deep ties to the community, was exactly where people would turn for comfort, clarity, and connection.

"Alright, Jack," Laura said, her voice steady now, "I'm ready. Let's do this." She took her seat behind the microphone and gave him a quick nod before pressing the button to start the transition. The gentle strains of Simon & Garfunkel continued, easing the tension that had settled over the studio.

As Laura prepared herself, Jack glanced back at his computer screen, watching the email notifications pop up, all confirming the same thing: the nation was holding its breath, and everyone in radio, from the smallest community stations to the biggest networks, was about to take on a monumental responsibility. He had been through his fair share of tense situations, but there was something uniquely profound about this one. The Queen was a constant, an institution that had been in people's lives for decades. This was not just breaking news; it was the end of an era.

He looked over at the clock. It was now 3:15 pm. Time felt like it was slowing down. He could see the other staff members at Radio Merseyside, some looking at the TV screens in silence, others murmuring in hushed voices.

Jack took a deep breath. The hardest part was not the uncertainty—it was knowing that, when the announcement came, everything would change in an instant. There was no room for error in this broadcast. Not today.

"Laura, just remember, we've got this. You're in control here," Jack said, trying to offer reassurance, but also to remind himself of the enormity of the task at hand. His role was to ensure everything ran smoothly, to keep the chaos of the outside world from intruding on their broadcast.

Laura gave a tight smile, her eyes focused, already slipping into her professional mode. "Thanks, Jack. I'm just waiting for that call. It's coming soon, I can feel it." She reached for the script, going over her notes once more. The last thing she wanted was to falter when the moment came. She had been in broadcasting long enough to know the impact of her words—today, they would matter more than ever before.

Jack took his seat behind the desk, reviewing the latest updates from the BBC News team. They were still waiting for confirmation from Buckingham Palace, but it was clear to everyone in the room that the announcement would be imminent. The BBC had already shifted into full coverage mode, with Radio 4 poised to take the lead. Once that news broke, Jack's job was simple: ensure the transition was smooth, the programming respectful, and the connection to the local community never wavered.

As the minutes ticked by, Jack could feel the tension mounting in the studio. He glanced again at the clock. It was now 3:25 pm, and the newsroom's usual buzz had given way to a subdued stillness. The atmosphere was one of anticipation, as though everyone was holding their collective breath.

Laura's voice broke the silence in the studio as she faded out *Bridge Over Troubled Water* with a soft, measured tone.

"That was Simon & Garfunkel with *Bridge Over Troubled Water*. You're listening to BBC Radio Merseyside. This afternoon, we're keeping you company with reflective music and updates as we follow the latest developments regarding Her Majesty the Queen's health. We know this is a moment that many of you will be reflecting on, and we're here to guide you through it."

Jack gave Laura a small nod of approval from behind the glass. Her tone was pitch-perfect—calm, steady, and reassuring. She leaned into her mic, her posture relaxed yet focused, as if she could feel the collective weight of the listeners who had turned to the station for guidance.

The newsroom phone rang, piercing the quiet. Neil, the producer, picked it up immediately, his expression tightening as he listened. Jack watched as Neil jotted down notes on his pad, his hand moving quickly. After a moment, Neil hung up and turned to Jack, gesturing for him to step out of the studio.

Jack slipped out of the room, his clipboard still in hand, and met Neil in the corridor. "What's the update?"

"That was the Mailbox. They were wanting to know if you had the email from Helen half hour ago?"

Of course, Jack thought, groaning, BBC Radio WM, the Birmingham based BBC Local Radio station was ringing round the other stations, probably needing their hand held by someone more experienced. It wasn't uncommon for the larger stations to lean on others during high-pressure situations, but today, it felt particularly exasperating.

"Yes, I've got the email," Jack said, keeping his tone measured. "It's the same protocol as always. Reflective music, no requests, local stories if appropriate, and stand by for the handover to Radio 4 when the announcement comes. What exactly do they need?"

Neil shrugged. "They were asking if there'd been any updates from Buckingham Palace. Sounded like they're on edge over there."

"Why don't they check BBC One or News 24. Huw's on both doing rolling news, so if they want to know what's happening, all they have to do is watch and listen like the rest of us," Jack said, exasperated but careful to keep his voice down. "Honestly, if they're on edge now, just wait until the announcement actually comes through. Tell them to stay calm, follow the protocol, and focus on their own broadcast. We've got enough to handle here without babysitting them."

Neil gave a small smirk, appreciating Jack's no-nonsense approach, and scribbled a quick note to pass the message back to Birmingham. "Got it. I'll relay that. And if they call again, I'll politely remind them that we're all operating on the same guidance."

Jack sighed, running a hand through his hair as he returned to his office. Looking at the BBC News 24 coverage, he noticed that the Breaking News bar stated that an update was expected at 6pm. Sighing, he knew that meant that the team had at least two and a half hours of preparation left before the most significant moment in recent broadcasting history. Still, the tension was palpable. Jack felt like he was holding his breath along with the rest of the nation.

He leaned back in his chair, taking a moment to collect his thoughts. He knew what lay ahead would be one of the defining moments of his career. Local radio wasn't just about news—it was about connection, community, and being the voice people trusted when everything felt uncertain. And if there was one day when BBC Local Radio needed to rise to that challenge, it was today.

The phone on his desk buzzed, breaking his moment of reflection. He picked it up and was greeted by the familiar voice of Helen Archer, the Head of BBC Local Radio.

"Jack," Helen began, her tone measured but carrying the weight of the day. "I just wanted to check in. How are things at Merseyside?"

"We're as ready as we can be," Jack replied. "Laura's on air, the team is focused, and we're fully aligned with the protocol. I'm tempted just to throw to Radio 4 anyway even if the Palace update is not coming at 6 and send Laura home, just in case, you know. I mean, I'd rather Salford and Broadcasting House take the heat for missing an update because we're midway through a handover to Radio 4, rather than risk a slip-up here. Oh, and the Mailbox lot need someone to hold their hand."

Helen let out a dry chuckle on the other end of the line, a rare moment of levity in what was an otherwise heavy day. "The Mailbox always needs someone to hold their hand, don't they? I'll make sure they're sorted. And as for throwing to Radio 4 early—don't worry, Jack. I know the temptation, but let's stick to the protocol. We've done this before, and the last thing we need is to complicate things further by deviating from the plan."

Jack sighed, rubbing his temples. "I know, Helen. It's just... the weight of it, you know? The Queen's been a constant for so many people, and if we're the ones who fumble this moment, it's going to stick with us forever. The stakes feel enormous."

"And they are," Helen replied, her voice softening. "But that's why you're in the position you're in, Jack. You're steady, you know your audience, and you know how to lead your team. Merseyside is lucky to have you, and I've got full confidence in you and your team to handle this with the dignity it deserves."

Jack nodded, though she couldn't see him. "Thanks, Helen. I appreciate that. And trust me, we're ready. Laura's on top of it, Neil's screening everything like a hawk, and the rest of the team knows exactly what to do when the time comes. We won't miss a beat."

****

CHAPTER 9 - A Breather
Thursday 8th September 2022

Link Thompson was just like any other 2 year old boy, a mixture of chaos, giggles and boundless energy. As the youngest member of the Thompson household, he had no awareness of the significance of the day unfolding around him.

The son of Toni Green and Kyler Thompson, he knew that some days he lived in his dad's home of Stratford, London, and other days he'd be with his mum in Liverpool , depending on their busy schedules and co-parenting arrangement. Today, however, was different. Link was with Kyler in Stratford, and while his infectious laughter and endless chatter filled the flat as usual, there was a tension in the air that even he seemed to pick up on.

His father, Kyler Thompson sat on the sofa, his phone in hand, trying to make sense of the messages pouring into his work chat. As a breakfast presenter on Manic Radio South Coast, and one of the target demographic for Manic's CHR stations, Kyler was used to navigating the fast-paced world of commercial radio. He had to admit that, yes, at 24, he was barely past puberty and was, like his colleagues on the CHR side of Manic, a cocaine, vodka and sex addict, and that no, he wasn't going to give them up anytime soon.

The irony that he'd only just seen out his latest conquest, Madison, one of the receptionists at the Stratford hub that Manic used for its London and the South East stations, as well as its more adult genres, like Blues, Jazz, Classical and Rock, was not lost on Kyler as he tried to focus on the unfolding news. The weight of the moment seemed at odds with his chaotic personal life and the usually irreverent culture of CHR radio. The messages in the work chat ranged from confusion to disbelief, with directives being issued in rapid succession.

Elena Stanescu: *We've been told to stay fully CHR, no tributes, no sombre vibes. Just business as usual. Does anyone else feel weird about this?*

Kyler read Elena's message and let out a dry chuckle. It was the kind of directive he expected from Manic Radio—a network so entrenched in its branding and demographic strategy that even the death of a monarch wouldn't make them deviate. He knew Elena, a Romanian born runner for Oxford Manic, the station which broadcast to the universities of Oxford Brookes and Oxford University, wasn't alone in feeling conflicted. The idea of maintaining the upbeat tone of CHR programming while the rest of the country was likely preparing for a moment of collective mourning felt surreal.

Kyler glanced at Link, who was busy arranging his toy cars in a line across the floor, blissfully unaware of the tension in the room. He envied his son's innocence. For Link, today was just another day of play and exploration, untainted by the weight of history or corporate mandates.

Kyler Thompson: *Honestly, I get it, Elena. But let's be real, this is Manic. They're never going to risk alienating the 18-25 crowd. The vibe is everything.*

Ellie Pendlehurst-Carpenter: *As long as I can do my society gossip segments, I'm happy!*

Kyler groaned, as Ellie, or Lady Pendlehurst-Carpenter, was from the aristocracy, a 19-year-old daughter of the Earl of Pendlehurst, who somehow managed to balance her privileged upbringing with a surprisingly sharp wit and irreverent charm. Her society gossip segments on Buckingham Vibes, the station that covered the exclusive areas of Buckinghamshire and its surroundings, were mainly featuring details of which Lordling was courting which heiress and who had been seen stumbling out of which private club.

The fact that she never even bothered turning up at the hub and insisted of presenting from her oak panelled library in the family estate only added to her mystique. She was the epitome of everything that seemed absurdly out of place in a CHR network that purported to cater to a youthful and relatable audience. Yet, her segments had a cult following, especially to fans of Bridgerton and The Crown, as it was the Manic equivalent of Hello! magazine meets Gossip Girl.

Kyler rolled his eyes but couldn't help smirking. Ellie's message had cut through the tension in the group chat with its characteristic lightness. Her ability to remain unfazed by even the most significant events was both irritating and oddly reassuring. It was classic Ellie to prioritise her society gossip over the gravity of the day.

Kyler Thompson: *Of course, Ellie, because the nation will be dying to know if Lord Whatsit will finally propose to Lady Thingy today.*

Ellie Pendlehurst-Carpenter: *Naturally, Kyler. It's the real news. Everything else is just noise.* 🌐 *Daddy said* *that he met the Queen once, and she invited him to go on a hunt.*

Kyler stared at his phone, shaking his head as the messages rolled in. The absurdity of Ellie's comment struck a chord, and for a brief moment, he let out a laugh—not the kind of laugh that came from genuine joy, but one that came from the sheer ridiculousness of it all. It was typical of the Manic culture: irreverence to the point of caricature, even on a day when the world seemed to be holding its breath.

Kyler Thompson: *And let me guess, the Count and the Queen shot a dozen deer and shared a bottle of the finest vintage in the palace afterwards? Classic Pendlehurst style.*

Ellie Pendlehurst-Carpenter: *Oh, darling, you're close, but not quite. It was grouse, not deer. And naturally, it was Château Margaux. What else would it be?*

Elena Stanescu: *Guys, seriously? Can we at least try to focus? This day is feeling surreal enough without Ellie giving us a glimpse of her next Netflix period drama.*

Tina Brown: *What? Netflix drama? Ellie, seriously, you're saying your old man is Lizzie's bestie? OMG, girl, spill the tea. Is she as loose as what Spitting Image make her?*

Kyler knew that Tina, an Essex Beats Drivetime host, was pure TOWIE in voice and personality, having been born in Brentwood, where the ITV2 and ITVBe reality show The Only Way Is Essex had been filmed for years. Tina's over-the-top energy and love for drama were infamous across the network. She thrived on chaos, and Kyler could practically hear her high-pitched laughter through the screen as he read her messages.

Kyler Thompson: *Tina, you're the only person who could turn a national moment into an episode of Love Island. I'm waiting for you to ask if Lizzie's corgis had designer collars.*

Tina Brown: *Babe, I was thinking Gucci! Or Hermès maybe?* 💅 *Nah, seriously though, Ellie, your old man must have some proper stories. Spill or it's a crime against radio.*

Ellie Pendlehurst-Carpenter: *Oh, Tina, darling, I wouldn't want to disappoint. But let's just say the Queen had impeccable taste—in both wine and company. A true icon, even by Daddy's standards.* 🥂 *Anyway, I'm doing my show from the library as usual-don't want to catch anything from the plebs.*

Kyler rolled his eyes so hard he thought they might stick. Ellie was exactly the sort of person who could breeze through any situation, dropping quips about Château Margaux and corgis wearing Hermès while the rest of the world held its collective breath. Despite her oblivious privilege, Kyler had to admit she added a certain flair to the chaotic patchwork of Manic Radio.

He glanced at Link, who was now climbing onto the coffee table with all the grace of a baby giraffe. "Oi, mister," Kyler said, scooping him up before the inevitable crash. "You've got no idea how mental today is, do you?"

Link giggled and patted Kyler's face, clearly more interested in playing than pondering the state of the nation. Kyler let out a sigh and plonked the boy back on the sofa, tossing him a stuffed toy to keep him occupied. His phone buzzed again.

Elena Stanescu: *Seriously, does no one feel weird about this? Like, the whole country is on edge, and we're acting like it's just another Thursday?*

Kyler Thompson: *Elena, welcome to Manic. You've got to stop expecting logic around here.*

Tina Brown: *Logic is boring, babes. Give me vibes and chaos every day of the week. I mean, the nation might be holding its breath, but the playlist ain't gonna fill itself, right?*

Ellie Pendlehurst-Carpenter: *Indeed, Tina. And speaking of playlists, I've checked Zetta2Go... we've got a classic on the playlist for the various drive shows... Dancing Queen!*

"Kyler, babe," a voice on the door speaker, and he groaned, as he knew it was Lisa Cowley, the Manic Radio Surrey Breakfast host, and another of his regulars, calling through the intercom. Lisa Cowley was known across the Manic network for her big personality and penchant for dropping by unannounced, often with an air of chaos trailing behind her. Kyler buzzed her in with a sigh, already dreading whatever nonsense she was about to bring into his already tense day.

The fact Manic had allocated Dancing Queen to a CHR show, despite having been released in 1976 and more suited for the national Manic Goldies network, was yet another example of their brand's unchecked, irreverent chaos. Kyler shook his head. At any other time, the choice might have been amusing, even in line with Manic's devil-may-care ethos. But today, with the world likely moments away from historic news, it just felt...off.

Elena Stanescu: *Oh, and get this, it's not just any track... it's a remix that's mashed up... with David Guetta's new track that charted last week, that I'm Good (Blue).*

Kyler stared at his phone, his jaw tightening as he read Elena's message. Of course, he realised, Manic would go there. A remix of Dancing Queen mashed with David Guetta's I'm Good (Blue) on what was rapidly shaping up to be one of the most solemn days in modern British history? It was the kind of audacious, tone-deaf decision that perfectly encapsulated Manic's "vibes first, think later" ethos.

Tina Brown: *Oh, and Zetta's showing no scheduled tracks between 6 and 7, apart from... Destination Calabria.*

Kyler groaned, running a hand through his already messy hair. "Destination Calabria" by Alex Gaudino? The sultry sax riff blaring through the speakers minutes after a possible historic announcement? That track would cause a scandal. It wasn't just tone-deaf—it was a full-blown car crash.

Kyler Thompson: *This is beyond parody. You can't write this stuff. Has no one at Speke thought to lock Zetta down yet? What time's it scheduled?*

Ellie Pendlehurst-Carpenter: *Oh, darling, it's all about vibes. Nothing says 'national reflection' like a sax solo that sounds like it belongs in an Ibiza pool party.*
It's straight after the half 6 news.

The absurdity of the situation hit Kyler all at once, and he laughed—a deep, frustrated laugh that carried with it the exasperation of someone who had seen too much of Manic Radio's antics. He could almost picture the headlines: *"Radio Network Plays Ibiza Classic Moments After National Announcement—Listeners Outraged."* And the tweets? They'd be relentless.

The intercom buzzed again, and Kyler rolled his eyes as he went to let Lisa in. She bounded through the door moments later, her energy palpable and her arms full of pastries from the bakery down the road.

"Kyler, babe, have you seen Zetta? It's like a rogue DJ programmed it today! Dancing Queen mashed with I'm Good? They've lost the plot!" Lisa dropped the pastries on the kitchen counter and threw herself onto the sofa, narrowly missing Link's carefully arranged line of toy cars.

"I've seen it," Kyler said, waving his phone at her. "Destination Calabria right after the half 6 news. It's chaos. Speke's asleep at the wheel, as usual. It's funny, really, as they've got to program Zetta for us and Dudley, Myriad for Huddersfield and Exeter, and PlayoutONE for Speke, Manc, Cardiff and Dundee. You know, I'm still struggling to use Zetta and GSelector, and I've been down here since July when Lite was brought and merged into the hubs."

Lisa leaned back, kicking off her trainers and propping her feet up on the coffee table as though she owned the place. "Honestly, babe, I'd love to be a fly on the wall in Speke right now. Can you imagine the chaos? It's probably like The Thick of It, but with less swearing and more passive-aggressive emails. Anyway, you think it's bad? I miss Myriad and its flexibility. Why they insisted on keeping Zetta at our hub when we're not even an ex-Breeze station?"

"I think it's because Breeze used Dudley as their network centre, but Stratford was the playout point for them. I come from the ex-Manic side, where Speke was the be all and end all of network operations. Because Goldies, Classical, Blues, Jazz, Soul, Rock and Metal all run out of Stratford Olympic Park, and we're now part of that chaos, they're having to do black magic to get the CHR shows that aren't from Breeze hubs to playout on the national CHR network," Kyler finished with a groan. "It's like they're holding the entire network together with duct tape and a prayer. I mean, why not just migrate everything to one unified system? Why do we need three different playout systems for the same group? No wonder Zetta's spitting out 'Dancing Queen' mashed with Guetta."

"Oh, yeah, you're an ex PlayoutONE guy, coming from Manc, aren't you?" Lisa interjected, smirking as she tore open a pastry bag. "Speke loves their Frankenstein setup. I'm telling you, one day the entire network's going to collapse, and they'll still be sat there going, 'Well, it worked in theory!'"

Kyler rolled his eyes as he paced the room, his phone clutched tightly in his hand. "Lisa, it's not even the system anymore. It's the fact no one seems to care about how this makes us look. If Zetta's been programmed with that playout, then Myriad and PlayoutONE have had the same absurd playlist shoved down their systems too. Imagine the chaos across the hubs when 'Dancing Queen' mashed with Guetta starts blaring right after what could be the most solemn announcement in living memory. This isn't just an embarrassment—it's a PR disaster waiting to happen."

Lisa took a massive bite of her pastry and grinned, crumbs already falling onto the sofa. "Kyler, babe, you're preaching to the choir here. But honestly, do you really think the execs care? As long as we've got the vibes and the numbers, they're laughing all the way to the bank. Anyway, their beloved protocol is funny... they flip Goldies to be a mini BBC News clone, the CHR lot stay on brand as if the world isn't turning upside down, and the rest of us? We're just collateral damage in their bizarre experiment."

Kyler sighed, dragging his hand down his face. "You've got a point. They'll probably argue that it's what the younger audience wants, to escape all the doom and gloom. But there's a difference between offering escapism and outright disrespecting the moment."

Lisa chuckled, reaching for another pastry. "True, but let's be honest—Manic's never been one for subtlety. I mean, we're the same network that had a DJ accidentally play Firestarter by The Prodigy after a story about a house fire. Do you remember that? Absolute classic."

Kyler laughed despite himself, shaking his head. "Yeah, that was Nelly Vixen on her Saturday Throwback40 chart show last year. To be fair, she didn't have a choice as the idiots at Speke had programmed it into the system and the playout was set to auto while she was shagging her producer, Jamie, I think his name was."

Lisa doubled over in laughter, nearly choking on her pastry. "Only at Manic, babe. Only at Manic. And I bet someone in Speke blamed her, didn't they?"

"Nah, but the CEO jumped before he was pushed, and we got Adam Banks running the place. To be fair, Dr Bennett was on his way out anyway as he did what no other Manic CEO did."

Lisa raised an eyebrow, intrigued. "What, actually give a toss about the stations? That'd be a first for Manic."

Kyler smirked, pacing the room again. "Nah, he went to the Ralph Bernard School of 'How to Sell Off Assets Without Burning the Whole House Down.' He downsized the hubs, merged everything under Speke's control, and even made some of the regional CHR stations network-driven. It was all to make us look shiny enough to be bought out by Lite. But, you know, Covid didn't help. I was with Toni Green then... married, surprisingly, and... well, as soon as Covid hit, he networked everything bar Breakfast and Drive. That and his history came out at the first bloody Manic-Breeze joint boot camp in 2019."

"History?" Lisa asked, confused.

"Yeah, one of the Breeze lot apparently worked at GWR in the 90s and 00s, and Bennett sacked him... because he'd had the cheek at GWR to report a potential perv... who turned out later that the person reported was an actual predator."

Lisa's laughter trailed off, replaced by an incredulous look as she leaned back on the sofa. "Wait... are you saying Dr Bennett booted someone out for reporting a predator? And that came up at a boot camp? What even is this company, Kyler? It sounds like a bad soap opera."

Kyler exhaled sharply, collapsing into the chair opposite her. "Oh, you haven't heard the best yet... Manic had their own predator up at the Preston station back in 2010... when Bennett left Global and joined Manic.

Lisa's eyes widened, her laughter replaced by a grimace. "Wait, hang on a minute. You're telling me that not only did Dr Bennett sack someone for reporting a predator, but Manic had one of their own too? And at Preston of all places? God, Kyler, this company's history just keeps getting worse."

Kyler leaned back, running a hand through his hair. "Yep, Preston in 2010. Rob Trowbridge. He was on Breakfast up there—25 years at the station, a bloody local legend. Then he got arrested for possession of indecent images and sexual assault. It was a scandal that rocked the place. And guess who was joining at the time of the Court case as Head of Legal?"

Lisa stared at Kyler, her jaw dropping in shock. "Oh my god... Dr Bennett? You're telling me he joined Manic during all that? As Head of Legal? And he still managed to climb to CEO?"

Kyler nodded grimly, the weight of the story settling over the room. "Yep. He joined just as the trial started, had to manage the fallout, and then climbed the ladder until he became CEO. But honestly, you think he'd have been kicked out after all that bad PR? Nah. In fact, he used it to streamline the entire network, saying it was time to 'modernise' and 'leave the past behind.' Classic spin."

Lisa shook her head in disbelief, leaning forward as though trying to wrap her head around it. "And no one thought that maybe, just maybe, having a CEO whose tenure started during a predator scandal was a bad look? Like, how does this stuff not blow up in their faces?"

Kyler smirked darkly, his voice laced with cynicism. "It's Manic, Lisa. The brand is chaos, and they wear it like a badge of honour. Our current CEO was... Promotions Coordinator back in 2003 at Brookes Vibes."

Lisa sat back, stunned, her jaw still slack as she processed Kyler's revelation. "Wait a second—are you telling me Adam Banks, the guy who's running the show now, started out as some uni promotions guy? Like, handing out flyers and organising pub crawls?"

"Worse... he's ex GWR Group himself... Trent FM. And half the board... either GWR, GCap or Global alumni. It's like a reunion for the old boys' club of radio chaos. I mean, I know I'm a walking red flag, and I fuck anything that moves, be they male or female, but even I draw the line somewhere. Manic seems to actively recruit disaster magnets. It's like they've got a special HR department just for hiring people who thrive in chaos."

Lisa let out a bark of laughter, wiping her eyes as she shook her head in disbelief. "You're telling me that Manic, this network of absolute shambles, has basically been run by a bunch of old GWR lads who decided to double down on their 'everything's a promo stunt' vibe? And you're still here, Kyler? Mate, what are you doing with your life?"

Kyler shrugged, smirking as he gestured towards Link, who was now attempting to use a toy car as a microphone. "Well, Lisa, I've got a kid to feed, a mortgage to pay, and, to be honest, chaos is all I know. Plus, where else can I get paid to roll my eyes at Ellie Pendlehurst-Carpenter's society gossip and Tina Brown's Essex glamour while occasionally pretending I'm still relevant in CHR radio?"

Lisa snorted, tossing him a pastry. "Fair enough, babe. But seriously, with the Queen's situation unfolding, don't you think Manic is about to hit its breaking point? I mean, we're literally on the edge of a national moment, and we've got Ellie tweeting about Château Margaux, Tina giggling about Gucci collars, and Zetta pushing Destination Calabria into the world's most inappropriate playlist."

Kyler caught the pastry and sighed, his expression softening. "Yeah, Lisa, it's a car crash waiting to happen. But that's Manic for you. It's like we're all part of some weird social experiment to see how far a radio network can go before it completely implodes. And you know what? I wouldn't be surprised if we actually gained listeners because of it. People love a good train wreck."

Lisa nodded thoughtfully, polishing off her pastry. "You're probably right. But when the announcement
124

comes, Kyler—when it really comes—do you think they'll actually get it together? Or are we going to be the ones trending on Twitter for all the wrong reasons?"

Kyler leaned back in his chair, his gaze drifting to Link, who was now trying to balance two cars on top of each other. "Honestly, Lisa? I don't know. But if there's one thing I've learned about Manic, it's that no matter how bad things get, they always find a way to survive. Even if it's just by leaning into the chaos and hoping for the best."

Lisa grinned, raising her pastry in a mock toast. "To chaos, then. And to Manic—because, love, we're all just along for the ride."

Kyler laughed, raising his pastry in return. "To chaos. And to the most dysfunctional radio network in the UK. God help us all when the clock strikes six."

****

CHAPTER 10 - Annoyance In Dudley
Thursday 8th September 2022

Jane Spearmore, the Regional Director for Central England was sat in her office that was part of The Waterfront complex, a modern business park overlooking the Dudley Canal. The sleek glass-and-steel building that was shared with HMRC, the taxman in common parlance, was a world away from the gritty, industrial heart of the Black Country, but it housed the regional hub for Manic Radio's Midlands operations. Jane's office was typically a place of calm efficiency, but today, it was anything but.

The fact that Studio 1, the prime studio which housed Midlands Manic, their Birmingham and the Black Country CHR brand had effectively been commandeered by Speke for the network feed of Manic Goldies, a brand that screamed geriatric nostalgia, was causing chaos among the usual team. Midlands Manic was one of the region's flagship stations, and its presenters were accustomed to being the stars of the show. Having their studio handed over for a national broadcast was an affront to their pride—and their schedules.

Jane rubbed her temples, staring at the flurry of emails on her screen. The directive from Speke had been clear: Pete Smith will broadcast the Queen's announcement live from Studio 1. Midlands Manic will be taking the Network Drive.

Jane knew that Pete, as the host of the Midlands Manic Drive, was being given, effectively, a Huw Edwards moment—an opportunity to be the voice of history. But for the Midlands Manic team, it felt like a slap in the face.

Pete was their guy, their local legend, and now he was being whisked away to Goldies for a sombre, national moment that had nothing to do with CHR radio. The resentment was palpable.

In the corridor outside her office, the hum of tension was building. Jane could hear the raised voices of Lyra Nott, one of the Northern Vibes Drive hosts, the CHR station for Staffordshire and Cheshire, which used Studio 2 for its broadcasts, and a junior producer named Thomas from the Midlands Manic team. Their argument echoed through the glass walls, a chaotic clash of frustration and confusion that seemed to mirror the day's events.

The fact it was just after half past 3, and she could see Pete going into his normal studio, Studio 1, not for his usual show but the grim responsibility of delivering one of the most significant announcements in modern British history, made Jane's stomach churn. It wasn't that she doubted Pete's ability—he was a seasoned broadcaster, professional and composed. But the incongruity of it all— Pete, a man known for his blokey, fast-talking style and decades of presenting pop radio, suddenly pivoting into the role of a national news anchor—felt bizarre.

"I need to get to Studio 1!" Thomas snarled with a frustrated edge in his voice, pushing past Lyra as she tried to block his way.

"Tom, what are you gonna do?" Lyra shot back, crossing her arms. "Storm in there and demand Pete comes back? He's reading the announcement, for God's sake! You think Speke gives a toss about Midlands Manic when Goldies is getting the full BBC treatment?"

Thomas scowled, rubbing his temples as he tried to compose himself. "It's not about Pete, Lyra. It's about the fact that they've shoved us onto the network feed like we're some second-rate regional opt-in! We're the bloody Midlands hub! And now we're sitting here, waiting for some generic presenter from Speke to do our drive show? The listeners are gonna know something's up."

Lyra exhaled heavily, running a hand through her short, bleached-blonde hair. "Look, I get it, alright? But Speke's running the show today. Even Jane can't overrule them."

Thomas turned to Jane, his expression pleading. "Can't we at least fight this? Tell them we'll take the national feed for Goldies, sure, but let Pete do his own show here for Midlands Manic once the announcement is done? It's bad enough that we've got a Brummie show being presented from Speke—Speke's taking the piss now."

"Right, everyone, listen up!" Jane's voice cut through the din, firm but composed. The bickering staff turned to face her, their expressions a mixture of frustration and uncertainty. Lyra, arms crossed, looked ready to launch into another tirade, but Jane held up a hand to stop her.

"I understand this is a difficult day," Jane began, her tone measured. "But we have a job to do, and we need to do it with professionalism and respect. Studio 1 has been allocated to Pete Smith for the Goldies broadcast because this is a national moment. This is not a decision I made lightly, but it's the directive from Speke, and we're going to follow it. Studio 1 has always been the main studio for this hub, even when it was part of Woody Bones's network, and whether we like it or not, Goldies is getting priority today. That's just how it is."

Thomas clenched his jaw, exhaling sharply through his nose. "And Midlands Manic? You're telling me we're just meant to roll over and let them pipe in some faceless presenter from bloody Speke?"

"Well, would you rather that then have Speke breathing down our necks for having dead air or taking a senior presenter from a broadcast?" Jane said with a smirk. "Anyway, as for your 'can't Pete do the announcement and then do Midland Manic drive, the answer is no, as we don't know when or if the Palace will be making the official announcement, and Pete can't be in two places at once. Once he's done with Goldies, he's staying with them for rolling news coverage. That means we're taking the networked Drive for Midlands Manic, end of story."

Thomas let out a frustrated huff and ran a hand through his hair. "So, we're just supposed to sit here and watch as Speke turns us into an outpost? What's next, our Breakfast show coming from bloody Liverpool too?"

Jane shot him a sharp look. "OFCOM would have our heads if they did that. Legally, we have to provide 7 Approved Area hours a day on the Stoke, Cannock, Stafford & Crewe, Nottingham & Derby and the Birmingham & Black Country licences, so that means that so that means that, for now at least, Breakfast and Drive have to stay local. But today isn't about playing politics with Speke or arguing about autonomy—it's about doing our jobs properly. Midlands Manic is still broadcasting, and as frustrating as it is, we have to trust that the audience won't abandon us over one show coming from elsewhere."

Lyra, who had been fidgeting impatiently, finally spoke up. "But what about our shows? Are we just supposed to carry on like nothing's happening? The Queen's health is all anyone's talking about, and we're here playing Dua Lipa and plugging the £500K Money Drop. I've looked at the programming Speke have made for the CHR stations, and Clive and I have to do the normal CHR shows as if nothing is happening! We're a Midlands station, Jane! People are expecting us to acknowledge what's going on!"

Jane sighed, pinching the bridge of her nose. She knew Lyra had a point as Lyra, despite having only been in radio a couple of years, and had been brought up on a diet of Bauer, Manic and Global's networked CHR, Hot AC and Classic Hits stations. Lyra understood how audiences reacted to major events. CHR radio thrived on energy, personality, and fast-paced banter, but today was different. Today was historic, and audiences would expect some level of acknowledgment—even from the stations that usually prided themselves on being non-stop party zones. She knew that Lyra had grown into the same sentiment that the older presenters like Pete Smith often voiced: a longing for radio that felt connected to its audience, rather than driven purely by corporate strategy. Lyra's question echoed the frustrations Jane had been hearing all day—not just in Dudley but across the entire network.

Thomas, on the other hand, Jane knew, was still young, and was obsessed with the trends, playlists and focus group requirements that defined CHR radio. He was the polar opposite of Lyra, and his response came swiftly, a mix of defensiveness and disdain.

"That's the job, Lyra," Thomas shot back. "People tune in to CHR for escapism, not obituaries. If we start acting like Goldies or some news channel, we'll lose listeners. The £500K Money Drop is what keeps the audience engaged. It's what we're here for. Anyway, did you see Ellie's WhatsApp message on the Stratford hub chat."

Jane noticed Lyra blank face, as she knew Thomas had moved up from the London studios in Stratford, and was part of that hub's specific WhatsApp group. Each hub, Jane knew, had its own specific WhatsApp group where presenters and producers exchanged updates, gossip, and, more often than not, rants about the chaos of Manic's operations. They had been set up back in January, when the former Breeze and Manic stations had started to move into hubs, and expanded when the former Lite stations, such as Manic Radio Kent, the former Garden County Radio, or Manic Radio Teesside, the former Tees Retro Radio, had joined the network. Stratford, as one of the largest hubs, had its fair share of unfiltered drama. Jane was wary of what was about to come.

"What's Ellie said now?" Lyra asked, rolling her eyes. "Something about how her family knew the Queen personally and they once had tea with Prince Philip at Sandringham?"

Thomas smirked. "Close. She's been going off about how 'Dancing Queen' is still in the playout for networked CHR shows—oh, and get this, the version that's been programmed is some mashup with David Guetta's I'm Good (Blue)."

Lyra nearly dropped her phone. "You're joking."

Jane groaned, rubbing her temples. "Please tell me that's a mistake."

Thomas shook his head. "Nope. Speke's apparently locked the playlist already, and unless someone manually changes it before the show goes out, it's staying."

"That's actually disgusting," Lyra snapped, crossing her arms. "It's not about being a news station, Thomas. It's about reading the damn room. If the Queen's death is announced before or even during Drive, and then we play Dancing Queen as if nothing's happened, do you know how bad that's going to look?"

Thomas shrugged. "People don't listen that closely. Anyway, if Speke locked it in, that's the end of it."

Jane had had enough. She turned on her heel, heading straight for her office. "No, it bloody well isn't," she called over her shoulder. "If they think I'm going to let any stations on my part of the network broadcast that mess of a playlist on this day, they can think again."

Jane had had enough. She turned on her heel, heading straight for her office. "No, it bloody well isn't," she called over her shoulder. "If they think I'm going to let any stations on my part of the network broadcast that mess of a playlist on this day, they can think again. Lyra, it's a minute to four, so your Stoke and Cheshire show is about to begin."

Marching back to her office, Jane felt her mobile phone vibrate. Looking at it, she saw it was Tom Hargrove, her North East counterpart from Huddersfield on the line. She knew Tom was a former Bauer station manager, running

TFM and Metro Radio, and so he'd most likely have a furious opinion on the playlist that Myriad, the system his hub ran, which was synced with PlayoutONE and Zetta.

Jane pressed the answer button with a sigh, already bracing herself for the inevitable tirade.

"Tom," she greeted curtly, "I'm guessing you're calling about Speke's latest masterpiece?"

Tom Hargrove's exasperated voice came through the speaker instantly. "Jane, have you seen the absolute dog's dinner they've programmed into Myriad for our CHR stations? Dancing bloody Queen! And a mashup with David Guetta of all things! Are they having a laugh? If this was the Hits Radio network, heads would bloody roll at Castle Quay and at Golden Square!"

Jane let out a deep breath, as she was a former Global regional programmer at one stage in her career, when Galaxy Birmingham had been converted to Capital Birmingham in 2011. She knew all too well the meticulous planning that went into a proper radio network operation. Global would never have let something like this happen—not in a million years. Every song, every transition, every moment of airtime would have been scrutinised. The idea that Manic's leadership in Speke had signed off on a playlist containing Dancing Queen mashed up with I'm Good (Blue) on a day like this was beyond belief.

"I know, Tom," she muttered, rubbing her temple. "You think I'm not fuming? It's been locked into the playout for all the CHR hubs—Zetta, Myriad, PlayoutONE, all of them. I've already got Thomas in my ear saying 'audiences want escapism,' and Lyra's about to riot because she actually cares about audience perception."

"You think that's bad... ever since Manic moved this lot in here, I've had a dozen sexual harassment complaints, 3 orgies and half a dozen presenters get a cocaine habit," Tom ranted, clearly wound up beyond belief. "I spent twenty years in this industry, Jane. Twenty years of proper radio—Bauer, Global, proper leadership. Now I'm babysitting a bunch of overgrown teenagers who think breakfast shows are just a warm-up for the afterparty. Your hub's alright, as you've got former Woody Bones stations and no Manic stuff at Dudley, but mark my words, when Speke sends their next bright idea to Dudley, you'll be having orgies in your break room quicker than you can say 'brand synergy,'" Tom finished, his voice full of pure exasperation.

Jane let out a bitter chuckle, rubbing her forehead as she slumped back into her office chair. "Tom, if I ever walk into this building and find an orgy happening in my break room, I swear to God I'll hand in my resignation on the spot."

Tom let out a dry laugh on the other end of the phone. "I wouldn't blame you. I had to send two of my presenters on 'sabbatical' last month after I walked in on them doing lines off the Myriad console at two in the afternoon."

Jane shook her head. "Jesus, Tom. At least my lot still have the decency to keep it to the pub after their shift."

"Give it time, Jane. Give it time," Tom replied grimly. "Anyway, about this playlist... have you spoken to Speke? Because if this goes out as scheduled and Ofcom come sniffing around, I'll be making damn sure my name isn't anywhere near this mess."

Jane sighed, tapping her nails against her desk. "I sent an email earlier, but you know how that lot operates. They'll just shrug it off, say it's 'what the audience wants,' and then shift the blame if it all goes south."

"Sounds about right," Tom muttered. "And what about Pete Smith? Any word on how he's handling this?"

Jane exhaled through her nose. "He's in Studio 1 now, and he should be live. I trust Pete as he's been here decades, even when I left Global and came here in 2015 as Deputy Head of Programming for Breeze."

Tom let out a knowing hum. "Pete's a pro. If anyone can hold it together, it's him. But you know what gets me, Jane? It's not just the playlist. It's the total lack of foresight from Speke. They're so obsessed with being edgy that they've lost sight of what actually matters. You'd think they'd have some level of contingency for a day like today."

Jane rubbed her temple, feeling the tension headache that had been brewing all day begin to reach its peak. "Tom, they don't do contingency. They do vibes. And right now, the vibe is absolute chaos."

Tom chuckled darkly. "That should be the bloody station tagline. 'Manic Radio: Absolute Chaos, All Day, Every Day.'"

Jane snorted despite herself, shaking her head. "Well, I've got half a mind to call Speke myself and demand they pull the track. We can't be the only ones who see how bad this looks."

Tom sighed. "Good luck with that. You know what Speke's like—they'll either ignore you completely or send back a smug email about how 'the data shows' that our audience doesn't want 'melancholy radio.' Honestly, Jane, they act like a bunch of toddlers in charge of a national broadcaster."

Jane scrolled through her inbox, noting the sheer volume of complaints and concerns coming in from presenters across the region. If even their own people were this riled up, she could only imagine what the reaction from listeners would be once *Dancing Queen*—remixed or not—went out on air.

"Alright, I need to go and make some calls before I end up screaming into the void," she muttered. "If you don't hear from me in an hour, assume I've been buried under an avalanche of passive-aggressive emails from Speke."

Tom laughed. "Noted. And Jane?"

"Yeah?"

"If you manage to stop this train wreck before it happens, I'll owe you a pint. Actually, screw that, I'll owe you an entire brewery."

Jane smirked. "I'll hold you to that."

She ended the call and immediately dialled the direct number for Manic HQ in Speke. The line rang for what felt like an eternity before a disinterested voice finally answered.

"Manic Radio, this is Chris, how can I help?"

Jane took a deep breath, bracing herself for battle. "Chris, it's Jane Spearmore from Dudley. Who's in charge of CHR programming today?"

****

CHAPTER 11 - The Cav
Thursday 8th September 2022

"Sir," Captain Tarquin Pendlehurst-Carpenter, an officer in the Household Cavalry, stood at attention in the imposing confines of the barracks at Hyde Park. The news of the Queen's health had filtered through unofficial channels earlier in the day, and now a palpable tension filled the air. As one of the ceremonial guards responsible for the monarchy's most visible traditions, Tarquin and his regiment were acutely aware that their role would soon take on profound significance.

Tarquin, older brother to the irrepressible Ellie Pendlehurst-Carpenter of Buckingham Vibes fame, was a stark contrast to his sister's playful irreverence. Where Ellie was cheeky and carefree, Tarquin embodied the stoicism and discipline expected of a Household Cavalry officer. Today, however, even he couldn't hide the unease in his usually impassive expression. The fact that there had been rumours ever since the Prime Minister, Liz Truss, had been appointed by the Queen at Balmoral rather than Buckingham Palace had already set the wheels of speculation turning. Now, with senior members of the Royal Family having flown to Scotland, it was all but certain: something historic was about to happen.

Ellie Pendlehurst-Carpenter: *Hey, big bro. Pity Lizzy's going to cop it before she can even sip her birthday Château Margaux. You lot all geared up for the big parade?"*

Tarquin frowned as he read his sister's WhatsApp message. Ellie was many things—provocative, infuriating, utterly incapable of self-censorship—but today, her usual irreverence felt particularly out of place. The gravity of the situation had begun to sink in across the barracks, and for once, Tarquin had no patience for her aristocratic flippancy.

Tarquin Pendlehurst-Carpenter: *Ellie, this isn't one of your bloody radio stunts. Keep it respectful.*

Ellie Pendlehurst-Carpenter: *Oh, come on, Tarq. You think she'd be offended? Woman had a wicked sense of humour. Pity Phil the Greek ain't around, as he'd have a few choice words about all this pomp and circumstance.*

Tarquin knew who his sister was talking about, the late Duke of Edinburgh—Prince Philip, known for his sharp wit and sometimes eyebrow-raising humour. He let out a slow exhale, shaking his head. Of course, Ellie would be like this. It wasn't that she didn't care—he knew she did, in her own way. But where he had been trained for formality and discipline, she had been raised in a world of scandal sheets and social circles where irreverence was currency.

Still, today wasn't the day.

Tarquin Pendlehurst-Carpenter: *Ellie, if you're going to carry on like this, at least keep it out of the family chat. This isn't a game.*

There was no immediate response, which meant one of two things—either Ellie was ignoring him, or she was concocting some even more outrageous remark. He didn't have time to care. He turned his phone off, shoving it into the pocket of his tunic.

Looking at his best friend, and technically senior to him by a few minutes because of the way they passed out at Sandhurst, Captain Barnaby St John-Smythe, Tarquin let out a low breath. He knew that, as they were both only just Captains, having passed out of Sandhurst two years earlier, they wouldn't be the ones leading the most significant ceremonial duties in the coming days. But as second-in-command of two companies within the Household Cavalry, they would play a vital role in ensuring everything ran flawlessly.

Tarquin knew that by addressing his close friend as 'Sir', all because of the order in which they had passed out of Sandhurst, was a matter of protocol, but it was something that always amused Barnaby.

"Sir," Tarquin repeated, his voice clipped but carrying the weight of an unspoken question.

Barnaby gave him a wry smile, tilting his head. "You know, Tarq, you really don't need to call me that when the brass are around. Come on, mate, we've been at Eton together, been to all the usual society balls, and, let's be honest, been utterly plastered together more times than I care to count. You calling me 'Sir' is bloody ridiculous."

Tarquin allowed himself the barest hint of a smirk, but his posture remained rigid. "Protocol, Barney. You outrank me, even if it is only because you happened to be born two minutes earlier and passed out of Sandhurst ahead of me."

Barnaby sighed, rolling his eyes. "Right, fine, I've had to get the Sergeant Major rip a few of your lads a new one."

Tarquin raised an eyebrow. "Which ones?"

Barnaby crossed his arms, leaning against the desk in the briefing room. "McAllister, Bailey, and that new lad, Rawlings. Rawlings wanted to nip down the NAAFI for a quick pint before things kick off. McAllister and Bailey were about to join him. Now, normally, I'd let it slide, but today? Not a chance. Sergeant Major was about two seconds away from ripping their spines out through their nostrils."

"The bloody-"

"WHAT IN THE NAME OF KING AND COUNTRY WERE YOU THINKING? YOU SCRAWNY, MILK-DRINKING EXCUSES FOR SOLDIERS THINK TODAY—OF ALL BLOODY DAYS—IS THE TIME TO POP DOWN FOR A PINT? I HAVE NEVER SEEN SUCH A DISPLAY OF PURE, UNFILTERED STUPIDITY IN ALL MY YEARS. DO YOU THINK HIS MAJESTY WANTS TO SEE A BUNCH OF HUNGOVER LAYABOUTS STAGGERING AROUND BUCKINGHAM PALACE? DO YOU THINK YOU'RE IN MAGALUF? YOU'RE IN THE HOUSEHOLD CAVALRY, YOU HORSE-RIDING HALF-WITS, NOT A BLOODY SQUADDIE HOLIDAY CAMP!

"OH, YOU THOUGHT I WOULDN'T NOTICE? YOU THOUGHT YOU'D SLIP AWAY FOR 'A QUICK ONE' AND COME BACK LIKE NOTHING HAPPENED? WRONG. YOU'RE MINE NOW. FOR THE REST OF YOUR BLOODY CAREERS, YOU ARE MINE. YOU WILL NEVER BREATHE WITHOUT ME HEARING IT. YOU WILL NEVER TAKE A SINGLE STEP WITHOUT ME KNOWING WHERE YOU'RE GOING. AND YOU SURE AS HELL WILL NEVER SEE THE INSIDE OF

THE NAAFI AGAIN UNLESS IT'S TO CLEAN THE
FLOOR WITH YOUR TOOTHBRUSH. DO I MAKE
MYSELF CLEAR?!"

Tarquin shuddered as he heard the booming voice of
Regimental Sergeant Major, Jules Halliday reverberating
through the corridors. It was a voice that could strip paint
from the walls, turn hardened soldiers into meek
schoolchildren, and, in this instance, make three
unfortunate troopers reconsider every life choice that had
led them to this moment.

"YOU'RE NOT IN THE BLOODY TERRITORIAL ARMY!
YOU'RE IN THE HOUSEHOLD CAVALRY! DO YOU
THINK THE EYES OF THE WORLD WON'T BE ON US?
THIS ISN'T SOME BLOODY COMMONWEALTH
GAMES PARADE—THIS IS HISTORY! AND YOU LOT,
YOU ABSOLUTE EMBARRASSMENTS, YOU THINK
NOW IS THE TIME FOR A QUICK PINT? YOU MAKE
ME SICK!"

Barnaby turned back to Tarquin with a knowing look. "I
think that's your answer, mate."

Tarquin pinched the bridge of his nose, exhaling slowly.
"McAllister and Bailey, I can almost understand. But
Rawlings? He's 36 and he only joined recently because
Manic let him go after their latest round of
'streamlining'—you'd think he'd have more sense."

Barnaby let out a dry chuckle, crossing his arms. "Mate,
he spent ten years reading the news for Manic's latest
purchase in Essex, didn't he? Bloody idiot doesn't know
what military discipline looks like. I'd wager he thought

this was just another day at the office—until Halliday made it abundantly clear otherwise."

Tarquin sighed, glancing towards the corridor where the distant echoes of Halliday's tirade were still reverberating. "Well, at least we know no one's sneaking off now."

Barnaby chuckled, straightening his tunic. "That's one way of putting it. You know, Tarq, in a way, I almost envy them."

Tarquin shot him a look. "Envy them? How, exactly?"

Barnaby gestured vaguely towards the window overlooking Hyde Park. "Ignorance, my friend. They're still wrapping their heads around what this means. For us, though? We already know. It's all been drilled into us for years. We know exactly what's coming. And we know we're going to be the ones making sure it all runs like clockwork."

Tarquin glanced at his watch. The Queen wasn't officially gone yet—not publicly, anyway. But he knew. They all did. He had been briefed just hours earlier on Operation London Bridge, the meticulously planned protocol for this very scenario. His regiment would be at the heart of it. The Ceremonial Troop of the Household Cavalry would take their place alongside the Grenadier Guards, the Scots Guards, and the rest of the regiments that had sworn their allegiance to the Crown. There would be no margin for error.

Hearing the telephone on the desk ring, Tarquin snapped back to the present. He exchanged a quick glance with Barnaby before striding over and picking up the receiver.

"Pendlehurst-Carpenter speaking."

"Tarq, it's Pinky up at Balmoral," came the clipped but familiar voice on the other end of the line. Lieutenant Alastair "Pinky" Pinkerton, a fellow Sandhurst graduate who was now stationed in Scotland, had been keeping them updated on any unofficial movement coming from Balmoral.

Tarquin knew that his friend, by rights, should have had his promotion to Captain at the same time as Tarquin and Barnaby, but his placement at Balmoral meant he was often caught between ceremonial duties and operational tasks. That, and the fact that, despite the British Army claiming to be a place where one's background shouldn't impact one's career trajectory, Pinkerton's lack of the usual upper-class connections had subtly slowed his progress up the ranks. Tarquin and Barnaby, on the other hand, being part of the aristocracy, his own father being an Earl and Barnaby's grandfather a Baron, meaning that their paths had been considerably smoother. It was an unspoken reality of the officer class—one that Tarquin had long since accepted, even if he didn't particularly like it.

"Pinky, what's the word?" Tarquin asked, gripping the receiver tightly. Looking at his watch, he saw it was only half past 3, meaning that Pinkerton's voice was quiet, but the urgency in his tone was unmistakable.

"Mate, it's happening. We've just had word from one of the staffers inside Balmoral. They're making preparations. All non-essential personnel are being quietly removed from the estate, and the senior royals are already inside. They've locked down comms, but the word is that it's just a matter of time."

Tarquin clenched his jaw. He'd expected this, but hearing it confirmed made it feel even heavier. Barnaby, who had been listening intently, straightened up, already processing what this meant.

"How long do you reckon?" Tarquin asked, his voice level, betraying none of the weight pressing down on him.

Pinkerton exhaled, the sound crackling slightly down the line. "No official confirmation yet, obviously, but the Palace is already drafting the announcement. If I were a betting man, I'd say we'll hear something publicly between six and seven. But internally? She's gone, Tarq."

Tarquin closed his eyes for a brief moment, inhaling sharply through his nose. He opened them again, focusing on Barnaby. No emotion. No hesitation. Just duty. "Right. Thanks, Pinky. Keep me posted."

"You'll know as soon as we do, mate," Pinkerton replied. "See you on the other side."

The line went dead. Tarquin placed the receiver down with deliberate care, straightening his tunic before turning back to Barnaby.

"Well?" Barnaby asked, his tone clipped but expectant.

"Nothing official, but Pinky said that Balmoral's already in lockdown. The staff are being cleared out, and the Palace is drafting the announcement. If he's right, we'll be hearing it publicly in the next few hours."

Barnaby inhaled sharply, nodding as he processed the weight of the moment. "So, that's it, then." His voice was quiet, devoid of the usual aristocratic drawl he slipped into during casual conversations. "The Queen is gone."

Tarquin didn't answer immediately. He turned towards the window, looking out over Hyde Park, where the late afternoon sun cast long shadows over the green. The Queen's ceremonial guard had spent centuries perfecting their discipline, their precision, their unwavering ability to carry out their duties no matter the circumstance. And yet, despite all the preparation drilled into him since Sandhurst, despite knowing that this moment had been meticulously planned for decades under the codename Operation London Bridge, he felt… unmoored.

The two had been present when Operation Forth Bridge had been executed the year before, following the passing of the Duke of Edinburgh. That had been a momentous occasion in itself, as he had passed at Windsor Castle, meaning that the ceremonial aspects had been centred around London and Windsor rather than Balmoral.

"Remember when we were Lieutenants last year, fresh in the Cav and witnessed Forth Bridge unfold for Prince Philip?" Tarquin said quietly, still staring out of the window. "I remember thinking then—this is what we were trained for. And now, it's happening again, only this time… this time, it's the Queen."

Barnaby, standing beside him, folded his arms and let out a slow breath. "Forth Bridge was one thing. That was a royal consort. But this—London Bridge—this is the Crown itself. This is the moment they drilled into us at Sandhurst, over and over again. And yet, knowing it was coming doesn't make it any less surreal."

"You know we'll have to start getting ready for Operation Menai Bridge soon, because Charles is in his 70s, so it's only a matter of time before we go through this again," Tarquin said, his voice heavy with the weight of reality. Operation Menai Bridge—the codename for King Charles III's eventual passing—was already in the planning stages, just as Operation London Bridge had been for decades.

Barnaby let out a humourless chuckle. "Bloody hell, Tarq. The Queen's not even officially gone, and you're already looking ahead to the next one."

"Hey, hopefully it won't be our problem, as we're doing the usual, aren't we?"

The usual, Tarquin knew, was what those who were in society called the well-trodden path of the aristocratic officer class. Serve your time in the Household Division, either in the Household Cavalry, the Foot Guards, or the Blues and Royals, gain experience, make connections, and then gracefully bow out to take up a well-paid corporate position, enter politics, or run the family estate. Very few stayed in for their full twenty years. Even fewer reached the upper echelons of the Army. The Household Division, for all its military prestige, was as much about maintaining tradition as it was about actual soldiering.

"That's the spirit, old boy. Keep the traditions alive—while ensuring the only battles we fight are over the best claret at Whites," Barnaby said, smirking. "Father's already got me a board position lined up at some ghastly finance firm in the City, but I suppose I ought to see this through first. Can't exactly abandon ship when London Bridge is falling down."

Tarquin gave a dry chuckle, the old Etonian humour slipping into place like a well-worn glove. "Wouldn't be terribly good form, would it? Imagine the scandal—Pendlehurst-Carpenter and St John-Smythe go AWOL on the eve of the greatest state funeral in living memory. We'd be blacklisted from Whites, and that's a fate worse than death."

Barnaby snorted. "And Mother would never forgive me. She still hasn't quite forgiven me for refusing to dance with that Viscount's daughter at Ascot last year. Said I embarrassed the family."

"To be fair, Barney, she had been in more scandals than what my dear sister has at manufactured on Buckingham Vibes," Tarquin finished, shaking his head. "And that's saying something."

"GET MOVING YOU USELESS WASTE OF SPACE! DO YOU THINK THIS IS A BLOODY TEA PARTY? MOVE LIKE YOU'VE GOT A PURPOSE!"

The bellowing of Regimental Sergeant Major Halliday sent a ripple of urgency through the barracks. Tarquin and Barnaby instinctively straightened, their ingrained military discipline overriding the dark humour of their conversation. Outside the briefing room, the sound of boots striking polished floors, orders being barked, and ceremonial kit being hastily checked filled the air.

Barnaby smirked. "I do love a Halliday meltdown. Almost makes me nostalgic for Sandhurst."

"You disgusting pathetic whimpering tree, just look at you! You can't even stand up straight! Is that how you're going to present yourself to the world? If you were in battle, you'd be the first casualty, and frankly, I'd let you rot where you fell!" Barnaby deadpanned, doing an impression of how Regimental Sergeant Majors must be trained. The exaggerated bellowing tone was near perfect, and for a brief moment, the tension between them broke as Tarquin let out an involuntary chuckle.

"You know, if you weren't an officer, you'd have made a bloody brilliant Sergeant Major," Tarquin quipped, shaking his head.

"Ah, but that would require actual work, and you know my philosophy, old boy—work smarter, not harder," Barnaby grinned.

Their moment of levity was short-lived. The barracks door swung open, and Halliday walked in, a frown on his face that could curdle milk. His uniform was impeccable, his boots shined to a mirror finish, and his glare could probably melt steel beams.

"Pendlehurst-Carpenter. St John-Smythe," Halliday barked, his voice carrying the authority of a man who had spent his entire career instilling terror in the hearts of recruits. "Why do I find you standing around like a couple of old Etonian wankers at a bloody wine tasting?"

Tarquin and Barnaby snapped to attention, their expressions immediately neutral. They knew better than to answer that question. Halliday was a legend in the Household Cavalry, a man whose voice had the power to make seasoned officers flinch. He had seen everything, from royal ceremonies to combat deployments, and he had little patience for the aristocratic officer class that filtered through Sandhurst and into the Cav. He tolerated them, of course, because he had to. But he did not like them.

"Sir," Tarquin said crisply, "we were awaiting further orders."

"Further orders?" Halliday scoffed, stepping closer. "What are you, a couple of schoolboys waiting for a bloody tuck shop to open? Do you think His Majesty is going to just pop in and tell you what to do? No, gentlemen, we are on the verge of executing the most important ceremonial operation of your pampered little lives, and you are standing around."

Barnaby, for all his usual charm, had enough sense not to reply. Instead, he kept his eyes forward, hands behind his back, and let Tarquin take the brunt of it.

Halliday exhaled sharply, shaking his head. "Right. Listen up. You two may only be captains, but you'll be leading your men through this, and I expect nothing less than absolute perfection. This is not some Tatler party where you can charm your way out of a cock-up. If I see one improperly shined boot, if one strap is out of place, if one man so much as breathes out of time, I will personally see to it that you are reassigned to ceremonial duty in bloody Colchester. Do I make myself clear?"

"Sir, yes, sir," Tarquin and Barnaby answered in perfect unison.

Halliday gave them both a hard stare, his jaw tightening. Then, with the faintest of smirks, he stepped back. "Good. Now get to work. The next time I see either of you, you had better be in full dress, leading your men, or so help me, you'll be polishing saddles until the next coronation."

With that, he turned on his heel and strode out, leaving behind an air of barely contained menace.

Barnaby let out a low whistle as soon as the door shut. "Well, that was fun."

Tarquin sighed, shaking his head. "You'd think we were fresh out of Sandhurst."

"To be fair, we did look like a couple of old Etonian wankers standing around."

Tarquin rolled his eyes. "Come on. Let's get this sorted."

Barnaby smirked. "Race you to the kit room?"

Tarquin arched an eyebrow. "We are officers, Barnaby."

Barnaby shrugged. "Doesn't mean I can't win."

With that, the two of them strode off, the weight of duty pressing down upon them as the world around them braced for history.

****

CHAPTER 12 - Vixen
Thursday 8th September 2022

Dr Nelly Vixen had never been one for decorum. Even before she became the face of Manic Radio's weekend network chart show, her reputation as a provocateur had been well-earned. A sharp tongue, an acid wit, and an almost pathological disdain for the stuffiness of traditional radio had made her a favourite with the young, the cynical, and the perpetually online.

Born Nelly Peterson, she had joined Worcestershire Beats in the early 2010s as a third member of the breakfast team, adopting the on-air persona of Dr Nelly Vixen, a sardonic agony aunt who dispensed brutally honest advice to listeners while making thinly veiled digs at her co-hosts, Mark Daniels and Lisa Roberts, two former Sunshine FM Breakfast hosts who had, in 2007 been sacked by the station for a competition scandal that had nearly brought OFCOM knocking at their door. Nelly had been the wildcard, the unpredictable element that had taken the sleepy Midlands station by storm.

Of course, Nelly had been sacked in 2016 by the former Woody Bones owned station, as her PhD thesis, she knew because she had written it, heavily plagiarised academic papers on media for her Film and Media PhD. Of course, the Breeze Media owned station fired her as soon as her old University friend, Toby Roberts, had dug up the evidence and gleefully handed it over to management. The scandal had been swift and brutal—her PhD revoked, her radio career seemingly in ruins.

Then, a week later, she had joined Manic, initially as a mid-morning presenter on Manic Radio Liverpool, the original station in the Manic CHR network. That was where she'd reinvented herself, honing her persona into something sharper, more brazen, and, crucially, impossible to ignore.

And then in 2019, Manic announced it was purchasing the Breeze Media network, and, Nelly, by then a host on Manic's UK40Chart, a national show produced in Speke and almost a clone of her idol's 1990s and 2000s show, Neil Fox and his Pepsi Chart Show. The irony of her situation was not lost on her—she had been sacked by Breeze only to end up one of the most prominent voices on their newly absorbed stations. The same management structure that had booted her out now had to pretend she was one of their shining stars. She revelled in it.

Of course, the Breeze merger had been thwart with issues, as the dinosaurs she hated, people like Pete Smith and Gary Holloway, had refused to go down without a fight. The Boot Camp in Liverpool had been an all-out war. Nelly had been prepared for hostility, but she hadn't quite expected the levels of resentment that oozed from the ex-Breeze presenters. She remembered Gary Holloway standing up in front of the entire Manic and Breeze contingent, accusing Dr Scott Bennett, then-Manic's CEO, of covering up the Peter Rowell scandal when he'd been at GWR. She remembered Pete Smith's cold, almost clinical takedown of her career, bringing up the plagiarism scandal with a precision that suggested he'd been waiting years for the chance. And she remembered her own response—laughing it off, mocking them for clinging to the past, before storming out in a blaze of righteous fury.

The fact that Holloway had been sacked, but had then announced Bauer had already hired him for their newly relaunched Greatest Hits Radio Swindon, only fuelled the animosity. Holloway had strutted out of Boot Camp like a victorious war hero, while Pete Smith had simply gone back to Birmingham, waiting for the next fight. The Breeze stalwarts had not gone quietly, and their resentment still simmered in every interaction.

Of course, she knew Pete Smith was still with Manic, 3 years later, still doing Birmingham Drive with the same smug, self-satisfied certainty that had made him a Midlands radio institution. But today, Pete wasn't on Birmingham Drive. Today, he was sitting in the main studio at the Midlands hub in Dudley, preparing to deliver the biggest announcement of his career on Manic Goldies—a station that, in Nelly's eyes, was the graveyard of old-school presenters who didn't know when to quit.

Nelly swirled the wine in her glass, leaning back against the booth in the restaurant she and her husband, Dr Nate Robinson, a Cheshire born plastic surgeon who she had met when her sister, Carla, had wanted to get a nose job and he had come highly recommended by a friend. They had hit it off immediately—Nate had found her irreverence refreshing, while Nelly had appreciated his calm, measured approach to life. He wasn't in media, which was a blessing; he didn't care about radio politics, or who was feuding with whom in the industry. His life was about scalpel work and aesthetics, not OFCOM complaints and station mergers. It made their relationship blissfully devoid of the nonsense that usually defined her professional life.

It was half past 3, and the couple were sat in one of those sleek, overpriced bistros in Manchester's Spinningfields—the kind that catered to footballers, minor celebrities, and media types looking to be seen. The kind of place where a bottle of wine cost more than a week's groceries, and yet here she was, idly sipping at a glass of Sancerre.

"Nelly, babes, how are ya?"

Nelly groaned as she saw Lisa Devonport, a media manager at Communicorp UK, who were based at the nearby XYZ Building, a media powerhouse that controlled a handful of regional stations across the UK. Lisa was the kind of person who thrived on industry gossip, always armed with the latest rumours, half-truths, and barely veiled digs about her competitors. She was also, unfortunately, someone Nelly couldn't completely avoid—Communicorp still had ties with Global, as it was, in Nelly's mind, Global's pet franchisee, having been forced by the Competition and Markets Authority to operate Capital and Heart under licence rather than outright ownership.

Unlike Manic and Bauer, who were the second and third biggest commercial radio groups in the UK, Communicorp was a curious entity—technically independent, but inextricably linked to Global's branding and operations. It meant that people like Lisa Devonport operated in a strange limbo, both part of the industry's biggest player and yet forever outside the decision-making powerhouses in Leicester Square.

Nelly didn't particularly like Lisa, but she tolerated her. Mostly because Lisa was useful. And because Lisa's presence meant she wouldn't be the one paying for the next bottle of wine.

And Lisa was married to a Hits Radio Programme Director, which meant that the incestuous ties within the British radio industry were as tangled as ever. If there was gossip worth knowing, Lisa would have it.

"Lisa," Nelly drawled, placing her glass down with a deliberate slowness. "Didn't expect to see you here. Thought you'd be in your bunker, prepping for Global's eventual world domination."

Lisa smirked, sliding into the booth uninvited. Nate, ever the diplomat, gave her a polite nod before returning his attention to his steak, wisely staying out of the inevitable media bickering that was about to unfold.

"You know me, babe," Lisa said, flagging down a waiter and ordering a gin and tonic without missing a beat. "Always got my ear to the ground. Darren's on his way, and he's got some hot goss about Hattie Pearson. Anyway, why did that Scouse lot let you Brummies over here? I thought Manic was allergic to crossing the M62?"

Nelly rolled her eyes, swirling her wine as she leaned back in her seat. "Please, Lisa, as if I'd let some Speke-based suits dictate my movements. Besides, I'm married to a Cheshire boy, which means I have diplomatic immunity north of Stoke."

Lisa snorted, flicking her nails against the side of her glass. "Sure, babes. But let's be real, you've been more Manic than Brummie since the day you sold your soul to Speke. Speaking of which, how's Pete enjoying his last hurrah over on Goldies? Must be a kick in the teeth for the old git, going from Birmingham's top dog to the network's obit reader."

Nelly arched an eyebrow. "If you think Pete's going anywhere, you're deluded. That man survives more management changes than a cockroach in a nuclear fallout. If anything, he'll be insufferable after this— probably thinking he's Huw bloody Edwards."

Nelly chuckled. "Oh, I know. Believe me, I've tried to take him down before. The man's like a relic from an ancient broadcasting civilisation—just when you think he's finally extinct, he pops up with another bloody RAJAR win, another long-service award, another reason for Birmingham to act like he's some sort of radio deity."

"Great. You know the Global bosses are miffed again, as he's got another bloody RAJAR win over Capital Birmingham?" Lisa finished, rolling her eyes. "Honestly, I don't know what it is about Pete Smith, but the bloke is like radio Teflon. He could announce the Second Coming live on air, and OFCOM would still find a way to fine someone else for it."

Lisa snorted, taking a sip of her gin. "Honestly, it's hilarious. You've got Pete Smith, radio's cockroach, still running Birmingham Drive like it's 2005, while you're here swanning about with a plastic surgeon husband and a primetime chart show. And now Pete's got to break the biggest bit of news since, what, Diana? He must be loving the drama."

Nelly smirked. "Oh, you know he is. Sitting in that Goldies studio in Dudley, all serious, all composed, probably rehearsing his 'this is a moment of national significance' voice. Meanwhile, some poor sod at Speke is trying to work out how to pull Dancing Queen from the playout before it makes history for all the wrong reasons."

Lisa nearly choked on her drink. "Dancing Queen? Oh, please tell me you're joking."

Nelly grinned. "Wish I was. But no, Speke's got it locked into the CHR playlist—Dua Lipa, David Guetta, a £500k giveaway, and, right on cue, Dancing Queen. If they don't pull it, I guarantee you there'll be a viral clip of some poor sod trying to transition from 'the nation mourns' into 'stream the latest Manic playlist on Spotify.'"

Lisa howled with laughter, shaking her head. "Oh, that's rich. And what are you lot doing over at Manic? Any major corporate statements? Or is it just business as usual?"

Nelly leaned back in her seat, tapping her nails against her glass. "Oh, the official line is all very dignified—Goldies goes full BBC-lite, CHR sticks to 'positive vibes,' and everything else gets a sombre playlist. Jazz is slated to be yeeted any minute now and replaced by an automated classic hits playlist. All because the PD for Goldies, Jazz, Blues and Soul is former Radio 2, so that means they're panicking about making sure everything sounds 'respectful'. Take a guess where the PD for Manic Classical is from?"

Lisa took a sip of her gin, already smirking. "Let me guess—Classic bloody FM?"

"Nope... Radio 3. It's a bloody Tory club at Classical, as half the hosts are ex Radio 3, half are ex Global and there's a token Scala host thrown in for good measure to make it look diverse. Honestly, you'd think they were running a Conservative Party fundraiser rather than a classical music station. Both report to an ex Radio 4 guy who got made redundant in the recent cuts."

"Wait, so the former Radio 2 and former Radio 3 guys report to a former Radio 4 guy? Bloody hell, no wonder Manic Classical and Manic Goldies sound like the BBC's retirement home. You lot really are just Global in a leather jacket, aren't you?" Lisa teased, taking another sip of her drink.

"It's like Absolute, Capital, Hits and Kerrang had an orgy and gave a bunch of Scousers the adoption papers," Nelly said with a smirk. "You know the CHR PD is ex Capital when Richard Park ran it... and Adam Banks, the CEO, used to be, in the 90s, a promo guy for GWR era Trent FM... and we've got a new owner thanks to Big Vlad getting on the Sanctions List. It's now a Sheikh who's the new majority shareholder, and the bloke hasn't even set foot in the UK yet. We're basically the world's most chaotic radio experiment, and honestly, I'm here for it."

"Wait... the PD for the CHR side of Manic is one of the old-school Capital lot from the Richard Park era?" Lisa asked, eyes wide with disbelief. "That explains so much. You lot have got that same never stop talking, energy at all costs kind of vibe. And let me guess, he's the kind of bloke who still thinks playing the same ten songs every hour is the key to radio success?"

"Well, he... lets us do what Hits do and have... throwbacks... on air. And not the usual ones but things that were on what half the Breeze lot still call the Hit Parade. Things like Steps, S Club, McFly, Busted, and even the odd Craig David track. You know, the stuff that your lot at Capital wouldn't touch with a bargepole unless TikTok decided it was cool again," Nelly smirked, finishing off her glass of wine. "But yeah, that's the culture at Manic CHR—relentless energy, big personalities, and a playlist that feels like it's been curated by a 2002 iPod that refuses to die. Anyway, I bet your lot must be busy with Lizzie getting ready to cark it?"

Lisa smirked, swirling the last remnants of her gin and tonic in her glass. "Oh, babes, you have no idea. The Global bosses are in absolute meltdown mode. Apparently, Ashley Tabor-King and that James Jenkins bloke, that guy who's his Head of Legal or something, are basically pacing around Leicester Square like caged animals. It's all hands on deck. Obit playlists locked, network-wide scripts issued, every presenter briefed down to the last syllable. If someone so much as sneezes on air during a sombre link, they'll be escorted out the building before their chair gets cold."

Nelly smirked, swirling the last of her wine in her glass. "Classic Global. Never anything less than military precision. Adam was saying he remembers when Jenkins was a runner at Brookes Vibes in the 2000s. Back in 2003, he was a runner and the only promo lad... a Brookes Vibes Hunk."

Lisa raised an eyebrow. "Hang on. James Jenkins? As in the James Jenkins? The one who's Global's legal Rottweiler now? You're telling me he started off prancing around in some ridiculous promo t-shirt, handing out keyrings and getting people to sign up for competitions rigged in favour of advertisers?"

Nelly grinned, sipping the last of her wine. "Oh, absolutely. He was the token 'Hunk' in the Brookes Babes promo team back in the early 2000s. Before he got his law degree, before he became the industry's favourite hatchet man. I'm pretty sure there are still pictures somewhere of him grinning like an idiot next to a bunch of girls in glittery bikinis at some godforsaken freshers' event in Oxford."

Lisa cackled, slapping the table. "That's incredible. Oh my God, please tell me someone has receipts on this. You know the man's practically untouchable these days—Mr 'No Comment', Mr 'I'll Have My Lawyers Send Over a Cease and Desist'. And care to guess who his old man drinks with?"

Nelly tilted her head, already sensing that Lisa was about to drop something juicy. "Go on, then. Who's Jenkins Senior knocking back pints with these days?"

Lisa smirked, leaning forward conspiratorially. "None other than bloody Ashley Tabor-King's dad, Michael Tabor. Old man Jenkins was a lawyer by trade, same with his old man, and they both ended up moving in the same circles as the likes of Tabor and the racing lot. That's how James got his foot in the door at Global—family connections, mate. He might have started off handing out flyers in Oxford, but the real reason he's Ashley's right-hand man now? Daddy's little network."

Lisa smirked, leaning forward conspiratorially. "None other than bloody Ashley Tabor-King's dad, Michael Tabor. Old man Jenkins was a lawyer by trade, same with his old man, and they both ended up moving in the same circles as the likes of Tabor and the racing lot. That's how James got his foot in the door at Global—family connections, mate. He might have started off handing out flyers in Oxford, but the real reason he's Ashley's right-hand man now? Daddy's little network."

Nelly let out a low whistle. "That explains so much. Jenkins always had that 'I was born to issue legal threats' energy, but I had no idea he had that kind of pedigree. Man's been playing the long game since day one."

Lisa smirked, swirling her glass. "Oh, absolutely. But don't get me wrong, he's good. Ruthless, but good. If you so much as breathe in Global's direction without their permission, he's already drafted an NDA and a lawsuit before you've finished your sentence. He's the reason half of the industry won't go on record about Global's more... let's say 'strategic' business practices. He's the one who tried to take the CMA to court when they blocked Global's attempt to outright buy Communicorp UK. And guess what? He almost won. That's the kind of bloke you're dealing with."

Nelly let out a low whistle, shaking her head. "I mean, fair play to him. If I had that kind of power, I'd be unstoppable. Imagine what I could do with a legal team like that backing me up. I'd be a god."

Lisa rolled her eyes, finishing off her gin. "Babe, you already act like you're untouchable. The only difference is, Jenkins actually is. Add to that his wife was a Brookes Babe, then went to Bauer before tapping out and becoming a DEI consultant, and you've got the ultimate industry power couple. You know she was working class, from Essex, before going to Oxford?"

Nelly raised an eyebrow, swirling the last dregs of her wine. "A Brookes Babe turned DEI consultant? That's one hell of a career pivot. Let me guess—she reinvented herself as a champion for industry inclusivity while sipping champagne at corporate networking events?"

Lisa smirked. "Pretty much. Carly Jenkins—she was Carly Hemsworth before she married James, obviously—did her time at Bauer, made a name for herself in HR, then jumped ship and started her own consultancy. She's been dining out on her 'rags-to-riches' story ever since. Grew up in Southend, got into Oxford on a scholarship, worked the promo circuit to pay her way, then married into media royalty. Now she's on every diversity panel going, lecturing about how women should be paid better than their male counterparts while conveniently forgetting that she's married to a man who's probably responsible for half the NDA clauses keeping those pay gaps under wraps."

Nelly saw her husband was on his tablet computer, looking at patient notes or some other work-related matter, blissfully ignorant of the radio industry gossip unfolding around him. She envied his detachment. Plastic surgeons didn't have to deal with media power struggles, corporate buyouts, or legal threats disguised as polite emails. His biggest stress was ensuring his scalpel was sharp enough.

"...Let me tell you, you know, aah, I need a miracle," the sound of a car radio pumped up to the top of its speakers blared through the restaurant's open-plan seating area. The unmistakable synth intro of Fragma's Toca's Miracle was followed by the voice of a Manic CHR presenter trying to keep the energy up despite the growing tension in the country.

Lisa rolled her eyes, taking another sip of her gin. "Jesus Christ, are they seriously still running normal programming? It's like watching a slow-motion car crash."

Nelly smirked, leaning back in her seat. "Oh, absolutely. Welcome to Manic. Where the vibe is 'denial' until it's physically impossible to ignore reality. If they could, they'd be running the £500K Money Drop and pretending nothing's happened."

Lisa let out a dark chuckle, shaking her head. "I'd kill to be a fly on the wall in Speke right now. Tabor-King's probably got Global's obit machine running smoother than a military operation, and meanwhile, your lot are still playing 90s dance classics like we're on a Hen Do in Magaluf."

"Listen, babe," Nelly said, tipping her empty wine glass towards Lisa. "We all grieve in different ways. Some people cry. Some people light candles. And some people play Toca's Miracle at full volume while plugging a free iPhone giveaway. Who are we to judge?"

Lisa cackled, setting her drink down. "Oh, you lot are so getting fined for this."

****

CHAPTER 13 - Returning from Ibiza
Thursday 8th September 2022

James Smith had to chuckle as he walked down the steps of his Easyjet flight at London Luton airport, the grey skies of England a stark contrast to the sun-soaked beaches of Ibiza he'd left behind. Having taken a gap year after finishing at Dudley College, he had done what any then 18 year old had done after the Pandemic had died down - booked the first flight he could to the party capital of Europe. Ibiza had been everything James had hoped for: sun, sea, and endless nights of music and revelry.

The irony that he had been a waiter at some of the most exclusive parties and done some DJ sets at a couple of beach bars, a few underground clubs, and one very memorable night playing at a villa party for a group of slightly unhinged Swedish tourists. Looking at his banking app, James grinned as he saw that he had come back with more money than he had gone out with, thanks to doing a waiting gig at a party hosted by Dua Lipa's entourage and a DJ set for an Arab businessman celebrating his daughter's engagement. Ibiza had been more than just a holiday for James—it had been an experience that blurred the line between work and pleasure, a whirlwind of beats and connections that felt worlds away from the overcast skies of Luton.

As he stepped into the terminal, James felt his phone buzz in his pocket. Pulling it out, he saw a flood of notifications from news apps and social media. The Queen's health dominated every headline. The mood in the airport seemed unusually subdued, with passengers clustered around televisions and scrolling through their phones.

"Well, that's not what I was expecting to come back to," James muttered to himself, tucking his phone away as he headed towards baggage claim. The contrast between the carefree nights of Ibiza and the gravity of what was unfolding back home was stark.

He knew that his dad, Pete, would no doubt be presenting the usual drive on Midlands Manic, the CHR station that covered James's native Pensnett, but as someone who preferred Capital to Free Radio or Manic, James knew that his dad's show wasn't exactly his style. Pete Smith, a stalwart of regional radio and a consummate professional, was the polar opposite of James in many ways. While Pete was an ILR veteran who was stuck in CHR, James preferred the polished networked vibe of Capital or the edgy, dance-heavy energy of Ibiza's underground music scene. They often joked about their differing tastes, but James couldn't deny his dad's talent behind the mic. Pete was the kind of broadcaster who could make even the most mundane topics sound engaging, a skill James secretly admired.

As James waited for his luggage, he checked his phone again, scrolling through the messages in the family group chat. His mum had sent a string of updates about the Queen's health, each one more solemn than the last. His sister, Chloe, James knew, was in her final year at Dudley College, the siblings being a year apart in age and having a relationship that oscillated between playful rivalry and genuine camaraderie. Chloe, never one for unnecessary sentimentality, had simply sent:

Chloe Smith: *Dad's on Goldies today. Big news coming. Looks serious.*

James frowned, rereading the message. That wasn't right. His dad never did Manic Goldies. He was Midlands Manic through and through—a CHR presenter, not a nostalgia host. If Pete had been shifted to Goldies, something major was definitely happening.

James Smith: *Goldies? Since when?*

Sarah Smith: *Since this morning. They've got him on standby for something big.*

James knew that his mother, Sarah, as a former Smooth Radio host, an occasional community radio host and founder of Reeves Radio Ltd, a production company which sold syndicated programming to various independent radio stations, had a deep understanding of the industry. If she said something big was happening, she wasn't being dramatic. She had seen the inner workings of radio far too long to get caught up in unnecessary speculation.

James's stomach tightened. He might not have been into radio the way his parents were, but even he could see what was coming. If his dad had indeed been pulled from his usual CHR slot and placed on Manic Goldies—a station designed for reflective, nostalgic programming—then the network was bracing for a major announcement.

James dragged his suitcase off the carousel and wheeled it towards the exit, his mind now completely out of Ibiza mode. The balmy nights of the White Isle, the deep house thumping through beach bars, and the hedonistic energy of the clubs felt like a different lifetime. His flight had landed at just past three-thirty, which meant, as it was quarter to four, the drive shows would be near to starting across the UK. If the Queen's passing was imminent, then everything was about to change.

Loading the Uber app up on his phone, he was shocked to see the price for an Uber was nearly £200, all because he was at Luton, where Easyjet had landed because Ryanair had wanted nearly £300 for his return flight direct to Birmingham. Cursing under his breath, James debated his options. The train was an alternative, but Luton Airport Parkway was a faff to get to, and the idea of hauling his luggage through London just to get a packed train home to the West Midlands didn't appeal.

It was then that he remembered that National Express did coaches from Luton direct to Birmingham's Digbeth coach station, and while it wouldn't be as comfortable as an Uber, it was a hell of a lot cheaper. The fact he could just get a bus round to Colmore Row from there, jump on a X10, and, as it stopped at Russells Hall Hospital before heading to Pensnett and Gornal was far more practical than spending a small fortune on an Uber.

He quickly searched for the next National Express departure and saw that a coach was leaving for Birmingham in thirty minutes. Perfect. He booked his ticket, grabbed a quick coffee from one of the overpriced airport cafés, and made his way to the coach bay.

As he settled into his seat, he plugged in his headphones, expecting to escape into a mix of Ibiza deep house. But as he glanced around the coach, he noticed that nearly every other passenger was glued to their phone screens, murmuring in hushed tones. A few had even turned on live streams from BBC News and Sky News, the muted footage showing aerial shots of Balmoral and Buckingham Palace.

A creeping sense of inevitability filled the air.

James hesitated, then opened up the Manic app on his phone. He wasn't normally one for live radio, preferring to stream music or catch up on podcasts, and when he did, it was Capital, Capital Dance, Radio 1 Dance or Manic Dance, the occasional exception. But today was different. Today, he needed to hear what was happening.

He scrolled through the list of stations and hesitated for a moment before tapping Manic Goldies UK. If his dad was really on, this would be the place to hear him. The app buffered for a few seconds before the stream kicked in.

"…our correspondent at Balmoral, Angus McKinley, reporting live on the situation at Balmoral. We now go to our correspondent at Windsor, Helen Jenkins, who's reporting from Windsor Castle, another focal point for Royal activity today. Helen, what's the atmosphere like there?"

"Thank you, Pete. Here at Windsor Castle, the atmosphere is one of quiet reflection. Members of the public have begun to gather outside the gates, laying flowers and standing in silent vigil. The historic walls of Windsor have seen centuries of change, and today they stand as a symbol of continuity during a time of uncertainty. While there is no official word yet, the mood here is one of reverence and concern. Helen Jenkins, for ITN... erm... Manic Radio News."

James had to groan at how the obvious slip up from a professional broadcaster had made it to air. It was hardly surprising—Helen Jenkins, like many of Manic's news staff, were contractors from ITN, the same company who did ITV's news bulletins. She'd probably spent years saying, "Helen Jenkins, ITN" and had gone into autopilot. It was a small, almost amusing mistake, but it underscored how unusual today was. Even the professionals were rattled.

James adjusted his headphones, leaning back in his seat as his dad's voice filled the airwaves again.

"Thank you, Helen," Pete said, smoothly transitioning. "We'll continue to bring you updates from Windsor, Balmoral, and beyond as they come in. As the nation waits, we invite you to share your thoughts and reflections. Our phone lines and text messages are open, and we'll be sharing some of your tributes throughout the evening."

James exhaled. This wasn't just speculation anymore. Manic Goldies had already shifted into full-on obit mode, especially as, he knew from his dad's mentioning, the classic hits station was effectively controlled by a former BBC Radio 2 senior staff member who reported to a BBC Radio 4 executive who had been let go during the last round of budget cuts. The way Manic Goldies was handling the situation felt eerily like the BBC's own sombre, measured approach—professional, dignified, and above all, prepared.

Switching over to Capital, James noticed that the Global Player app had crashed on his phone when he launched it, and he groaned, as the iPhone that he had been given three

172

years earlier, when he was 16 was starting to struggle under the weight of multiple apps running at once. He closed everything else, rebooted the Global Player, and tried again.

This time, it worked.

Capital FM's breakfast host, Roman Kemp, was long gone for the day, and instead, James was greeted by an unusually subdued voice from Tom Watts and Claire Chambers, the two Birmingham drive hosts. Normally, they were upbeat, fast-talking, and full of energy, but today, their tone was muted, their usual banter replaced by careful, measured words.

"…and we know this is a moment of great concern for many of you," Claire was saying. "We'll keep bringing you updates as soon as we get them, and in the meantime, we'll continue with the music you love while keeping you informed on this developing situation."

James frowned. The playlist wasn't its usual relentless stream of high-energy pop and dance tracks. Instead, it had shifted into something far more restrained— Coldplay's Fix You was playing, a far cry from the usual hyper-produced pop anthems.

Having a father in the industry, James knew that Capital in the Midlands was the former Galaxy network, and its team had been honed under the relentless, polished machine of Global's programming team. That meant that, unlike the barely controlled chaos of Manic, Capital's response was precise and deliberate. They wouldn't break the news first—they would instead simulcast LBC, Global's own news powerhouse, or switch to rolling updates from their Leicester Square newsroom the moment the official announcement came through.

James closed his eyes for a moment, exhaling as the coach pulled out of Luton Airport. He'd been expecting to come back home to a hangover and a few funny stories to tell his mates about his year in Ibiza. Instead, he was returning to a country on the brink of a historic moment.

His phone buzzed again—another message from Chloe.

Chloe Smith: *Dad just did a massive sigh after that last report. Think he knows what's coming.*

James didn't reply. He just kept listening, as Pete Smith, the voice of Midlands radio for as long as he could remember, carried on broadcasting into history.

The next couple of hours would change everything.

****

As the coach went up the M1 motorway, James decided to tune into some of the other Manic stations in their CHR network, some which were branded as Manic Radio and then the region they served, and some branded with their heritage names, something with James found curious, as the Manic Radio branded stations were ones that, a year ago, he had not seen on the Manic Prime app.

"Manic Radio South Coast, Manic Radio Ayrshire, Manic Radio Essex?" he muttered to himself as he scrolled through the app. These were new. Or, at least, new to the Manic branding. The fact that all of them, plus the legacy stations such as Midlands Manic, which had been a Breeze Media station, and Bee Manic, one of the original

Manic stations from the old network, were all playing the same tracks, as the network, like the Hits network and the Capital networks, used similar playout systems. That, James knew, was standard, and his dad, before he had left for Ibiza, would moan that ever since Manic had took over the Breeze stations, which allowed presenters to curate their own hourly clocks, CHR programming had become far more rigid, stripping away the individuality that once defined local radio.

"That was The Vamps with their 2013 hit, Can We Dance," the voice of Hallie Young, the former Breakfast host, said. "It's me, your girl, Hallie, back on Brum's airwaves for one day only, and yes, I'm here in Manc, wishing I was back on Broad Street with a pint instead of stuck in a studio full of panicking execs! Now, I bet you're all wondering where Pete is, right?"

James sat up a little straighter as he listened, his interest piqued. Hallie Young had been a staple of Midlands radio, and he had been unaware that there was a reshuffle, or that she was now the Bee Manic drive host, a Manchester based station in the Manic network. The fact that she was covering Midlands Manic from Manchester was an obvious sign that something big was happening behind the scenes.

"Well," Hallie continued, her voice carrying that same mischievous edge she always had. "Our Pete's been called up to the big leagues for today, covering on Manic Goldies. So you're stuck with me! And no, before anyone asks, I have no idea what's happening either, and the bosses are all running around like headless chickens. But don't worry, we'll keep things moving, keep things positive, and if you fancy a shoutout, send me a WhatsApp on 0161 496 0999—yes, it's a different number today, as I can't log into the normal Brum WhatsApp, or just fire me a tweet, I'm on @HallieBeeManic, and I'll be keeping an eye on your messages. But yeah, bear with us today, folks—things are a bit mad behind the scenes."

James let out a low chuckle. He had to give Hallie credit— she was handling the chaos with the kind of wit and blunt honesty that had made her a favourite among Midlands Manic listeners before she had moved north. The fact that she was openly admitting she had no clue what was going on spoke volumes about the state of Manic's internal communication.

He checked Twitter, searching for mentions of Midlands Manic, Manic Goldies, and Pete Smith. Sure enough, listeners were already noticing something was off.

@BrumRadioLad: *Pete Smith NOT on Midlands Manic? Wtf is going on? Hallie's great but this feels WEIRD. #RadioShakeUp*

@CharlotteMUAx: *This sounds like when that Capital DJ got COVID, and they had to scramble someone in last minute. But Pete's a MACHINE. Something's up. #MidlandsManic*

@Sarah_Jane78: *Pete is on Manic Goldies??? That's like Ant turning up without Dec. What is going ON.*

James smirked at that last one. It was true—his dad *was* Midlands Manic, and the fact he had been moved over to Goldies for the day was not only unexpected but, to radio-savvy listeners, a clear indicator that something big was happening.

It was then that he noticed a tweet which was about Bee Manic, and one that he knew Manic would hate.

@ManicWatcher: *Seems @JJDennisonManc has announced the Queen has died and then gone into @DuaLipa's Physical #ManicFails*

James read the tweet twice, blinking in disbelief. JJ Dennison was not a name he knew, as he had been in Ibiza for most of the past 12 months, with some Dubai visits in order to make up the maximum 180 days he could stay in Spain under the post-Brexit rules. But even so, he knew that screwing up an announcement like this was the kind of thing that could kill a career.

He also knew that, as Manic used, according to his dad, PlayoutONE at the former Manic stations and Zetta at the former Breeze stations, meaning that playlists and automation were, like Global and Bauer, centralised, the fact that Dua Lipa's Physical had played right after an apparent announcement meant that something had gone seriously wrong.

But he knew that the BBC would have been likely the first to make the official announcement. The fact that JJ Dennison had apparently jumped the gun was either a rogue moment or a colossal error in Manic's handling of the entire day. James quickly scrolled through Twitter, trying to find a clip or more context.

@ManicWatcher: *Audio from @BeeManic is now on SoundCloud.*

James tapped the link, his curiosity overtaking any lingering exhaustion from his journey. The page loaded, and sure enough, there it was—JJ Dennison's moment of infamy. He hit play, the audio crackling into life.

"So yeah, Lizzy is brown bread. Anyway Manchester, here's Dua Lipa with her 2020 hit Physical."

He instinctively checked the timestamp. It had gone out minutes ago—which meant that if the Queen's death hadn't been officially announced yet, JJ Dennison had just committed one of the biggest broadcasting blunders in recent memory. James' stomach twisted. He knew enough about the industry from growing up around it to understand just how serious this was. Manic had just broken the story of the century incorrectly—or, at best, prematurely.

It didn't take long for the backlash to start flooding Twitter.

@Sam_Caldwell90: *Did that Manic DJ just say 'Lizzy is brown bread'?! Actual OFCOM-worthy behaviour. Someone's getting fired.*

@NewsWatcherUK: *If JJ Dennison's announcement is true, then he's just scooped the BBC. If it's false, he's just ended his career. Either way—what an absolute mess from Manic.*

@Capital_Jay: *I work in radio. I cannot stress how massive this screw-up is. You DO NOT announce something of this magnitude unless the Palace or the BBC confirms it first. Manic have fucked it.*

James shook his head, scrolling down to find clips of other stations. He knew that if the Queen had passed, the BBC would be the ones to break it.

He switched apps, loading up BBC Sounds. He scrolled to BBC Radio 1 first, expecting to hear something different from its usual output.

But it was still the usual programming, meaning that the BBC hadn't been informed of the official announcement yet. That meant that JJ Dennison had jumped the gun— and not just by seconds or minutes, but potentially by an entire hour or more.

James exhaled sharply, switching over to BBC Radio 4, the station that would be the first to break the news officially. If anything was happening, this was where it would be confirmed.

A calm measured voice filled his headphones—not a breaking news tone, not rolling updates, just a quiet, poised conversation about a completely unrelated topic. A discussion about Britain's energy crisis was unfolding, with no sense of urgency or interruption.

No obit mode. No announcement. No change in tone.

JJ Dennison had completely fucked up.

And that meant Manic were going to face issues with OFCOM.

****

CHAPTER 14 - Hallie
Thursday 8th September 2022

Hallie Young was sat on the 142 bus from East Didsbury to Piccadilly Gardens, her halter top and dolphin shorts a contrast to the teens in Rusholme who were still dressed in oversized hoodies and joggers, clutching iced coffees despite the temperamental Manchester weather. Hallie's outfit was unapologetically bold, just like her personality. Her oversized sunglasses perched on the bridge of her nose, shielding her eyes from the occasional burst of sunlight breaking through the clouds.

A former member of the Dudley team at Midlands Manic, the Birmingham and Black Country hub, Hallie had made the leap to Manchester after being offered the coveted drivetime slot at Bee Manic, replacing Toni Green, she had already made her mark on the Mancunian station, with her Brummie sass, infectious laugh, and ability to connect with her audience. Hallie's shift to Manchester was a fresh start, but today, the energy of the city felt different.

She knew that it was only lunchtime, and that she had 4 hours until her Bee Manic show with JJ Dennison. The duo had become a local favourite in Manchester for their on-air chemistry, with JJ's cheeky humour bouncing off Hallie's no-nonsense attitude. But as the bus trundled down Wilmslow Road, Hallie couldn't shake the feeling that today's show would be anything but normal.

Checking her phone, she decided to text a friend of hers who was based at Hits Radio, in the Castle Quay area of Manchester, to see if they fancied meeting up for lunch before she had to go in to work. It was traditional for Hallie, in the 4 months she had been based at Piccadilly Gardens, to get an earlier bus, have a Nando's, her only meal of the day due to her cocaine habit dulling her sense of hunger, and head into the Bee Manic studios early to prepare for her show.

She fired off a quick text to her mate Alex at Hits Radio:

Hallie Young: *Nando's before work? Usual time?*

The reply came within seconds.

Alex Peacock: *Can't. Chaos here. All hands on deck. Have you seen the news?*

Hallie frowned, lowering her sunglasses and scrolling through Twitter. That was when she saw it.

BREAKING: Buckingham Palace issues statement on Queen's health.

Her stomach twisted. She tapped on the link, skimming through the formal wording. "The Queen remains under medical supervision at Balmoral. The Royal Family has been informed."

Hallie didn't need to be a political analyst to know what that meant. She might not have been a royalist, but she understood the weight of this moment. The Queen had been an unshakable constant in Britain her entire life. If the Palace was being this direct, things were bad.

She quickly flicked to WhatsApp, opening the Bee Manic Work Chat, where the station's producers, presenters, and managers messaged about everything from playlist changes to who was nipping out for a Maccies run.

Buzz Campbell: *Not long til Lizzy drops, eh, lads?*

Hallie knew that Greg "Buzz" Campbell, the newly minted Regional Director for Greater Manchester, a small region compared to the other Manic outposts, but still important due to the fact Manic was still, at heart, a Scouse operation even though a Sheikh was the owner of the station, and Hits Radio, despite being a Bauer operation, was a Manchester group of stations, so naturally with Scousers and Mancunians being in a perpetual state of rivalry, Bee Manic had to prove itself as the dominant CHR station in Manchester, especially as Hits Radio, the Bauer station which formed the key opposition, had deep roots in the city as the spiritual successor to Key 103. Buzz had been pushing hard to get Bee Manic more recognition, more influence—more wins—against Hits Radio.

Hallie rolled her eyes at his crass comment but wasn't surprised. Buzz was the kind of boss who thought he was still one of the lads, despite now being in charge. She flicked through the rest of the chat.

JJ Dennison: *So what's the deal if she... you know?*

Buzz Campbell: *Protocol says business as usual, unless Speke says otherwise. No doom and gloom, we're a CHR station, not the BBC. Let Global and Bauer do the weepy stuff.*

Hallie had to chuckle at what Buzz had said, even though she knew the corporate directive was absolutely serious.

Bee Manic, like all Manic Radio stations, had a strict brand identity—high-energy, upbeat, and irreverent. It didn't matter if the Queen was on her deathbed, Bee Manic wasn't going to turn into Radio 4 overnight. Still, the way Buzz phrased things was peak Manic Radio: no filter, no subtlety.

She glanced back at Twitter. Journalists were already gathering outside Balmoral. The BBC had suspended all regular programming on BBC One. LBC and Times Radio were filled with speculation and cautious analysis. Global's Capital FM was still playing Harry Styles like nothing was happening, but that would change soon. Bauer's Hits Radio was playing a slightly older track— Coldplay—perhaps a sign they were already softening their playlist.

Bee Manic, however? She could already imagine the pre-show brief: *Business as usual, keep the tempo high, and no mention of it unless absolutely necessary.*

Hallie sighed and looked out of the window as the bus crawled towards Piccadilly Gardens. The streets were their usual chaotic mix of workers, students, and shoppers, but something in the air felt different. A weird, anticipatory hush beneath the usual city buzz. Even the man ranting outside Boots about 5G and lizard people didn't seem as loud as usual.

Her phone vibrated again.

JJ Dennison: *We still doing the Birthday Game in Hour 2 or do we swap it out?*

The Birthday Game was a game where Hallie would act as quizmaster, and JJ, along with Wahab Hussain, former late-night producer on Bee Manic who was their new their producer, would compete against each other and listeners in guessing the ages of various celebrities who had birthdays that day. It was a segment that thrived on light-hearted banter and quick-fire jokes—something that might not land well if the nation was collectively preparing to mourn.

On the other hand, Hallie knew, keeping things normal for the CHR demographic, the 18-to 34-year-olds who made up the core audience, was crucial. Most of them weren't glued to rolling news. They weren't obsessing over every minor detail coming out of Balmoral. They were scrolling TikTok, sending WhatsApps, and getting on with their day.

The irony that Hallie, being 26, was firmly within the demographic that Manic, Hits Radio and Capital were fighting over, wasn't lost on her. She was their audience, their key listener, and yet she had one foot in the world of media insiders who knew exactly how the radio machine worked.

She stared at JJ's message for a moment before typing.

Hallie Young: *Let's see how things go. If Speke sends an update, we might need to tweak the clocks. But for now, Birthday Game stays. No mention of anything unless we get told otherwise.*

A few seconds later, Wahab chimed in.

Wahab Hussain: *Just had a quick word with the duty PD. No changes for now. Playlist as normal. No sombre stuff. No breaking news tone if we do mention it. We're not BBC Manchester.*

Hallie snorted. Of course they weren't. Manic's CHR stations had been built on the idea that young listeners didn't want news, and if they did, they'd check their phones. Bee Manic's format was all about energy, hype, and pop culture nonsense. Even on a day like today, the brand came first.

But still, it felt... odd.

The bus juddered to a halt at Piccadilly Gardens, and Hallie climbed off, adjusting her bag as she walked towards the tram stop. Seeing the tram with an all-over wrap for Capital Manchester, with Roman Kemp, the networked Breakfast host's grinning face staring down at her, Hallie couldn't help but smirk, especially as the building the other side of Piccadilly Gardens tram stop, One Piccadilly Gardens, was, along with several restaurants and businesses, the studios for Bee Manic, as well as its recently moved in siblings, Manic Radio Rochdale, Manic Radio Bolton and the Manic Metal UK national DAB station. Seeing Capital's branding loom over the square like some dystopian advert only fuelled her competitive spirit.

As she crossed over into Piccadilly Gardens itself, Hallie had to chuckle as she saw the on street adverts in the Gardens for Bee Manic, not just for the local drive show with her and JJ, which said "Hallie and JJ, driving the whole of Greater Manchester Manic every weekday between 4 and 7pm," but also for Toni Green, saying

"Toni Green, Alty's own Queen of Sass, every evening across the Manic Radio network. Get it now on Manic Prime," and also the generic Bee Manic branding, saying "Bee Manic - Greater Manchester's Hit Music Station - Download the Manic Prime app now!" It was a reminder of the ongoing battle for Manchester's CHR dominance— Hits Radio, Capital, and Bee Manic all jostling for position, all trying to win over the same listeners. And today, with the Queen's health dominating every news feed, it was about to become even messier.

Hallie knew that she had over an hour until she and JJ needed to start their show prep, which for Hallie, as a former Midlands Manic breakfast host, meant doing it diligently, ensuring no mistakes slipped through. She prided herself on her ability to keep a show running smoothly, even if JJ sometimes preferred a more chaotic, off-the-cuff approach. Their dynamic worked because it was a balance—her professionalism tempered by his mischief, his quick wit bouncing off her sharp, no-nononsense delivery. Looking at her iPhone, she decided to go for her usual Nando's—after all, just because the country was in a state of anxious anticipation didn't mean she had to skip her only proper meal of the day.

As she walked towards the Piccadilly end of Piccadilly Gardens, where Nando's, nestled underneath a Travelodge, was, she glanced at her phone again. The Bee Manic Work Chat was still buzzing.

JJ Dennison: *Bet Capital are bricking it. You know they're gonna have to throw out the whole network playlist when the big news drops. Global don't do 'vibes' when it comes to obits.*

Wahab Hussain: *They'll cut to LBC the moment the BBC confirms it. Bet you £10 Roman Kemp isn't on air tomorrow morning.*

Hallie Young: *Not taking that bet, Wahab. Too easy. Capital'll go to rolling news before we even get our first song intro out.*

Buzz Campbell: *See, this is why Bee Manic wins Manchester. Global's like an AI bot running a playlist from London. We're actually here. We get the city. We know what they want. And right now? They want to forget about the outside world and listen to us take the piss out of JJ's shite dating life. Anyway, the protocol is that Midlands Manic drive gets yeeted as Pete Smith's on our network announcement and Goldies is rolling obit. If it happens, Speke will tell us what's what. Till then, crack on like normal.*

Hallie frowned, as she knew that Birmingham, lie Manchester, was a key market for Manic, as both Global's Capital, formerly Galaxy, and Bauer's Free Radio, formerly BRMB, two Brummie powerhouses, had deep roots in the city. Having been a teen in the 2000s, living in West Bromwich, when BRMB, Beacon FM, Heart 100.7 and Galaxy were all battling for dominance, she knew that, like Manchester, the authenticity of local radio, despite people like Ashley Tabor-King pushing for networked dominance, still mattered. That was why Bee Manic was able to carve out an audience in Manchester— because it wasn't just another voice-tracked network feed from London. And Buzz, for all his posturing, had a point. When the moment came, Capital Manchester wouldn't be breaking the news themselves. They'd be waiting for orders from Leicester Square.

Hallie sighed and pocketed her phone, stepping into Nando's. The usual post-lunchtime lull meant she got her food quickly— Half a chicken, extra hot, peri fries, garlic bread, macho peas, and a bottomless Coke, not the sugar free or fake sugar nonsense either, just straight-up full-fat Coke. A proper meal before she had to go into work and pretend like everything was normal while the world outside held its breath.

As she took a bite of her chicken, the work chat was still buzzing.

JJ Dennison: *Right, but seriously, how much chaos is this gonna cause if it happens mid-show?*

Buzz Campbell: *Mate, we ride the storm. Manic doesn't do the 'BBC-lite' approach. We're the station people come to for an escape, not for rolling misery. We don't break the news—we react to it. So until Speke calls it, you two do what you do best.*

Wahab Hussain: *Yeah, but if it drops mid-link and JJ's talking about which Love Islander's got an OnlyFans now, we're gonna look like pricks.*

Hallie smirked. Wahab had a point. Bee Manic thrived on *chaotic good* energy—quick-witted, unfiltered, always teetering on the edge of what was acceptable. But there were limits, and today was one of those days where stepping over that line could have actual consequences. She popped another peri fry into her mouth and sent a reply.

Hallie Young: *We just need to be ready to pivot if needed. If Speke gives the go-ahead, we tone it down and go semi-respectful. If not, we act like it's a normal day. We're walking a tightrope here, lads. Hang on… if Speke pulls Pete off Midlands Manic, who'll be doing it?*

Hallie knew that it'd probably go to the network feed from Speke, Danny O'Neil, a show which was aimed more to the secondary CHR stations in the Manic network—places like Rochdale and Bolton, Warwick and Rugby, Burton-upon-Trent and the High Peaks, places where there were no universities or major metropolitan hubs. The fact that the playout of music was standardised across the whole CHR network, meaning that even though there were local hosts in different regions, they were all playing the exact same songs, meant that the differentiation of stations relied on the personalities of their presenters. Bee Manic had the advantage of being in Manchester, where competition was fierce, so it was given more freedom to develop a unique identity compared to the smaller CHR outposts. If Pete Smith was off Midlands Manic, it meant one of two things: either they were going to network Danny O'Neil, or they were scrambling for another solution.

Looking at her watch, she noticed it was half past 1, and that, as she was a Brummie… well, West Bromwich (which, in the grand scheme of things was near enough to count), and she had only moved from the Midlands to Manchester 2 months earlier, she was still known on the Birmingham scene, which meant that she knew that she could easily do the drive show for Birmingham remotely, even if it meant using her Zetta2Go credentials, as even though the majority of hubs used Myriad or PlayoutONE, the Dudley and Olympic Park hubs had full RCS Zetta and GSelector integration, so she could access the Midlands Manic playout remotely if it came to it.

Hallie sipped her Coke, letting the sugar and caffeine kick in as she considered the implications. It wasn't unusual for presenters to cover shows from other hubs remotely—especially after COVID had normalised remote voice-tracking—but doing it *live* while also juggling Bee Manic's drive show? That would be chaos.

She pulled up her contacts and fired off a quick text to her mate Carl Richards, a producer at Midlands Manic.

Hallie Young: *Oi, mate. Heard Pete's off drive. Who's covering?*

The typing bubbles popped up almost instantly.

Carl Richards: *Don't even bloody start. We don't know yet. I've got Tommo from breakfast sat in the office refusing to do it, and Jane is on the warpath. If it's Danny bloody O'Neil I swear to God...*

Jane Spearmore, the Regional Director, was not someone to be crossed. Hallie knew from experience that if Jane was "on the warpath," it meant that Midlands Manic was in complete disarray behind the scenes. The fact that Tom Greaves, her former co-host, was outright refusing to step in only added to the mess.

Hallie took another sip of her Coke, considering her options. It wasn't her problem, technically. She had Bee Manic to think about. But at the same time, she hated the idea of the Birmingham station, the one she had built a career on, falling apart like this.

She fired off another message.

Hallie Young: *If it's that bad, just tell Jane I'll do it from Manc. I've still got my logins.*

The reply came within seconds.

Carl Richards: *You serious? You'd do both shows?*

Hallie Young: *Nah, I'll throw JJ under the bus and have him do Manc drive on his own while I hold down Brum's drive remotely. He can handle it—might actually stop him from embarrassing us all live on air for once.*

****

It was half past three when the decision was made, not locally, but by Speke. JJ was to do the Manchester drive on his own, while Hallie would handle Midlands Manic remotely from Studio 2, what was normally the Manic Radio Rochdale studio since the move from local studios to hubs, with Rochdale and Bolton only having local breakfast and the rest of the shows being the network feed with split links, or for Drive, they would simulcast the Manchester drive show with split links, ensuring that local branding remained intact. The uniqueness of those two stations not taking the network small market feed was a quirk of Manchester's size—Bee Manic was allowed to extend its influence on nearby areas rather than force them into the generic network.

Hallie sat in the studio, quickly configuring her logins for Midlands Manic while balancing a half-finished bottle of

Diet Coke on the desk. She'd already checked the playout logs—Midlands Manic's clock was still running its usual CHR cycle, packed with upbeat hits, mostly the same as Bee Manic's but with slight variations to cater to a Birmingham audience. She flicked through the music log: Harry Styles, Lizzo, Joel Corry, Ed Sheeran… the standard fare. As she was known to audiences in Birmingham, and when she was down there, she had her own segments, not the Manchester ones, she would be expected to slot into her familiar style without missing a beat. It was a strange kind of homecoming—just not the one she'd imagined.

Her phone buzzed again.

JJ Dennison: *Fuming. Properly fuming. I've been mugged off here. You get to do the Brummie show, and I'm left here solo?*

Hallie smirked, quickly tapping out a response.

Hallie Young: *Oh, come on, JJ. Think of it as a chance to prove you can actually host a show without me carrying you.*

JJ Dennison: *Piss off.*

She rolled her eyes. He'd be fine. He might be an absolute menace, but he was a pro when it counted. Wahab would make sure he didn't completely tank the show.

The irony that the studio was fitted with PlayoutONE, but thanks to having Google Chrome on the computer and access to her old Zetta2Go logins, as she did the occasional cover shift on Manic Dance when Dr Manic, the evening show host who was based out of Speke but was a genuine A&E doctor, was on call, meaning that she had to make sure that she had access to the system whenever necessary. That meant she could manually override and control Midlands Manic's playout directly from Manchester. The thought made her laugh. The whole radio industry was built on illusion—listeners assumed everything was live, local, and seamlessly produced. In reality, half the country's radio was being run from a few hubs with presenters juggling multiple shows across multiple regions.

She knew that she wouldn't be presenting the Manchester show today, so she knew that she could put all her efforts into making sure Midlands Manic ran smoothly, even if it meant she'd be broadcasting to her old Birmingham audience from a studio in Manchester. The absurdity of it wasn't lost on her.

The clock ticked closer to 4 PM. JJ would be going live on Bee Manic soon, and she needed to be in place for the Midlands Manic show. She did a final check of her playout settings, making sure her mic was patched correctly through the remote system. A quick glance at the WhatsApp chat showed no new updates from Speke. That was a good sign—it meant no sudden changes to protocol. At least, not yet.

She put her headphones on, adjusted her mic, and leaned back in her chair, watching the final seconds tick down on the playout screen.

****

CHAPTER 15 - Rolling News
Thursday 8th September 2022

Pete Smith knew that this was much unlike his usual shifts, where he'd be jovial, upbeat, and lacing his links on his usual drivetime show on Midlands Manic, the CHR station within the Manic Radio Group for the Birmingham, Coventry and Black Country areas, with his typical Dudley humour and quick wit. But today was different. Pete had been called upon to anchor the rolling news coverage for Manic Goldies, the group's nostalgia-driven station, known for its playlist of hits from the 60s, 70s, and 80s. The weight of the assignment was not lost on him. This wasn't just any day. The passing of Queen Elizabeth II was a moment that would resonate across generations, and it was his voice that would carry the news to millions of listeners.

The fact it was half past 3, and that he'd been told 5 minutes earlier that he'd be starting early and not finishing until 8pm, a straight on-air shift of four and a half hours, was almost secondary to the gravity of the situation. Pete had spent years navigating the quirks and chaos of commercial radio, but today felt different, quieter.

Officially he knew that he was not to mention anything to do with the passing of the Queen, which was at the moment "rumours" and "embargoed news" but to state for, however long the Palace said, that she was ill, and that the nation was holding its breath. Pete knew that once the embargo was lifted, everything would change. He would be the voice that broke the news to listeners across the Midlands and beyond—a responsibility he both dreaded and honoured.

The irony that no tracks were being permitted to be played on Manic Goldies for the duration of the rolling news coverage was not lost on Pete. For a station built around music, it felt jarring to strip it away entirely. Instead, the airwaves would be filled with his voice and that of the correspondents, analysts, and pre-recorded tributes carefully curated for the occasion.

Sitting in the studio at the Manic Midlands hub in Dudley, Pete adjusted his headphones and glanced at the clock. It was now 3:35 pm, and he could feel the weight of the nation's collective unease settling over him. The newsroom was a hive of muted activity, with producers and researchers darting back and forth, their faces set in serious expressions. Pete's producer for the day, Laura, handed him the latest script, her face betraying a mix of nervousness and focus.

"Pete," Laura said, her voice low but steady, "this is the running order for now. We're sticking with updates about the Queen's health until the embargo lifts. After that, you'll go straight into the official announcement, followed by the pre-recorded tribute package. Just remember—keep the tone measured and respectful. You've done this kind of thing before."

Pete nodded, offering her a small smile. "Thanks, Laura. I'll be fine. It's just… well, it's not every day you get handed something like this."

Laura gave him a reassuring pat on the shoulder before returning to her workstation. Pete scanned the script, his mind racing as he tried to internalise the flow of the programme. The announcement would be followed by a montage of listener tributes, pre-recorded reflections from
196

historians and public figures, and updates from Manic's correspondents stationed across the UK.

At precisely 3:45 pm, Pete leaned into the microphone and spoke, his voice calm and steady.

"Good afternoon, and thank you Louise for passing over to me. I'm Pete Smith, live and across Britain on Manic Goldies, on FM, AM, DAB and the Manic Prime app. Her Majesty the Queen, Elizabeth the Second, is currently under medical supervision at Balmoral, as announced earlier by Buckingham Palace. Members of the Royal Family are gathering at her side, and the nation waits for further updates. We'll be bringing you rolling news coverage throughout the evening, reflecting on the life and reign of Her Majesty, while keeping you informed as events unfold."

He paused, letting the weight of his words settle, straightening his black tie, which he had stored in his locker as he knew that today would demand a sombre tone, even before the full gravity of events became clear.

Pete glanced through the glass panel into the producer's booth, where Laura gave him a thumbs-up. The small gesture of support steadied him. Taking a breath, he continued, his voice unwavering.

"At this moment, the thoughts of millions across the country and around the world are with Her Majesty and the Royal Family. This is a time of reflection, unity, and respect. Angus McKinley, our local reporter for Manic Scotland is at Balmoral, Angus, can you provide an update?"

Pete watched as Zetta automatically loaded an only just recorded bulletin from ITN's news service, voiced by Angus McKinley, one of ITN's correspondents stationed near Balmoral. The recording played seamlessly, his professional yet sombre tone filling the studio.

"Thank you. Here at Balmoral, there's a noticeable air of quiet anticipation. Members of the public and press have gathered nearby, watching as senior members of the Royal Family continue to arrive. While official details remain limited, the presence of close family members at Balmoral underscores the seriousness of the situation. This is Angus McKinley for Manic Radio News."

Pete had to silently chuckle at how ITN were the main supplier of news for Manic, and that Angus, one of ITN's staff, was trying to pretend he was a Manic reporter, whereas Bauer and Global used IRN and Sky News Radio for their news services. The distinction was both amusing and sobering; it highlighted the patchwork nature of Manic's operations, even during moments of national significance.

"That was our correspondent at Balmoral, Angus McKinley, reporting live on the situation at Balmoral. We now go to our correspondent at Windsor, Helen Jenkins, who's reporting from Windsor Castle, another focal point for Royal activity today. Helen, what's the atmosphere like there?"

Pete noticed that Laura and some of the Speke network centre people were updating both his Zetta system and his script in real time, with conflicting edits that reflected the chaotic coordination typical of Manic Radio's sprawling operations. It was a delicate balancing act, navigating the demands of live broadcasting while maintaining the gravitas required for such a momentous occasion. The irony that while he and Laura were in Dudley, at the former Dudley FM studios and former headquarters of both the Breeze Media and Bones Radio Network operations, they were reliant on edits from Speke—a hub that had historically been the heart of Manic's frenetic CHR operations—was not lost on Pete. It was a logistical tangle, but one he had come to expect after years in the industry.

Helen Jenkins's report came through clearly, her voice calm but tinged with the solemnity of the moment.

"Thank you, Pete. Here at Windsor Castle, the atmosphere is one of quiet reflection. Members of the public have begun to gather outside the gates, laying flowers and standing in silent vigil. The historic walls of Windsor have seen centuries of change, and today they stand as a symbol of continuity during a time of uncertainty. While there is no official word yet, the mood here is one of reverence and concern. Helen Jenkins, for ITN... erm... Manic Radio News."

Pete had to groan at the slip up of the namecheck, of Helen saying ITN before remembering that she was acting as a Manic correspondent for the day. It was a small detail, but it spoke volumes about the rushed and somewhat chaotic nature of Manic Radio's operations. Still, Pete knew better than to dwell on it. His job was to keep the broadcast moving seamlessly, maintaining the dignity and professionalism the moment demanded.

"Thank you, Helen," Pete said, smoothly transitioning. "We'll continue to bring you updates from Windsor,

Balmoral, and beyond as they come in. As the nation waits, we invite you to share your thoughts and reflections. Our phone lines and text messages are open, and we'll be sharing some of your tributes throughout the evening."

Pete glanced at the clock. It was approaching 4 pm, and he knew the minutes were ticking down to the inevitable announcement. The studio, usually buzzing with the energy of producers, engineers, and presenters, felt eerily calm. Laura was now in constant communication with the central newsroom, her voice low but firm as she coordinated updates and ensured the script was aligned with the latest developments.

At a minute to 4pm, Pete saw that he had a minute or two break, as the regular news at the top of the hour was about to play. He knew that as Goldies was based out of the Olympic Park hub, and that the news bulletin at the top of the hour would originate from there, it would follow the standard format, unlike his regular CHR drive show that originated from the studio he was in, Studio 1, at Dudley, where like news at the top and bottom of each hour was produced by Dudley staff who were, like the Olympic Park staff, still on Breeze Media terms and conditions—a relic of the chaotic mergers and acquisitions that had shaped the Manic Radio Group over the years. Pete allowed himself a brief moment of reflection as the hour struck, and the familiar tones of the Manic Goldies news jingle faded into the opening lines of the bulletin.

"From the Manic Radio newsroom, this is the latest news on Manic Goldies."

The newsreader's voice was calm and measured, delivering updates on the Queen's health and the global reaction to the Buckingham Palace statement. As Pete listened, he prepared himself for the next segment of rolling coverage, mentally rehearsing the words he might need to say when the inevitable announcement came through.

The bulletin concluded, and Pete took a deep breath, leaning into the microphone once again. "Thank you for joining us here on Manic Goldies. I'm Pete Smith, bringing you rolling news coverage as we await further updates on Her Majesty the Queen. Coming up, we'll hear more from our correspondents at Balmoral and Windsor, as well as reflections on the Queen's life and service from voices across the nation. As we await further updates, we will continue to bring you live coverage and reflections on the extraordinary life of Her Majesty. For now, we'll hear from historian Dr Eleanor Marlowe, who has shared her thoughts on the Queen's enduring legacy."

The pre-recorded segment played, Dr Marlowe's voice resonant and thoughtful as she spoke of the Queen's steadfastness through decades of change. Pete leaned back slightly, using the brief respite to glance at Laura, who was now juggling a flurry of messages from Speke and ITN. She caught his eye and mouthed "You're doing great."

The reassurance helped. Pete adjusted his posture and prepared for the next segment, knowing that the real test would come when the embargo lifted. For now, it was about maintaining composure and providing a steady presence for listeners who were likely tuning in for both information and solace.

At around half past 4, Laura sent Pete a message which made him frown.

Laura Turner: *Bee Manic just broke the embargo with an ad-libbed announcement about the Queen's passing. Someone from their Manchester studio apparently said it live on air during a link. Speke is scrambling to contain the fallout. Just stick to the plan—we're solid here.*

Pete knew that his microphone was off, as a pre-prepared audio package was being played, and that he had to keep his frustration in check. The sheer recklessness of breaking the embargo was unfathomable to Pete. An announcement like this demanded coordination, respect, and precision—qualities that clearly weren't in abundant supply at Bee Manic's Manchester studio.

Pressing the internal intercom, Pete sighed. "Seriously, Laura, which moron in Manchester thought this was a good idea? They've basically thrown a grenade into the middle of this whole operation."

Laura's voice came through the intercom, steady but tinged with exasperation. "Apparently, it was JJ Dennison. The same presenter who managed to say 'moment of history' before veering completely off-script. Speke's trying to get a formal apology lined up, but honestly, Pete, it's a disaster."

Pete thought back to the year before, when he had been struck down with Coronavirus, and the death of Prince Phillip had been covered by IRN, as they had, until the

Manic and Lite Group merger, been the contractor for Manic's news services until one of the former Lite executives who had joined the combined board pointed out that Manic was paying Bauer and Global substantial fees for a service they could replicate in-house. The decision had led to ITN being contracted as the sole news provider, but incidents like Bee Manic's gaffe made Pete question whether the new arrangement had been worth the cost-cutting.

Pete exhaled, gathering his thoughts as the pre-recorded package concluded. The microphone light blinked red, signalling he was live again.

"Thank you, Dr Marlowe, for those insightful reflections on Her Majesty's legacy. As we continue our rolling coverage here on Manic Goldies, our focus remains on providing thoughtful and respectful updates during this significant moment for the nation. It's half past 4, and here's your Manic Goldies news update."

Looking at his script, it said that he had to lead with the news that the Palace were now going to be issuing an update at half past 6, not 6pm as was originally planned. Pete mentally adjusted his pacing for the next couple of hours. It meant extending coverage with more of the pre-prepared content and carefully navigating the emotional weight of the day without tipping into speculation. He jotted down a few notes as the bulletin ended.

"Thank you for that update," Pete began, his voice steady, projecting the calm authority listeners expected from him in moments like this. "It has just been announced that Buckingham Palace will issue a further statement at 6:30 pm. Until then, we will continue to bring you live coverage, reflections, and updates as they come in. Coming up, we'll hear more listener tributes, but first we're going live to Westminster, where Manic Radio sources have been informed that the day's session at the House of Commons had ended early, with our Political Editor, Robert Peston, Robert, what can you tell us about the atmosphere at Westminster today?" Pete's voice remained calm and measured, but there was a faint edge of curiosity as he handed over to ITV's Political Editor and famed correspondent, whose voice came through the feed with its usual distinctive tone.

Internally though, he knew that what audience he had would find it ironic that the ITV Political Editor—a staple of commercial television news—was now reporting live on a station known for nostalgic music, and the fact he was actually live and not prerecorded like his ITN colleagues.

"Thank you, Pete," Robert Peston's familiar voice carried a weight of seriousness, underscored by his characteristic intonation. "The atmosphere here at Westminster is, as you'd expect, subdued and reflective. MPs were informed of the Queen's health earlier this afternoon, and there's a sense of quiet anticipation as everyone awaits further updates. While the Commons has adjourned early, there's a significant presence of MPs and Lords in the Palace of Westminster, many of them staying to offer their support and to be present should any formal statements or actions be required. Across the street, Downing Street has been eerily quiet, with senior officials remaining indoors. It's clear that this is a moment unlike any other, one that transcends politics and party lines."

"Robert," Pete then said, looking at his script which had highlighted a note about rumours the Palace had pulled the Prime Minister, Liz Truss, into a confidential meeting earlier in the day, "there have been unconfirmed reports that Prime Minister Liz Truss has had a direct briefing with senior Palace officials. Is there any indication of what this might entail or what role she might be playing in the events unfolding today?"

Peston responded carefully, his words deliberate. "Pete, while I cannot confirm specifics, it is not unusual for the Prime Minister to be closely involved in moments of national importance such as this. The relationship between the Prime Minister and the Sovereign is one of the pillars of our constitutional system, and it would make sense for the Prime Minister to be kept abreast of developments. From what I understand, this meeting was private and focused on ensuring that all necessary preparations are in place, both administratively and ceremonially, should the nation need to transition into a period of official mourning. But again, the Palace remains tight-lipped, and no official statement has corroborated this as of now."

Pete nodded, his voice even as he thanked Peston for the update. "Thank you, Robert. As ever, your insights are invaluable during this time. We'll be checking back in with you later for further updates from Westminster."

Switching gears, Pete turned back to his audience, glancing at the clock and seeing that Zetta had got scheduled a pre-recorded report. "It's now coming up to 4:40 pm, and here on Manic Goldies, we continue our rolling coverage of this significant moment in our nation's history. We now head over to our Scottish Political editor, who is at Holyrood, Paul McAndrew. Paul, for our Scottish audience on Manic Goldies, what is the situation in Edinburgh?"

Paul McAndrew's voice came through the feed, calm and with a distinct Scottish lilt that brought a sense of local connection to the broadcast.

"Here at Holyrood, the atmosphere mirrors much of what we're seeing across the UK—one of solemnity and anticipation. Members of the Scottish Parliament have been informed of the Queen's condition, and while proceedings have officially adjourned, many MSPs remain in the building, quietly discussing the implications of today's events. Outside the Parliament, the mood is reflective, with members of the public beginning to gather. There's a tangible sense of respect here, given Her Majesty's deep connection to Scotland, particularly Balmoral, which she has always considered a sanctuary. While we await further updates from the Palace, the people here are preparing for what feels like the end of an era. This is Paul McAndrew, for Manic Radio News."

Pete nodded slightly as he leaned into his microphone. "Thank you, Paul. As you mentioned, the Queen's connection to Scotland runs deep, and it's fitting that such reflections come from Holyrood today. We'll return to Edinburgh later in the hour for more insights as we continue to bring you the latest updates."

****

CHAPTER 16 - Breaking the Network
Thursday 8th September 2022

"This is the Manic Radio Group across Britain. It is my duty to inform the nation that Her Majesty Queen Elizabeth II has passed away. The Queen died peacefully at Balmoral this afternoon. The King and The Queen Consort will remain at Balmoral this evening and will return to London tomorrow."

The words hung in the air like a dense fog, heavy with the weight of history. Pete Smith, sitting in the Manic Goldies studio in Dudley, had just delivered the announcement that would echo across the nation for generations. His voice, steady but solemn, carried the gravity of the moment as millions of listeners tuned in to hear the news they had been dreading.

Pete knew that he needed no script to deliver that specific line, as he had rehearsed it several times over the past year, and had, in the past week, done intensive rehearsals of it as part of the Senior Presenter role, with the news that the Queen had been not as well as the Palace had hoped. His delivery, a culmination of those rehearsals and years of experience, was flawless. But even so, as he removed his headphones and adjusted his posture, the reality of what he had just said began to settle over him like a heavy blanket.

The studio was silent, save for the faint hum of equipment and the occasional muffled voice from the production booth. Laura Turner, his producer, looked pale but composed as she coordinated the next steps with the network centre in Speke. Pete could see her mouthing instructions into her headset, her professionalism a steadying presence amidst the surreal atmosphere.

He knew that Manic Goldies would remain rolling news, with Manic Blues and Manic Soul joining for the remaining hour and half of his emergency show, and that Manic Classical, after the National Anthem played out, would return to their London based Obit playlist, Manic's CHR and Manic Dance stations not even staying for the national anthem, and Manic Rock and Manic Metal taking his announcement and then resuming their usual programming. The stark differences in how each station under the Manic Radio Group handled the announcement highlighted the network's chaotic and inconsistent approach to a moment of national significance. Pete couldn't help but feel a twinge of frustration at how disjointed it all seemed.

"This is Manic Goldies, Manic Blues and Manic Soul, live and ad-free for the next 10 days, I'm Pete Smith, and I'll be bringing you all the latest following the sad passing of Her Majesty, Queen Elizabeth the Second," Pete said as God Save The King, as it would be now known, played softly in the background, marking the transition to a new chapter in British history. Pete felt a lump rise in his throat as he uttered those words—"God Save The King." It was a moment that symbolised profound change, one that every listener would remember for the rest of their lives.

As the anthem faded, Pete leaned into the microphone, his tone measured and reflective.

"The Queen's passing marks the end of an era, a reign spanning more than seventy years, during which she became a symbol of unity, resilience, and dedication.

Tonight, we'll reflect on her extraordinary life, her service to the nation, and the legacy she leaves behind. We'll also bring you tributes from across the country and beyond, as we come together to honour Her Majesty. Now, I was born in 1972, 20 years after Her Majesty ascended to the throne. Like many of you, I grew up knowing no other monarch. Her face was on our coins, her speeches marked our Christmases, and her presence was a constant in an ever-changing world. I remember being on the air in the Midlands when Her Majesty The Queen Mother had passed, when the late Princess Diana tragically died, and during the Golden Jubilee celebrations in 2002. Yet, today feels different—a moment both deeply personal and shared by millions. For so many of us, she was not just the Queen; she was a symbol of continuity, a steady hand guiding us through decades of change."

Pete paused, allowing the moment to breathe, the weight of his words resonating across the silent studio and through the airwaves. He glanced at the clock; it was 6:40 pm. The next segment, a pre-recorded tribute featuring historian Dr Eleanor Marlowe and royal biographer Richard Armstrong, was queued and ready to air. Pete took a sip of water, his throat dry from the emotional intensity of the announcement.

"Up next, we'll hear from some of the country's most respected voices, reflecting on Her Majesty's remarkable life and her impact on the world. But before that, we go live to Westminster, where Robert Peston, our political editor, is standing by. Robert, what's the atmosphere like in Westminster right now?"

The familiar voice of Robert Peston came through the feed, calm yet layered with a gravitas that matched the moment. "Thank you, Pete. Here in Westminster, the mood is sombre, reflective, and profoundly respectful. Flags have been lowered to half-mast, and MPs from all parties have gathered in quiet discussion, their usual divisions set aside in recognition of this historic moment. Prime Minister Liz Truss is expected to make a statement shortly, and preparations are already underway for a period of national mourning."

As Robert spoke, Pete allowed himself a moment of reflection. The contrast between the composed professionalism of Robert's report and the chaotic reports trickling in from Manic's CHR stations—where upbeat music had resumed almost immediately—was striking. Pete knew that listeners would notice the disparity, and he silently hoped that the gravity of the moment would prompt changes across the network.

"Thank you, Robert," Pete said, his voice steady as he resumed. "We'll return to Westminster later in the hour for further updates. For now, let's reflect on the extraordinary legacy of Queen Elizabeth II with this tribute."

****

"This is the Manic Radio Group across Britain. It is my duty to inform the nation that Her Majesty Queen Elizabeth II has passed away. The Queen died peacefully at Balmoral this afternoon. The King and The Queen Consort will remain at Balmoral this evening and will return to London tomorrow."

Hallie was sat in Studio 2 at the Piccadilly Gardens hub when the network-wide announcement came through. Her headphones pressed firmly against her ears, she sat back in her chair, watching the monitors in front of her as the Manic network fractured under the weight of history.

Looking at her Zetta2Go setup, Hallie noticed that the clock was half past 6, and that she had only 30 minutes left to fill before the Bee Manic show was scheduled to finish. But in reality, nothing about this show was normal anymore. The network-wide announcement had just aired, yet Manic's playout system was still rolling forward, as if nothing had changed.

She refreshed the music log. The next track lined up was Destination Calabria by Alex Gaudino. Hallie knew that the protocol for Midlands Manic, like the rest of the CHR network, was to air the regular playlist, barring any major updates from Speke, but she also knew instinctively that playing a high-energy club banger moments after the Queen's passing had been announced would be catastrophic.

She knew that she couldn't turn it out of the playlist, as it had already been preloaded into the automation system, and Midlands Manic's playout was centrally controlled from Speke. If she didn't act fast, that saxophone riff would blare out across Birmingham at precisely the wrong moment.

Hallie took a deep breath, her mind racing. She had seconds—seconds—to stop the worst possible transition in live radio history. *Destination Calabria* was about to come crashing in after a national moment of reflection, and she had no power to stop it directly. But she *did* have one trick up her sleeve.

She slammed the talkback button to her producer, Carl Richards, who was overseeing Midlands Manic's remote feed from the Dudley studios.

"Carl—fader kill. Now. Trust me."

Carl didn't hesitate. On the other end, she heard a quick *click*, followed by a sigh of relief as the monitor in front of her showed MIDLANDS MANIC – FADER MUTED. *Destination Calabria* had been silenced before it could wreak absolute havoc.

"Quickly, cue up something like anything acoustic, instrumental, or neutral," Hallie continued, still gripping the talkback button. "Something safe—don't let us be the station that plays Destination Calabria right after the biggest news of the century."

Carl's voice came through her headphones, slightly frazzled but clear. "Hang on, I've got Chasing Cars by Snow Patrol lined up. That work?"

"Yes. Perfect. Play it and keep it low going into an ID or something," Hallie exhaled, her heart still racing. "I won't be doing any more live links, so just play some filler music when I'm supposed to be talking, as I'm going to go to JJ and see if he's fucked up yet."

Hallie leaned back in her chair, her heart still racing from the near-miss with Destination Calabria. She could hear Chasing Cars fading in softly on Midlands Manic, a far more appropriate choice in the circumstances. The

Manchester air felt heavy, not just with the weight of history but with the knowledge that Bee Manic—her station—had already royally screwed up once today with JJ Dennison's reckless announcement.

Standing up and walking into Studio 1, Hallie saw that JJ was recklessly bantering on about Love Island Australia spoilers, acting as if it were a standard evening show.

Her stomach twisted.

This wasn't just tone-deaf—it was catastrophic. The biggest moment in modern British history had just unfolded, and here was JJ, grinning as he rattled off behind the scenes details of the upcoming season, while Destination Calabria was still set to play next on Bee Manic.

She knew that the instructions were to keep it normal after the announcement, and that Bee Manic's directive was business as usual, but this? This was suicide.

The fact that Wahab was looking like he was enjoying the normalcy infuriated her, as she knew, from what Wahab had told her when he came back to Bee Manic, when he was producer for the Calvin Prosner show back in 2017, when the Manchester Arena bombings happened, he had been the one to ensure that Bee Manic reacted properly, overriding the usual playlist and getting Calvin to speak from the heart. As a Sunni Muslim, he had experienced the horrors of that night from a deeply personal perspective, knowing that his own community would be affected by both grief and the inevitable backlash. He had acted with professionalism and dignity then—so why was he sitting back and letting JJ make a complete fool of the station now?

****

"This is the Manic Radio Group across Britain. It is my duty to inform the nation that Her Majesty Queen Elizabeth II has passed away. The Queen died peacefully at Balmoral this afternoon. The King and The Queen Consort will remain at Balmoral this evening and will return to London tomorrow."

Lord Cedric Ashcombe was sat in the Mayfair Private Members club that he and several other members of the House of Lords belonged to when the announcement rang out from the small digital radio perched on the mahogany bar. The weight of the moment settled over the room like a thick fog, muting the usual clink of glasses and hushed conversations. A silence fell, unnatural and heavy, as the well-heeled patrons, many of whom had spent their lives in service to the Crown in some form or another, absorbed the news.

"Ah, well, old chap," Lord Alistair Finch-Fletchery said, holding a glass of scotch neatly between his fingers, "we knew this was coming. Got your speech ready for the next Session?"

Cedric took a measured sip of his whisky, the amber liquid catching the dim club lighting. His normally jovial, rich baritone was tempered with a quiet solemnity. "Indeed, Alistair. I've also prepared to swear allegiance to His Majesty King Charles III, as we must all do in due course."

"As have I, Cedric, old chap," Lord Michael Banks, a fellow Life Peer who, much like his surname, was a banker who had long been a fixture in the financial corridors of power, added with a solemn nod. "Parliament will be suspended, of course. The Prime Minister will need to make a statement, and the country will enter official mourning. I expect the broadcasters will be in chaos right now."

Cedric leaned back in his chair, his fingers tapping lightly against the polished wood of the armrest. "Indeed, though I imagine the BBC and Times Radio are handling this with the utmost decorum. Commercial radio, however…" He trailed off, allowing the weight of implication to hang in the air.

"So says the former Radio 3 host who moved to Manic Classical," Lord Alistair said with a smirk, swirling the last of his scotch. "One can only assume your dear colleagues at Manic are making an absolute pig's ear of it."

Cedric sighed, setting his glass down with an air of resignation. "Indeed. While I suspect Manic Goldies is handling itself with some measure of dignity—owing to Pete Smith's steady hands—the same cannot be said for the CHR stations. If the Bee Manic debacle earlier is anything to go by, then I imagine it's already an absolute catastrophe."

Cedric sighed, setting his glass down with an air of resignation. "Indeed. While I suspect Manic Goldies is handling itself with some measure of dignity—owing to Pete Smith's steady hands—the same cannot be said for the CHR stations. If the Bee Manic debacle earlier is anything to go by, then I imagine it's already an absolute catastrophe. Anyway, I've had my secretary draft a statement along the lines of *'With the deepest sorrow, I pay tribute to Her Majesty The Queen, whose decades of service defined an era of stability and grace. I offer my allegiance to His Majesty King Charles III as he assumes the heavy burden of duty.'*"

"That's a good one, Cedric," Michael said approvingly, setting his glass down on the polished wood table. "Measured, respectful, and with just the right amount of gravitas. Of course, we'll all have to say something in the coming days. The Lords will be expected to lead in setting the tone for the nation. Mind if I borrow the statement for my own purposes? A touch of refinement, of course, but it encapsulates the moment well."

Cedric offered a nod of approval, lifting his glass in a small toast. "By all means, Michael. If ever there was a moment for unity in service, it is now. This transition will be one of great historical consequence, and we must ensure our words reflect that."

As the radio continued its rolling coverage, Cedric glanced at his pocket watch—a habit inherited from his late father, who had served in the Royal Household. He knew that by morning, the political and media landscape would shift dramatically. The BBC would move seamlessly into its well-rehearsed schedule of tributes, Global and Bauer's networks would tread carefully with respectful programming, and Manic… well, Manic would be Manic.

The quiet solemnity of the private club was a stark contrast to the chaos that was surely unfolding across the airwaves. Cedric took another sip of whisky, knowing that by the next day, he would likely have to step in to ensure that Manic Classical—his own domain—remained a bastion of dignity amid the inevitable corporate missteps elsewhere in the network.

****

"This is the Manic Radio Group across Britain. It is my duty to inform the nation that Her Majesty Queen Elizabeth II has passed away. The Queen died peacefully at Balmoral this afternoon. The King and The Queen Consort will remain at Balmoral this evening and will return to London tomorrow."

Jess Taylor was sat in Studio 5 of the Huddersfield hub, her Manic North East Drive show, despite the orders from Speke to remain business as usual, going from the announcement, Jess knew that, like her boss, the regional director for the North East region, Tom Hargrove, did, a more softer CHR schedule of tracks for the last half hour, something like what Smooth Chilled or Magic Radio might air, would be far more appropriate than the usual CHR fare.

Unlike the Dudley, London, Manchester, Cardiff, Dundee and Speke hubs, Huddersfield, like its Exeter sister, used a piece of software called Myriad, which, despite its age, was known for being incredibly reliable and flexible, something that had allowed Jess the ability to make quick changes without waiting for Speke to issue a centralised command. It was a small mercy in a day that had already been filled with more chaos than she had anticipated.

As she glanced at her playlist, she saw that the next track was Destination Calabria by Alex Gaudino.

Jess groaned.

It seemed that no matter how prepared she was, the spectre of an inappropriate dance banger was haunting the entire network.

Quickly, she clicked into Myriad and searched for an alternative. She knew she couldn't veer too far from the CHR sound—Speke would have a fit if she suddenly started throwing in tracks from the Smooth playlist—but she also knew that a pulsating club anthem would be an unmitigated disaster. Her eyes scanned the options, and she made a snap decision.

Coldplay – Fix You.

It was still pop. Still within the realm of what Manic North East's audience might expect. But it carried enough emotional weight to land properly in the moment.

Without hesitation, she dragged the track into the log, overriding Destination Calabria before it could cue. The screen flickered, Myriad processing the change. Then, finally, the playout confirmed the switch.

She looked at her producer, Carl Reed, a 50something who had been on Midlands and Yorkshire radio since the mid-1990s, and so was used to short notice changes. He raised an eyebrow but nodded in approval.

"Good call," he muttered, adjusting his headphones. "Speke might not like it, but sod them. The audience will."

Jess exhaled, the tension in her shoulders easing slightly. "Yeah, well, if they give me grief for not leading into a national mourning period with a bloody saxophone dance banger, they can take it up with OFCOM."

Carl let out a chuckle, shaking his head. "You're not wrong, love. Back in the day, we'd have had a producer in the studio pulling those tracks before they could ever hit air. These days? We're lucky if anyone at Speke even notices before it's too late."

Jess watched the waveform of *Fix You* appear on the playout system, the slow, mournful intro already a stark contrast to what had almost played. She allowed herself a moment to breathe before cueing up her mic.

"It's 6:35 on Manic Radio North East," she began, keeping her voice steady, calm. "If you're just joining us, the nation is reflecting on the news that Her Majesty Queen Elizabeth II has passed away this afternoon at Balmoral. Unlike some of our sister stations who have decided to stick with the regular schedule, here at Manic Radio North East, we'll be adjusting our music slightly for the rest of Drive, offering a more reflective tone as we remember the life of Her Majesty. For now, a song that feels appropriate for the moment. Coldplay, Fix You, here on Manic Radio North East."

Jess exhaled as Fix You faded into the distance, the gentle swell of Chris Martin's voice carrying the mood of the moment. She glanced across the studio at Carl, who nodded in quiet approval.

"Nice save," he murmured, tapping his pen against his notebook.

Jess smirked, shaking her head. "I swear, if I see Destination Calabria in this playlist one more time, I'm driving to Speke myself and deleting it from the servers."

Carl chuckled, rubbing his temples. "Speke's probably too busy trying to explain JJ's monumental cock-up to worry about us up here."

Jess grimaced. "Yeah, I need to check in with Tom about that. He must be losing his mind."

She reached for her phone and opened her messages. Tom Hargrove, her regional director, was usually a picture of calm, but if Jess knew him well enough, he'd be pacing the Huddersfield office, muttering about how Manchester had once again made the entire Manic Radio network look like a joke.

Sure enough, when she opened their chat, his last message was only one word:

Tom Hargrove: *Disgraceful.*

Jess sighed. It wasn't like she could argue with him. She typed out a quick reply.

Jess Taylor: *We've adjusted the tone here. No issues. I changed the log—went with Fix You instead of whatever nonsense was scheduled.*

A minute later, the three dots appeared.

Tom Hargrove: *Good call. If Speke moans, I'll deal with them. Just keep it tight, professional. The last thing we need is OFCOM crawling up our backsides over this.*

Jess put her phone down and turned back to Carl. "Speke's still running regular programming, aren't they?"

Carl snorted. "Business as usual, apparently. I mean, it's not like we've just had the biggest news in living memory or anything."

Jess groaned. "I bet Global and Bauer have already switched to rolling tributes. Meanwhile, we've got stations still playing Becky Hill and David Guetta."

Carl leaned back in his chair. "I'll say this much, kid— you've got your head screwed on. If we were still back in the old Breeze or Bones days, there wouldn't be any debate. Someone with common sense would be in charge. But Manic? It's a bloody free-for-all."

Jess shook her head. "Well, whatever happens, at least we're doing it right here. Next song's Somewhere Only We Know by Keane. Should buy us some time before Speke notices I've gone rogue."

Carl chuckled. "Rebel."

Jess just smirked and cued the next track.

****

CHAPTER 17 - Toni
Thursday 8th September 2022

Unlike most Manic presenters, Toni Green wasn't in a studio when the announcement came. Instead, she was sat in the Speke hub's prep area, doing the preparation for her evening show which, she knew was due to start in a mere few minutes. The irony wasn't lost on her. She had spent years building her brand as a no-nonsense, sharp-tongued radio host, thriving on scandal, pop culture, and snarky comebacks.

Born Cassie Longton, her life had been one of chaos, heartbreak and cocaine, as the young black Altrincham woman had clawed her way up from the toxicity of Bee Manic to land a national gig on Manic Radio's evening slot. Having been born in 1997, Cassie remembered Key 103, the EMAP, then Bauer, station that had dominated Manchester's airwaves during her childhood and its competitor, Bee Pic Gdnz, both based at the time in different parts of Piccadilly Gardens.

At 14, she had fell in love with a fellow Altrincham lad, Callum Ellington, who went to the same secondary school as her. Their relationship was intense, messy, and ultimately disastrous. By the time she was 16, Cassie had fallen pregnant and had given up the child, a daughter, for adoption, as her mother had intervened, declaring that neither Cassie nor Callum were in any state to raise a baby.

Callum, of course, ran off, moving to Middleton on the other side of Manchester, conveniently distancing himself from the situation. At the time, Cassie, as a teen, enjoyed the bad boy image that Callum, who was two years older than her, had cultivated. He was reckless, charming in that rough-edged way, and had a habit of making promises he never intended to keep. When she told him she was pregnant, he had nodded along, feigning concern, but within weeks, he had stopped responding to her messages. The final straw had been seeing him in the Arndale Centre with a new girlfriend, acting as if nothing had ever happened. That was when Cassie's mother had stepped in—arranging everything, making sure the baby would be placed with a stable family, ensuring Cassie could still have a future.

And then, a few years later, in 2019, she met him again at Bee Manic, when she was starting out in commercial radio, and he was a producer of the Emma and radio. Callum Ellington, now a producer at the station, had waltzed back into her life like nothing had happened. He still had that cocky grin, still exuded the same self-assured arrogance that had once pulled her in. But Cassie—now Toni Green—wasn't the same girl he had abandoned in Altrincham. She had hardened, sharpened by experience, by betrayal, by the sheer grit it took to survive in an industry that chewed up people like her and spat them out.

Monday 24th June 2019

Buzz stopped at a cluster of desks near the production booth. "This is where you'll be working," he said, pointing to a spare seat cluttered with old headphones, a tangle of cables, and a sticky note that read Fix This Mic. "Don't worry about the mess—nobody actually owns that desk, but it's yours for now."

Cassie set her bag down carefully, trying not to displace anything. "Thanks," she said, feeling like she was standing on the edge of a precipice, about to plunge into the unknown.

Buzz leaned casually on the edge of the desk. "Right, Green. First assignment's easy. Sit in with Emma and Kyler for the mid-morning show. Observe, take notes, soak it all in. You'll see how the magic happens. Oh, and hooking up with your colleagues is more than OK, it's practically expected, be it casual or long term relationships. Unlike the boring lot at Bauer and Global, we aren't stuffy about 'HR violations.' We're all adults here. As long as it's consensual, we don't care if you're fucking in the studio, as long as you don't swear or orgasm on air. You aren't a virgin, am you?"

Cassie—or Toni—felt her cheeks flush even deeper, the room suddenly seeming warmer than it had moments ago. The bluntness of Buzz's question was jarring, a stark reminder that Bee Manic wasn't a typical workplace. She opened her mouth to respond, but the words tangled in her throat. How was she supposed to answer that? Did they really expect their presenters to share that kind of personal detail?

The fact she'd lost her virginity at 14 to her secondary school boyfriend felt irrelevant, but she could sense that Bee Manic operated by its own set of unorthodox rules, where personal boundaries blurred into the professional. She straightened her shoulders, deciding to meet Buzz's audacity with her own composure.

But before she could answer Buzz, she saw him... Callum Ellington, her former secondary school boyfriend. He had been two years older than her, and Cassie knew exactly who he was the moment their eyes met. He looked older but still carried that effortless swagger that had made him the heartthrob of their school. Cassie froze. Of all the places, she hadn't expected to run into him here.

He was leaning casually against a desk on the far side of the office, scrolling through his phone. His trademark smirk, the one that used to send butterflies racing through her stomach when she was fourteen, was nowhere to be seen, replaced by a look of focus that made him seem more grounded, almost unrecognisable. He wore a fitted black t-shirt that hugged his frame and a pair of ripped jeans that screamed Manic uniform.

"Buzz," Callum called, his voice cutting through the hum of the office. "Have you sorted the newbie yet, or is she just standing there collecting dust?"

Buzz rolled his eyes. "Patience, Ellington. I'm getting her up to speed. Anyway, meet Toni Green. She's shadowing Emma and Kyler this morning. Maybe you could give her some pointers—y'know, if you're not too busy being Manchester's biggest pain in the arse."

Callum's gaze shifted to Cassie—or Toni. His eyes flickered with recognition, but he didn't let on. If he remembered her, he didn't show it. Instead, he extended a hand, his expression neutral. "Cal Ellington. I'm Kyler and Emma's producer."

Cassie frowned, as she knew Callum, like her, held a secret, but she had to act cool. Taking his hand, she mustered a smile. "Toni Green. Nice to meet you, Cal."

His grip was firm but brief, and for a moment, she thought she saw a flicker of something—curiosity, perhaps—but it vanished as quickly as it appeared.

"You'll survive," he said, his tone clipped but not unkind. "Buzz, I'll take Toni to the studio ready, as there's half hour until Em and Kyler's mid-morning show starts."

Buzz gave a mock salute, smirking as he turned back to his laptop. "Knock yourself out, Cal. And Green—" he pointed a finger at her as he settled into his chair— "remember, it's a jungle in there. Don't let anyone eat you alive."

Thursday 8th September 2022

Things, however, had got worse for Cassie, as, following Buzz dismissing her, Callum had escorted her to a studio, Studio 2, where he had forced a confrontation she hadn't been prepared for. The ghosts of her past had cornered her that day, wrapped in the smirk of the boy she had once loved and the man he had become.

And then there was Kyler.

The one who she ended up marrying.

Cassie... Toni... remembered the first thing he had ever said to her after walking into that studio.

"Is she a whore like the other presenters you've trained, Cal?"

And she remembered why.

When Callum, or Cal as he called himself, had ordered her to give him a blowjob in exchange for keeping quiet about their child, she had been cornered, desperate, unsure of how to navigate the cutthroat world of Bee Manic. And Kyler had walked in just as she was fighting to resist. The words had dripped from his mouth like poison, laced with smug amusement, and she had realised then that Bee Manic wasn't just a radio station. It was a game, a hierarchy of power and control, and she had just stepped onto the board as a pawn.

A few weeks later, a few drinks in, she and Kyler had had unprotected sex, which caused her to miss her period. By the time she realised, it was too late. She was pregnant.

Toni exhaled sharply, running a hand through her dark curls as she stared blankly at the show prep notes in front of her. It was a surreal moment, sitting in the Manic Speke hub, waiting for her evening show to start, while the nation was about to plunge into mourning. And yet, all she could think about was how far she had come from that scared 22-year-old, trapped between Callum's threats and Kyler's reckless charm.

She had married Kyler in 2020, at the height of the pandemic, in a small, rushed ceremony at a registry office. She had been eight months pregnant, her bump making the already hurried proceedings feel even more surreal. The marriage had been one of convenience rather than love—Kyler had been the safer option, the one who hadn't tried to manipulate her like Callum had. But safety had never equated to happiness, and two years on, Toni wasn't sure if she had made the right choice.

It was during that marriage that she changed her name, that Cassie Longton had died, and Toni Green had been born.

She had shed her past like a snake's skin, rebranded herself into someone sharper, someone untouchable. Toni Green wasn't a scared girl from Altrincham who had been backed into corners by men who thought they owned her. Toni Green was a name that commanded respect on the airwaves, a name that carried weight in the industry. A name that made listeners sit up and pay attention.

And then Lincoln, or Link for short, had been born.

Her son. The one true, tangible thing she had created out of the mess of her past. Link was the reason she had kept going, the reason she had fought tooth and nail to rise through the ranks. He had been born into a world locked down in fear, but to her, he had been the only thing that mattered. For all of Kyler's flaws—their late-night arguments, his refusal to fully leave behind the hedonistic lifestyle that came with radio—he had been a decent father. At least, in the moments when he was sober enough to be present.

In 2021, she and Kyler divorced, as he had hit her, he had crossed the one line she could never forgive.

It had been a Friday night, after another one of their endless, circling arguments—this time about his late-night habits, the women whose names she never asked for, the drugs he swore he wasn't still doing. She had called him out, told him she knew, told him she was tired. And in the heat of the moment, as she had turned to walk away, he had grabbed her arm and, before either of them knew what was happening, his hand had cracked across her face.

There had been a moment of silence after, a split-second where even Kyler had looked shocked at what he'd done. But then, just as quickly, he had tried to downplay it, tried to pretend it wasn't as bad as it was.

"Don't look at me like that, Cass," he had said, as if *she* were the one being unreasonable.

She hadn't looked at him at all.

By Monday, she had filed for divorce.

Of course, they were stuck together on the drive time show, which had returned from being a home based show to a studio based ow once COVID restrictions had lifted. Bee Manic had thrived on chaos, but even by their standards, forcing a freshly divorced couple to co-host a show together was a new level of dysfunction. Toni had swallowed her pride, buried the pain, and performed, because that's what she did. The listeners didn't need to know that the two people bantering on-air could barely stand to be in the same room once the mics were off.

And then Manic had handed her the golden ticket in May 2022, a golden ticket that she grabbed with both hands. Lucy Harrison, the host that had been installed following the forced COVID networking scheme which Manic had put in place when the first lockdown restrictions had been put in place, had decided to step down from the networked evening show, Manic Prime Nights. It was a high-profile slot, a nationwide gig across the entire Manic Radio network. It was the kind of job that put you on the industry map. And they had offered it to her.

For Toni, it had been a way out. A chance to finally break free from Bee Manic, from Kyler, from the memories of what had happened between those walls. It meant moving to Liverpool, to the Speke hub, and leaving Manchester behind, but that was a small price to pay for something bigger. Something better.

Of course, the custody arrangements for Link were ones that Cassie couldn't stand as, for some bizarre reason, Kyler had been granted full custody, despite his history. It had been a bitter pill to swallow, one that still made her stomach turn every time she thought about it. The courts had deemed her "too unstable," citing her career, her cocaine use—something that had been thrown in her face despite the fact Kyler was also a user—and the so-called "unconventional nature" of her lifestyle. Meanwhile, Kyler, the man who had hit her, who had spent nights high out of his mind, was considered the more "stable" parent, purely because he had a house with a garden in Chorlton and the ability to fake sincerity in a courtroom.

And then in July 2022, when Manic and the Lite Group merged, Kyler had took a position in London at Manic Radio South Coast, a pan-regional station which merged 4 different local stations into one during the restructuring. He had packed up, moved to London, and taken Link with him. Toni had fought, argued, screamed into the void that it wasn't fair, that it wasn't right, but the law didn't care. The law had already made its decision. The best she could do was visit Link on weekends, travelling down to the capital whenever her schedule allowed.

As a staunch Republican, someone who was of the opinion that the UK should elect its own leaders rather than rely on hereditary privilege, the passing of the Queen wasn't something that hit Toni on a personal level. But she understood its gravity, understood that for millions of people across the country, this was a moment that defined a generation. It was history unfolding in real-time. And it was her job to handle it professionally, even though her instructions were to be business as usual.

Toni knew that Capital was simulcasting LBC, Global's rolling news powerhouse, while Hits Radio had switched to an emergency tribute format, their usual CHR energy dulled down to reflect the magnitude of the moment. But as a staunch republican, she was of the opinion that Manic's business as usual was the right choice.

Why should radio stations grind to a halt for a monarch that people hadn't even voted for? Why should she have to sit there and pretend to care when, frankly, she didn't? This wasn't some beloved artist or cultural icon who had changed the world—this was just the latest chapter in Britain's never-ending obsession with deference and ceremony.

"I bet Camilla's cackling with glee," she muttered as she walked to Studio 1, the network studio, where Danny O'Neil was finishing up his small market Network Drive, which catered not to the likes of Birmingham or Manchester, but to the smaller markets—places like Rochdale, Bolton, Warwick, Burton-upon-Trent, Rugby, and the High Peaks. Being part of the Speke hub, both Toni and Danny knew that the building next door on the Speke Hall Road industrial estate was where all the execs were gathered, no doubt nervously refreshing Twitter and waiting for the fallout from the Queen's death to settle. The Speke Hall Road estate was the heart of Manic's operations, a place where executives dictated the network's every move, from the playlists to the presenters' public personas. And yet, despite the chaos unfolding across the nation, despite the gravity of the moment, Toni Green was walking into Studio 1 with the intention of keeping things as normal as possible.

She knew that Danny, like her, was a staunch Republican, and so he wasn't about to launch into a teary-eyed tribute to the monarchy. As Toni stepped into the studio, Danny was leaning back in his chair, arms folded, his expression one of mild disinterest as he spoke into the mic.

"And that's your drive time done. If you've been with me from four o'clock, cheers for sticking around. And if you're just tuning in, welcome to Manic Prime Nights. Up next, Toni Green is here to take you through the evening, and I'm off to the pub to drink to... well, whatever the opposite of 'The Queen is Dead, Long Live the King' is."

Toni stifled a laugh as she grabbed her headphones and settled into the chair opposite him. Danny muted the mic and shot her a grin.

"Got the memo?" he asked.

Toni smirked, adjusting her mic as Danny swung his chair to face her. Got the memo? Of course, she had.

"Yeah, business as usual," she muttered, rolling her eyes. "Don't mention it unless absolutely necessary. Keep the playlist rolling. Pretend like nothing's happened."

Danny let out a dry chuckle, rubbing his temples. "Mad, innit? The whole country's losing its mind, Hits and Capital have switched to tribute mode, but here we are, about to play some Dua Lipa like it's just another Thursday."

"Good. I've got my running order on my tablet," Toni said with a grin, "Nothing but pure bangers. Anyway, fancy staying on for a bit to watch the listener WhatsApp blow up?"

Danny smirked, leaning back in his chair. "Oh, absolutely. This is gonna be car crash radio, and I wouldn't miss it for the world."

Toni adjusted her headphones, watching as the automation system ticked down to the start of Manic Prime Nights. She had seen the group WhatsApp earlier— Speke HQ had reiterated the "business as usual" approach for Manic CHR, ensuring that, despite the gravity of the day, their network wouldn't sink into the same solemn tributes as Global and Bauer's stations.

She tapped at her tablet, scrolling through her first link. The playlist was unchanged. The next song cued up was Levitating by Dua Lipa, and honestly? That suited her just fine.

Danny was still grinning as he glanced at his phone. "Capital's switched to LBC. Hits have binned their entire playlist and gone full 'Queen and Country' mode. Smooth's practically broadcasting from inside a candlelit vigil at this point."

Toni let out a short laugh. "Meanwhile, we're about to bounce into Levitating. Can't say Manic's ever been known for subtlety."

Danny raised an eyebrow. "Think we'll get a listener backlash?"

Toni snorted. "Danny, the average Manic CHR listener probably found out the Queen died through a TikTok edit with Industry Baby playing in the background. You think they're tuning in for solemn tributes?"

Danny shook his head. "Mad world, innit?"

The studio clock hit 7pm. The network imaging rolled in—its usual bright, punchy branding—completely at odds with the sombre mood gripping the country.

"Live across the Manic Radio network, from Speke to the South Coast, it's Manic Prime Nights with Toni Green!"

Toni cleared her throat, adjusting her mic as the bed music faded in. Her voice came through smooth, confident, unfazed.

"Alright, you lot. Thursday night, let's get into it. You're with me, Toni Green, on Manic Prime Nights, across the country on FM, DAB, and the Manic Prime app. It's been… well, a day, hasn't it? But listen, you know the deal here. We're keeping things rolling, keeping the energy up, and making sure your Thursday night still sounds like a Thursday night. First up, it's the news, where you are."

****

CHAPTER 18 - The Overnight
Thursday 8th September 2022

Roland Waters was sat at his desk in the Executive Building, next door to the Speke Hall Road studios, the nerve centre of the Manic Radio Group. It was half past seven, and, having started at lunchtime, his shift was nearly coming to a close.

As one of Manic Radio's Complaints Officers, it was his job to field the inevitable backlash that would flood in from listeners, advertisers, and regulatory bodies. And tonight? Tonight was a disaster.

The Queen was dead. Global and Bauer had switched into their well-rehearsed obit mode, Capital was simulcasting LBC, Hits Radio was running rolling tributes, and Smooth sounded like it had been broadcasting from a cathedral since lunchtime. Meanwhile, Manic?

Manic had JJ Dennison speculating about Love Island Australia on Bee Manic, Toni Green pretending the Queen's death wasn't even worth a mention, and at least two stations still playing club bangers when the network-wide announcement had dropped.

His inbox had exploded.

There were complaints from listeners accusing Manic of being disrespectful, tone-deaf, or—ironically—too politically correct because they hadn't gone all-in on the monarchy. There were furious advertisers, threatening to pull sponsorships if they didn't issue an apology.

And the common factor?

All of the complainants were outside of the CHR demographic range, outside of the 15-34 target that Manic CHR stations catered to. Roland knew that Manic had long since stopped worrying about the "over-40s brigade" who still wrote into OFCOM every time a presenter said bloody hell before the watershed. But this? This was something else.

He skimmed through the emails.

From: *Maggie.Hemsworth@trainbasher.com*

To: *complaints@manicradio.group*

Subject: *Complaint*

I am appalled by the utter lack of respect shown by Manic Radio. While the rest of the nation is in mourning, your stations continue to play trashy club music and teenage drivel. An absolute disgrace.

Roland chuckled at the sheer predictability of it. Trainbasher.com, a railway enthusiast forum, was a haven for people who spent their days arguing over signal failures and whether Northern Rail was worse than Avanti. Why was she listening to a CHR station in the first place?

Still, he logged it, marking it under "Generic Outrage - Not Our Demo" and moved on.

From: *carpernter344@busphotography.co.uk*

To: *complaints@manicradio.group*

Subject: *Complaint*

I turned on my radio expecting solemn reflection, and instead I got some idiot discussing Love Island spoilers. Unbelievable. Hits and Capital are managing to be respectful—why can't you?

Roland sighed and marked it under "Bee Manic Disaster – JJ Dennison." That one wasn't surprising. He had already flagged JJ's segment for review after the first reports started rolling in. The fact that Bee Manic—a station designed to be chaotic—was handling the Queen's death with all the subtlety of a nightclub PA system was hardly shocking.

He continued scrolling.

From: *kentish121@yahoo.co.uk*

To: *complaints@manicradio.group*

Subject: *Complaint*

I am disgusted that Manic Prime Nights has not even acknowledged this historic moment. I switched on at 7pm expecting some kind of tribute, and what did I get? Dua bloody Lipa. Sort yourselves out!

Roland let out a low whistle. Dua bloody Lipa—that was going to be the phrase of the night, wasn't it?

He marked it as "Manic Prime Nights – Business As Usual Strategy Backlash" and forwarded it to the relevant execs in programming. Not that it would make much difference. The decision to keep the CHR stations running as normal had come straight from the top. Even if Toni Green had wanted to do a tribute—which, knowing her, was laughably unlikely—her hands were tied.

His inbox kept filling.

From: *tombrant407@yahoo.co.uk*

To: *complaints@manicradio.group*

Subject: *Disgusting Disrespect*

If I hear one more dance track on Bee Manic tonight, I swear I'll complain to OFCOM. Your presenters should be ashamed of themselves.

Roland sighed, rubbing his temples as he leaned back in his chair. The complaints were relentless, pouring in at a rate he hadn't seen since the infamous "WAP" scandal of 2020, when a Bee Manic presenter had played the explicit version at 8:30 in the morning. Back then, the outrage had mostly been from parents on the school run. This time, it was different.

This was national mourning.

This was Manic CHR deciding to ignore it.

From: *pinny3443oldie@yahoo.co.uk*

To: *complaints@manicradio.group*

Subject: *Complement*

I would like to say thanks to Toni Green for keeping things real while the woke softies at Capital and Hits Radio have turned into a state funeral broadcast. Not everyone in this country worships the royals, and it's refreshing to hear a presenter who isn't pretending to be heartbroken.

Roland chuckled at that, as he knew that Toni Green, who was currently on air, was a Republican, someone who was likely rolling her eyes at the entire concept of national mourning while queuing up the next banger. He knew her reputation—sharp, unfiltered, unapologetic. Of course, she'd have her fans in all this chaos.

He glanced at the internal Slack chat, where a thread titled "Obit Fallout - CHR Strategy" had descended into open warfare. The Speke HQ Programming team were defending the business as usual stance, while some of the regional directors—especially the ones overseeing stations like Midlands Manic and Manic Radio North East—were frantically trying to do damage control.

Tom Hargrove - RD North East: *We had to override the log manually. The next song after the announcement was Destination Calabria. Do you have ANY idea how bad that would've looked?*

Buzz Campbell - RD Manchester: *Oh, come on Tom, live a little. You don't work for Bauer now, so loosen up, you boring sod. Maybe the Queen would've loved a bit of Alex Gaudino, you never know.*

Roland chuckled at that, as, like Tom Hargrove, he was a former Bauer employee, having worked on the complaints side at H Bauer Publishing, the magazine division, before moving into radio. He knew how much the Bauer mindset clashed with Manic's more reckless, rebellious approach. Tom Hargrove was fighting a losing battle.

The Slack thread was still going.

Tom Hargrove - RD North East: *Buzz, this isn't about "living a little." It's about avoiding a PR disaster. Have you SEEN the complaints rolling in? We're getting dragged by the Daily Mail, the Express, and I'm fairly certain some bloke from The Telegraph just called our office demanding an interview.*

Buzz Campbell - RD Manchester: *Mate, The Telegraph doesn't even know we exist. Our audience doesn't read broadsheets. They watch TikToks and listen to podcasts about whether Kanye is a genius or just lost the plot. The only people complaining are people who don't even listen to us.*

Sally Harper - Head of Compliance: *Let's keep this professional. There are now formal OFCOM complaints being logged. While the CHR stations have followed the directive, the level of listener backlash is higher than anticipated. We need to consider adjustments overnight.*

Looking at his watch, Roland saw it was only 15 minutes until his shift ended, and he had no intention of staying longer than necessary to deal with what was clearly going to be a full-scale OFCOM headache by morning. He knew that as soon as he logged out, the night team—poor sods—would have to deal with whatever fresh hell awaited in the inbox.

As the minutes passed, Roland carried on sorting out the emails that were coming in quicker than a flooded inbox on Black Friday. The volume of complaints had reached the point where Roland had to create new categories just to keep track of them.

- *Bee Manic - JJ Dennison Disaster*
- *Toni Green - Business As Usual Backlash*
- *Manic CHR Playlist Inappropriate*
- *General Royalist Outrage*
- *Republicans Applauding Toni Green*

It was a mess. A glorious, chaotic, very Manic mess.

As the clock showed 7:57, Roland was ready to clock out, when his phone rang. Not the one that was his private line which was used for internal messages, but the main Manic Radio Group complaints line, which was a Cisco based loop, where him, as well as the agents who were the first line of defence against irate listeners, usually took the calls.

Sighing, Roland debated ignoring it—his shift was nearly over, and whatever this was, it could probably wait for the overnight team. But he knew he would receive overtime pay for every minute past his shift, so with a resigned sigh, he picked up the receiver.

"Manic Radio Group, complaints department, Roland speaking."

The voice on the other end was already mid-rant before Roland could even finish his introduction.

"DISGRACEFUL! ABSOLUTELY BLOODY DISGRACEFUL! WHO DO YOU LOT THINK YOU ARE?"

Roland pinched the bridge of his nose. *Here we go*.

"Sir, can I start off by taking a few details so I can log your complaint properly?" Roland asked, keeping his voice as measured and professional as possible.

"I DON'T BLOODY THINK SO!" the man roared. "I'M SICK TO MY BACK TEETH OF THIS—OF YOU LOT! I TURNED ON THE RADIO EXPECTING DIGNITY, RESPECT, MAYBE EVEN A BIT OF DECENCY! BUT NO! WHAT DID I GET? DUA BLOODY LIPA!"

Roland closed his eyes for a second, exhaling through his nose. Dua bloody Lipa strikes again.

"Sir, which station were you listening to?" he asked, flipping to his complaints log.

"Bee Manic! Or whatever it's called! And that absolute cretin JJ Dennison! It's a national disgrace! A moment of history and he's talking about Love Island! What's wrong with you people? My wife's in tears!"

Roland clicked into the "Bee Manic Disaster – JJ Dennison" category. "I understand your frustration, sir," he said, even though he didn't. "We're logging all feedback, and I assure you your concerns will be passed to senior management."

The man wasn't done. "I don't WANT my concerns passed on! I want ACTION! That man should be SACKED! In fact, forget sacking him—he should be banned from broadcasting! He's a liability! The Queen is DEAD and this clown is talking about bloody reality TV!"

Roland checked the call duration. *Four bloody minutes this git's shouting.*

"I appreciate your feedback," he said again, hoping to move this along. "If you'd like to make a formal complaint to OFCOM, you're entitled to do so—"

"DON'T WORRY, I'LL BE DOING THAT TOO!" the man snapped. "AND I'LL BE WRITING TO MY MP! THIS NEEDS TO BE SORTED!"

Roland resisted the urge to ask whether his MP had nothing better to do. "Understood, sir. Is there anything else I can help you with?"

"A refund!" the man barked.

Roland blinked. "I'm sorry?"

"A refund! I pay my licence fee, and I have to put up with this?"

Roland sighed. Not this again. "Sir, the BBC is funded by the licence fee. Manic Radio is a commercial broadcaster."

There was a brief pause.

"Well, it's still unacceptable!" the man huffed. "I'll never be listening again!"

"Sir, you have the right to decide which radio station you listen to. Are you a Manic Prime subscriber?" Roland asked, as Manic Prime, the app which Manic used for its radio stations offered both a free tier, which basically took the standard radio feed and had a limited set of stations, and then there was the Prime tier, which offered exclusive content, ad-free streams, and specialist music channels.

The man scoffed. "Why the bloody hell would I pay for this rubbish? I demand to speak to a manager, not a cretin like you, if you're not going to sort this out."

Roland knew that technically, as a Complaints Officer and not a Customer Services Agent, he was deemed to be a manager in the Customer Services department, but as the overnight Customer Service Manager had just logged in, he decided to transfer the call over. There was no point arguing with a man who clearly thought he was personally funding Manic Radio with his licence fee, and he wasn't about to let his own blood pressure rise over an issue that was very much above his pay grade.

"Sir, I understand your frustration. Let me transfer you to my manager, who can discuss this further with you." Roland pressed a few buttons on his Cisco handset, routed the call to the overnight shift lead, and muted his headset just in time to hear the distant bellow of, "AND ANOTHER THING—" before it cut off.

"Hey Annie," Roland said as the overnight manager, Annie Patel, picked up her headset on the other end of the line. "You're getting a special one to start your shift. Proper irate bloke, reckons he funds us with his licence fee."

Annie groaned. "Oh, for—Roland, it's literally been 90 seconds since I logged in."

"Welcome to Obit Fallout, where the complaints never stop and people still don't understand how commercial radio works," Roland replied dryly, clicking out of his queue. "He's all yours."

He could hear Annie sigh heavily as she unmuted her line. "Hello, sir, I understand you have a complaint—"

Roland didn't need to hear the rest. He flicked his headset off, stretched his arms, and closed his inbox for the night. He was done. This mess was now the overnight team's problem.

****

Like most of the employees at Manic, Roland had 3 vices—sex, cocaine and booze, and tonight he was indulging in all three.

Stepping out of the Executive Building and into the cool Liverpool night, Roland pulled his phone from his pocket and fired off a quick message to his dealer.

Roland: *You around? Need a pick-me-up. Long shift.*

Leo (Dealer): *Gotcha, usual spot?*

Roland: *Yeah, give me 20 mins.*

That was the first order of business sorted. The second? He scrolled through his recent WhatsApp messages, landing on one from Tasha Kemp, a PR rep for one of Manic's advertising partners and, more importantly, his current on-again, off-again distraction.

Roland: *You out? Need a drink and some company. Night shift nearly killed me.*

Tasha: *Thought you'd never ask. Baltic Market?*

Roland: *See you in 30.*

With that settled, he loosened his tie and started towards his car, parked in the lot behind the Speke studios. The irony of working for a company so deeply embedded in the UK's chaotic commercial radio landscape, only to need this level of personal decompression afterwards, wasn't lost on him.

The Queen was dead, the country was mourning, and Manic Radio was… still being Manic. He chuckled to himself. This was exactly why he had taken the job in the first place.

For all its faults—for all the corporate chaos, the complaints, the near-constant fire-fighting—there was something about Manic that made it different from Bauer, Global, and all the sanitised, PR-heavy stations that played it safe.

Manic didn't care about tradition. It barely cared about rules.

It was a station that had been built by Scousers who had a chip on their shoulders from when Emap had brought Radio City in 1991, held together with gaffer tape and pure chaos.

And deep down?

That was exactly why Roland loved it.

****

CHAPTER 19 - Independent View
Thursday 8th September 2022

Woody Bones was sat in the comfort of his Longbridge home, a glass of scotch in his hand, the 70 year old former ILR operator had spent decades navigating the turbulent waters of British commercial radio, and now, in the twilight of his career, he had found a certain peace in running community radio stations across the Midlands. He had long since left behind the cutthroat politics of corporate broadcasting, but tonight, as he flicked through the dial on his DAB radio, he couldn't help but shake his head at the chaos unfolding on the airwaves.

The Queen was dead. The nation was in mourning. And Manic Radio was… still being Manic.

It was 7pm, and he knew that on Midlands Manic, an amalgamation of 4 of his former ILR stations in the West Midlands County plus a further station, a former employee of his, Pete Smith, would normally have handed over to the network…

Yet tonight, Pete wasn't on Midlands Manic. He was on Manic Goldies, anchoring the network's rolling tributes. Woody had tuned in earlier and had to admit—Pete was handling it well. Steady, composed, respectful. He wasn't reading from a corporate script like the Bauer lot, nor was he treating it as a circus like some of the Manic CHR hosts seemed to be doing.

"You're listening to Manic Goldies, and to repeat our earlier news, Her Majesty Queen Elizabeth II has passed away at the age of 96. We'll be here throughout the evening with rolling coverage, tributes, and reflections on her extraordinary reign."

Woody took another sip of his scotch, letting the weight of the words settle. Pete Smith was an old-school professional, a voice that commanded trust without artifice. If there was anyone at Manic who could handle a moment of this magnitude with dignity, it was Pete.

He flicked the dial to Manic Classical, curious to hear how that station was holding up.

"And now, a reflection on the Queen's lifelong patronage of the arts, featuring performances from the Royal Philharmonic Orchestra and the BBC Singers. Iain Davies will be up after this, with The Queen at 75 Years, a retrospective about the late monarch's impact on British culture and music."

Woody nodded approvingly. Manic Classical was handling it the way you'd expect—measured, respectful, fitting. No drama, no nonsense. Mary Thomas, their evening host, was a former Classic FM presenter before Manic lured her away with promises of creative freedom and a healthier playlist budget. She had the kind of soft, authoritative voice that made everything sound important without over-sentimentalising. It was, in short, exactly what you'd expect from a station catering to an older, more refined audience.

Woody switched stations again, this time landing on Three Towns Radio, one of his own stations, which was based in Kidderminster and served the Wyre Forest area. Unlike the corporate networks, community radio had the freedom to decide its own tone, and Woody had instructed the team to find a balance—respectful, but not wall-to-wall mourning. After all, this was local radio. It wasn't about competing with the national networks; it was about serving the community.

Sarah Smith, or Reeves as she preferred to be on air, a former Wolverhampton FM and Smooth West Midlands presenter, was handling the evening shift, her normal Midlands Rock show, one which was networked across Woody's portfolio of community radio stations which spread the length and breadth of the East and West Midlands, had been paused for the night. Instead, she was hosting a special programme dedicated to the late Queen, reflecting on her impact both nationally and locally.

"-Three Towns Radio-"

"-Godiva FM-"

"-Derbonian Sound-"

"-Worcester Waves-"

"-where we're reflecting on the life and legacy of Her Majesty Queen Elizabeth II."

Woody had to chuckle at, despite having only community licences, he had had the full RCS suite of Zetta, GSelector and even the ability to override local logs remotely—a luxury many smaller operators could only dream of. His empire of community stations might not have had the reach of the big boys, but they were well-run, efficient, and most importantly, still local.

All because he had invested the money from when he sold his former ILR portfolio to Breeze Media in 2010, 14 radio stations which netted him a small fortune, enough to fund his retirement comfortably. But retirement had never really suited Woody Bones. He was too much of a radio man to walk away entirely, and so he had funnelled his money back into community radio, creating a network of stations that still gave presenters the freedom to be themselves—something that was rapidly disappearing from the industry.

As he swirled his scotch, he listened as Sarah Smith continued her programme across his network.

"In a moment, we'll hear from some of our listeners sharing their own memories of The Queen—perhaps you met her on a royal visit or remember watching her Christmas messages with your family growing up. We want to hear from you. Text us on 81400, starting your message with Sarah, I'm here until 10pm, and I'll be reading out some of your messages throughout the evening."

Woody nodded approvingly. Sarah was good at this sort of thing—striking the right balance between warmth and professionalism. He had known her for years, ever since her early days at Wolverhampton FM, and she had always had that natural ability to make listeners feel like they were part of the conversation.

The fact that her husband was Pete Smith, meaning that she had an inside track on both the local and national radio scenes, only added to her credibility. Pete was up in Dudley, guiding Manic Goldies through rolling coverage, while Sarah held down the fort on the Midlands' independent airwaves. Between the two of them, they were practically covering both ends of the industry.

Woody remembered hiring her back in 1992 for Dudley FM as a newsreader, back when she had completed a Journalism degree at the University of Birmingham, and had put her on the early Breakfast and Breakfast shifts, with the early breakfast show being helmed by Pete, who had been, until his Business degree had completed, a runner and jack of all trades around the station. The two of them had been thrown together by pure chance, but their on-air chemistry had been undeniable from the start.

Thursday 5th November 1992

Woody was walking through the Dudley FM studios at The Waterfront, a business complex in the Brierley Hill area of Dudley, where the station had been based since its launch in 1981, Cuban cigar in his mouth, the smoke of his usual vice drifting through the hallway as he made his way towards the breakfast studio. It was just after 4am, and he wanted to check in on Pete and Sarah, who were on the early breakfast shift, running the prelude to Dudley FM's main Breakfast Show. Pete, a 21 year old Wolverhampton Polytechnic graduate, and Sarah, a Birmingham graduate, had only been working together for a few weeks, but Woody had already seen potential in them as a duo.

As he pushed open the studio door, the scent of stale coffee mixed with the ever-present tang of audio equipment. What he saw, however, was a shock.

Sarah was completely naked, and Pete was behind her, pressing up against her, his hands on her waist, their bodies tangled in the dim glow of the studio's equipment lights. The only thing between them and the mic was a LP

253

playing a 12 minute Aretha Franklin medley, something Pete had clearly lined up to buy them some time.

Woody chuckled, as it was an unwritten rule in the radio industry that you're not a proper jock unless you've shagged someone in sales, someone in promos and someone in news.

"Well, well, looks like you've both found a unique way to prepare for the show," Woody quipped, leaning against the studio doorframe, Cuban cigar still smouldering between his fingers.

He knew that Pete had been, until then, a singleton, and that he had been living the typical post-university life—working odd hours, hitting the pubs with colleagues, and figuring out where he fit in the world of commercial radio. Sarah, on the other hand, had been focused, driven, the kind of person who planned out her life with precision. And yet, here they were, tangled in each other's arms, completely unbothered by the implications of their actions.

Pete froze, his hands still resting on Sarah's hips, his face draining of colour. Sarah, however, was quicker on the recovery, reaching for a nearby hoodie that had been draped over the back of her chair.

"Woody," she said, her voice calm despite the situation. "You've got terrible timing."

Woody exhaled a plume of cigar smoke and gave a low chuckle. "And you've got about eight minutes before that Aretha Franklin medley runs out. Unless you fancy doing the next link stark bollock naked."

Pete finally seemed to snap out of his stunned silence, running a hand through his dishevelled hair. "Uh—yeah. Right. Sorry, Woody. We, um—"

"Save it," Woody waved a hand, cutting him off. "I don't care who's shagging who. This is radio. It happens. Just don't let it affect your work."

Sarah, now dressed in the oversized hoodie, gave him a nod. "Understood."

Woody smirked, taking one last drag of his cigar before stubbing it out in the ashtray by the door. "Oh, and Pete— if you're going to pull stunts like this in the studio, at least make sure the soundproofing's up to scratch. The engineers don't need to hear you breaking in the new girl."

With that, he turned on his heel and walked out, leaving the pair scrambling to compose themselves before the Aretha Franklin medley hit its final crescendo.

Thursday 8th September 2022

Woody chuckled to himself, taking another sip of his scotch. That had been thirty years ago. Pete and Sarah had lasted longer than most radio couples—hell, longer than most radio stations, if he thought about it.

They'd gone through different employers, formats, company mergers, and still, somehow, they had endured. Sure, they'd had their moments—Pete's ego had always been a sticking point, and Sarah was never one to back down from a fight—but they'd made it work. Even now, in the twilight of their careers, they were still at it. Pete, holding down Manic Goldies' tributes, Sarah keeping community radio grounded.

The fact that they had two children, one who had gone off on a gap year to Ibiza, the normal

The fact that they had two children, one who had gone off on a gap year to Ibiza, the normal route for any child of radio parents, and the other, Chloe, who was a college student, only made Woody smile even more. It was like the Smith family had radio inked into their DNA.

He leaned back in his chair, flipping through the stations again. He had seen it all in his time—station buyouts, closures, the transition from ILR to national brands, the death of local radio, the rise of automation. Hell, he had been there in the '90s when GWR swallowed up half the stations in the Midlands and replaced everything with "Better Music Mix" branding. He had watched the same thing happen with Breeze Media, then again with Manic, and yet, through it all, radio still found a way to survive.

Tuning into Boom Radio, the 70 year old knew that there were still pockets of radio that stayed true to the original spirit of ILR. Boom Radio, run by and for the generation that had built commercial radio in Britain, was offering exactly what he expected—a measured, heartfelt tribute to the Queen, with carefully chosen songs reflecting the moment, interspersed with presenters who understood their audience.

He recognised the voice on air—David Lloyd, one of the great ILR veterans, who had spent decades in the industry. His tone was calm, dignified, weaving personal reflections with history, the kind of thing you wouldn't hear on corporate radio anymore.

"This is a moment of history, and for so many of us, it's hard to put into words. Queen Elizabeth II has been a part of our national fabric for seventy years—longer than many of us have even been alive. Tonight, we reflect on her life, her legacy, and what comes next for Britain. If you'd like to share your thoughts, you can text or email in, and we'll be reading some of them throughout the evening."

Woody nodded in approval. Boom Radio was doing what the likes of Beacon, BRMB, Mercia and Hereward would have done back in the day—serving their audience, giving them a place to reflect. No overblown mourning, no corporate nonsense. Just radio, done properly.

He flicked back to Manic CHR.

"It's Thursday night on Manic Prime Nights, and we are keeping things rolling! Got a request? Drop me a message on the Manic Prime app! Next up, it's Tiësto and Ava Max—The Motto!"

Woody let out a chuckle. Of course, Toni Green was carrying on like nothing had happened. He couldn't decide whether it was bold, stupid, or both. But then, that was Manic CHR all over—unpredictable, chaotic, and completely at odds with everything else in the industry.

He checked his phone, scrolling through WhatsApp, where his old mates from the ILR days were weighing in, including his sister-in-law, Lucy Kildare, who he had brought her network of 6 stations back in 2005 from, expanding his own 6 stations to 12.

Lucy Kildare: *Well, that was a bold move from Manic CHR. Someone in Speke must be off their head.*

David Lloyd: *Boom's audience has been incredible tonight. People just want a space to reflect. Manic? They're on another planet.*

Steve Penk: *I'd have played 'God Save The Queen' by the Sex Pistols just to see what happens.*

Phil Riley: *Pete Smith's doing a solid job over on Manic Goldies. The CHR side is a disaster, but at least there's some dignity left in the group.*

Ralph Bernard: *If this was back in the GWR days, I'd have had half of the PDs sacked before they even got through the second chorus of Levitating.*

The irony, Woody knew, of Ralph Bernard, the King Borg of ILR who had spent years sanitising local radio into oblivion under GWR, was now criticising Manic for being too reckless. Back in the day, Bernard had been the architect of the dreaded "Better Music Mix" and the centralised playlisting that had killed off individuality in ILR. Now, in his retirement, he was offering wisdom like some sort of radio Yoda. Woody chuckled at the thought.

Woody Bones: *Come on Ralph, we all know you'd have had a six-page memo sent to every station by now, outlining exactly how many times presenters could say the word 'Queen' per hour."*

Ralph Bernard: *GWR would have handled this with dignity, I'll have you know.*

Steve Penk: *Dignity? Mate, in 1997 you had stations still playing ads for DFS sofas the night Diana died.*

David Lloyd: *Meanwhile, Boom is getting messages from people sharing stories of meeting the Queen in the '60s. No complaints here.*

Lucy Kildare: *Look, Manic CHR was always going to be a disaster. This is a station where their breakfast show once got fined for calling the Prime Minister a 'wet wipe'. What did anyone expect?*

Phil Riley: *The thing is, it's not just Speke that looks bad. It makes commercial radio, as a whole, look bad. When Bauer and Global switch to tribute mode and you're still blasting Tiësto, it doesn't send the best message.*

Woody sighed, swirling the last of his scotch. The group chat was right—Manic CHR was an embarrassment tonight. Say what you wanted about Ralph Bernard's corporate approach, but at least GWR would've had a plan. They would've switched to a soft AOR playlist, brought in a voiceover from a safe pair of hands, and made sure no one on air said anything stupid. But Manic? Manic had never been a company that played it safe.

The worst part was, Woody knew why. It wasn't just arrogance from the Speke executives—it was a fundamental refusal to be seen as another Bauer or Global clone. Manic's whole brand was built on the idea that they weren't like the big corporates. They prided themselves on being rebellious, on being the 'alternative' in commercial radio. And on most days, that worked for them. It made them feel fresh, unpredictable, like a rogue player in an industry increasingly dominated by identikit formats.

But tonight wasn't most days.

Tonight, the entire country was mourning, and Manic's refusal to adjust was making them look not just irreverent, but incompetent.

Woody checked the chat again.

Lucy Kildare: *Word is, OFCOM's already getting formal complaints about Bee Manic and Toni Green. One of my mates at Global says they're loving this. They think it makes them look like the 'trusted' ones.*

Steve Penk: *That's hilarious, considering Global literally fires their breakfast hosts every 18 months and runs on autopilot 90% of the time.*

Phil Riley: *Toni Green is going to ride this out just fine. She thrives on controversy. JJ Dennison, on the other hand? Finished.*

David Lloyd: *And rightly so. There's being irreverent, and then there's being a moron.*

Woody put his phone down and leaned back in his chair, exhaling slowly. He had no stake in this mess anymore—not really. He was out of corporate radio, running his own thing, answering to no one. But he still cared about the industry, about what it had once been, about what it still could be.

He thought about Pete and Sarah, still holding the line after all these years. About the old ILR stations, the ones that had real personalities before the networks took over. About the young presenters coming up now, who would never know what it was like to work in a station where you could actually make your own playlist.

Radio had changed. Some of it for the better, a lot of it for the worse.

But if tonight had proved anything, it was that the soul of British radio—the thing that made it magic, unpredictable, human—was still there, buried somewhere beneath the corporate nonsense.

It just needed the right people to bring it back.

And, perhaps, a little less Tiësto.

****

Books by Thomas Brant

Broadcasting Boundaries Series
BROADCASTING BOUNDARIES
BROADCASTING CHAOS
BROADCASTING DISRUPTION

The Wirral Gal Series
THE WIRRAL GAL... IN SPEKE
THE WIRRAL GAL... NOW A MAM

Standalone Stories in the Manic Radio Universe
THE BROOKES BABES
THE DAY THE QUEEN DIED